THE
RICH
AND THE
DEAD

THE
RICH
AND THE
DEAD

Liv Spector

WM

WILLIAM MORROW

An Imprint of HarperCollins*Publishers*

THE RICH AND THE DEAD. Copyright © 2014 by Alloy Entertainment, LLC. All rights reserved. Printed in the United States of America. No part of this book may be used or reproduced in any manner whatsoever without written permission except in the case of brief quotations embodied in critical articles and reviews. For information address HarperCollins Publishers, 10 East 53rd Street, New York, NY 10022.

HarperCollins books may be purchased for educational, business, or sales promotional use. For information please e-mail the Special Markets Department at SPsales@harpercollins.com.

PRODUCED BY ALLOY ENTERTAINMENT, LLC
1700 BROADWAY, 4TH FLOOR, NEW YORK, NY 10019

Designed by Diahann Sturge

Library of Congress Cataloging-in-Publication Data has been applied for.

ISBN 978-0-06-225839-7

14 15 16 17 18   OV/RRD   10 9 8 7 6 5 4 3 2 1

To WW, for everything

ACKNOWLEDGMENTS

I WOULD LIKE to thank everyone at Alloy Entertainment and William Morrow for bringing this book into being—especially Joelle Hobeika, Katie McGee, and May Chen for their invaluable guidance, warmth, and enthusiasm.

I would also like to thank:

My father, for being a quiet but powerful voice of encouragement.

My sister, for a lifetime of unflagging support, gentle nudging, and laughter.

My mother, whose love, wisdom, and passion for life are the foundations upon which my life is built.

Sonia Verma, David Bell, Jeff Oliver, Ayla Teitelbaum, and Corey Kohn, for friendships that have buoyed me during the good times and, even more so, the bad.

Tim Foy, whose undying faith and joyful love have made me braver and stronger than I ever thought possible.

Behind every great fortune there is a great crime.
—Honoré de Balzac

PROLOGUE

STAR ISLAND, FLORIDA, is not so much a location on the map as a fantasy come to life. The hundred or so people lucky enough to live on its man-made shores exist as if in a waking dream—a dream as seductive, dangerous, and illusory as a mirage.

Nestled upon the turquoise waters of Biscayne Bay, a mere stone's throw away from that wild and wicked boomtown, Miami Beach, Star Island has been home to movie stars, corporate titans, drug runners, and even a cult leader named Brother Louv, all of whom prized both its opulence and its isolation. But today, Star Island is synonymous with one thing, and one thing only.

The massacre.

All of the sins and scandals that took place on the island before the murders now seem like nothing more than child's play.

By now, the details of the crime have been fervently hashed and rehashed so many times, on TV talk shows, around kitchen tables, and over cubicle walls, that everyone in the world knows the intricacies of the murders: On New Year's Day 2015, twelve bodies were discovered on the Star Island estate of hotel magnate Chase Haverford, whose body was recovered among the dead. The victims were all, like Chase, high-profile fixtures in Miami's social scene. Each had been murdered execution-style with a single bullet shot directly through the forehead.

The moment the news broke, the Star Island massacre took over the attentions of the world like a collective fever. From Tampa to Tokyo, from Kentucky to Kenya, the international media were breathless with talk about what many called the crime of the century.

For months, the hunt for the Star Island killer consumed the best and brightest investigators across the country and around the world. The CIA and the FBI each devoted a team to the case. A $10 million bounty offered by the father of one of the victims inspired countless home-brewed investigations. Yet even with the entire world on the hunt, the identity of the killer remained unknown.

And then, like any fever, the obsession with the Star Island massacre eventually broke. The press turned its attentions to another scandal. The cadre of investigators, tired of insurmountable dead ends and anxious to flee Miami before the summer humidity made the city unbearable, went off looking for new bloodstained bogeymen.

Long after everyone else had moved on, one local detective was left following leads, checking and rechecking evidence, and searching for a break in a case so cold even she knew there was little hope in catching the killer.

Only one detective was foolish enough to care, and it nearly cost her everything.

CHAPTER 1

THE INSTANT LILA Day knocked on the door to room 3746, the yelling from inside stopped. On the other side of the door, she could hear the hustle of loud whispers and shuffling feet—the sound of bad behavior being frantically covered up.

"Security!" Lila bellowed as she pounded on the door.

She looked at her watch: 4:13 A.M. "Figures," she muttered under her breath as she knocked again, landing three sharp strikes upon the door. "Open up, now!"

One thing all her years as a cop had taught her, and this crap hotel security job had merely confirmed, was that the hour from 4:00 to 5:00 A.M. was always when the ugliest shit went down. By four in the morning, most of the partyers, drunks, and fun-seeking idiots had passed out, and the early birds were still asleep in their beds. Anyone awake at this ungodly time was, without fail, up to no good.

Lila had been working night security at the Hotel Armadale for the past eight months, and in that time, not one notable thing had happened. Usually her job meant busting hotel guests smoking cigarettes in the stairwell, or searching under couch cushions for watches reported as stolen. Tonight, though, things were different. She felt it in her gut.

A sharp and sudden smash came from inside the room. Once again, Lila banged on the door.

"Hotel security. Open the door!" she shouted.

She reached down for her weapon, an automatic impulse after years on the force. But there was no gun there—nothing but a flashlight. Hotel security officers were strictly prohibited from carrying weapons. Bad for business, her manager said.

"Christ," Lila muttered. She settled for her flashlight, which she could use as a stand-in bludgeon if it came to that.

She banged on the door a final time. Then she heard a muffled cry, followed by what sounded like a heavy object being dragged along the floor. Someone was in danger. In an instant, Lila had swiped her universal key across the touch-screen door lock, kicked the door open, and stepped cautiously inside the room.

It was one of the hotel's most expensive suites, with jaw-dropping ocean views and sleek furniture. Even on an off-season night like tonight, mid-July in Miami, when the vast majority of tourists were long gone, this room went for $5,200.

But tonight, the suite looked like a war zone. A TV had been torn off the wall and smashed against the dining room table. The white marble floor was covered in broken glass and empty booze bottles. A chartreuse raw silk curtain had been ripped off the window.

Slowly, Lila skirted along the perimeter of the room, keeping her back to the wall.

She heard a door slam on the west side of the suite and followed the sound into the bedroom, where she saw a long trail of blood staining the white carpet. The blood stopped at the closed bathroom door. From behind the door, she could hear rushing water and heavy footfalls.

"Hotel security. Open the goddamned door!"

There was no response.

With all of her strength, Lila slammed the butt end of her flashlight repeatedly into the doorknob until the metal ripped away. She took a deep breath and then, using all 125 pounds of her body weight, shouldered her way into the bathroom.

Two men, stripped down to their underwear, stood frozen in a Jacuzzi tub at the far end of the cavernous marble bathroom. A woman's bare legs, tapering down to a pair of leopard-print high heels, hung limply over the tub's side. The crimson trail of blood continued across the floor toward the tub.

One man was quite short, no more than five four, with a bleached Mohawk and a muscular gym body. The other was a hulking presence, about a foot taller than his friend, paunchy and covered in thick tufts of body hair.

A strong smell of vomit hung in the air. The sink and tub faucets poured with steaming hot water.

"Hands up," Lila shouted.

"We weren't doing nothing," the short man said in a thick accent that Lila couldn't quite place. He raised his hands slowly and stepped out of the tub. He took several steps toward Lila, close enough that she could smell the soured alcohol escaping from every pore on his body.

"Don't move," Lila warned, standing her ground. The small man stopped within arm's reach of her. From his red-rimmed eyes and raw nostrils she could tell he'd been buried in drugs for hours. The woman's legs had not moved.

"This has nothing to do with you," the large man said in a tone so calm and measured that it made Lila's skin crawl. "You should turn around and go."

"That's not going to happen, sir," Lila said. If that woman was still alive, the water flowing into the tub would drown her within seconds. "Now, can you tell me if the woman is still breathing?"

The large man stepped out of the tub. "Everything is under control," he said.

"That's not what it looks like from here." She inched closer to the tub, her hand wrapped around the flashlight.

"I wouldn't do that if I were you," the short man said, grabbing her left arm.

"Hands off!" Lila snapped. She tried to pull her arm away, but the man only tightened his grip, burrowing his fingers deep into the muscle of her biceps.

Lila could see from his eyes and the tense twitch of his jaw that the man had no intention of letting her go. She glanced over at the taller man, who was now standing shoulder to shoulder with his buddy. Two against one. If she was going to get the upper hand, she would have to strike first.

In one swift movement, she spun around, using the momentum of her torqued body to crack the flashlight across the short man's cheekbone. He let go of her as he fell diagonally, clutching his face. Then she darted to the side as the larger man lunged for her, bringing her foot down on his leg, right above the ankle. She heard the stomach-churning sound of his bone breaking.

Howling in pain, the man collapsed to the floor, and Lila ran to the tub. The woman was naked, her arms akimbo like those of a rag doll. Her long blond hair was wet and hung in clumps around her bloody face. Grabbing the woman's life-less arms, Lila attempted to hoist her from the tub, but her wet, unresponsive body slipped out of Lila's grasp. The woman crumpled to the floor with a thud.

Lila called 911 for help. Her boss had been more than clear that calling the cops was absolutely the *last* resort. Even though this was a matter of life or death, she knew he'd still give her shit for it. "This is hotel security requesting police and EMT at Hotel Armadale, room thirty-seven forty-six. I have a medical emergency and two detained suspects."

As she was talking, she pressed her fingers to the inside of the woman's wrist and was relieved to find a pulse. She was still alive, but she wasn't breathing.

Just then, the short man got to his feet, stooping down to help his larger friend.

Lila shot back up, ready for round two. But the men weren't coming toward her. They were shuffling frantically away in the direction of the door.

"Freeze!" Lila shouted. They stopped, looked at her, looked at each other, and took off for the hallway as quickly as they could, the large man dragging his mangled leg behind him.

Lila hesitated for a split second. Should she chase after the men, or try to get this woman breathing again?

"Fuck it," Lila said. She brushed the blond hair from the woman's face, used a wet towel to wipe away the blood and vomit, and bent down to hold the woman's nose closed as she blew two long breaths into her lungs.

By the time the EMTs arrived, the men were long gone, and the woman was barely responsive. But at least she was breath-ing again.

After the woman had been placed on a stretcher and taken

to the hospital, a couple of fresh-faced cops arrived on the scene. They were young enough that Lila didn't know them from her years in the Miami Police Department; and if they knew of her, they didn't say. For that, she was thankful.

Her cell phone rang while she was in the middle of giving the police a description of the men who'd fled the crime scene. It was her boss. "Get to my office, now."

"I'm talking to the police," she replied. "I'll be down when I'm done."

"Which is right this minute. Get your ass here, now."

She took the elevator down to the basement, where her supervisor had his small office just off the kitchen. When she opened his door, he was on the phone.

"I got it. It's taken care of. Not a problem," he said, waving Lila in. She knew from the throbbing vein in the middle of his beet-red forehead that she was in deep shit.

"Yes, thank you, sir," he said into the phone, glaring at Lila. "Sorry that you had to be disturbed in the middle of the night over this."

Danny Ramirez, her superior, was an unshaven smudge of a man with a phlegmy cough and an allergic reaction to hard work. Like Lila, and most of the other shlubs who worked hotel security, he was an ex-cop. The difference was that he was retired with full pension, while Lila had been asked to leave the force. It was a distinction he never let her forget. He was a kiss-up, kick-down kind of guy. In other words, a complete prick.

Lila sat stiffly on a metal stool wedged between a wet vac and a fifty-gallon drum of olive oil, waiting for him to get off the phone.

"That's right, sir. I'll handle it. Yes, my pleasure." Danny hung up the phone, then let out an enormous sigh, rubbing the heel of his meaty hand across his forehead. "Do you have any idea who that was?" he asked Lila.

She shook her head no.

"Thanks to you, I just had the distinct pleasure of getting my ass chewed out by none other than Jonathan fucking Golding, the owner of this very fine establishment. Do you know how many times he's called me? Just guess."

Lila shrugged. Saying anything right now would only be digging herself deeper into whatever hole she was currently in.

"In my six years of working here, I've only spoken to that man once before tonight. And that was on the day he hired me."

"You're acting like I did something wrong."

"Do yourself a favor and shut your mouth!" he shouted. "I'll take bullshit from Golding 'cause that's my job. But I won't take it from you. Do you have any idea whose fucking ankle you broke tonight?"

"I don't know. A rapist's? A murderer's? I walked in on him and his little friend trying to kill a woman. If I wasn't there, you'd have a homicide on your hands right now. Is that what you want?"

"She's a whore who overdosed. That's the end of the story. The cops that are with her down at the hospital right now told me she's not pressing charges. She's staying very tight-lipped about the whole thing. Poor girl is just trying to keep out of jail herself. On the other hand, those guys you had so much fun bashing around already have their lawyers calling Jonathan fucking Golding demanding that you be brought up on aggravated assault charges."

"*Me?*"

"Yes, you. And now I've got Golding up my ass saying how bad this looks for the hotel. He's trying to keep the whole thing contained. If this is leaked to the press, it'll be a total shit show."

Lila sat there stunned. The worst she had expected was to be called out for letting the guys get away. But this wasn't the first time she'd been read the riot act for simply doing her job.

"I was warned not to hire you. But did I listen?" Danny shook his head. "You were a good cop. And you needed work, so I did what I thought was right and gave you the job."

"And I'm grateful for that. Really I am." Lila gave Danny a forced smile. "What I did tonight is part of the job you hired me to do."

"For as long as I've known you, you've had a rotten habit of fucking with the wrong people," he said.

"You mean rich people."

"That's one way to put it. Most people just call them the boss. And most people learn early to play nice with the guys who call the shots. It seems to me those are the folks you like to go after."

Danny stood up, walked around his desk, and stopped in front of Lila. "I'll need your hotel ID. Leave your uniform and flashlight in your locker. You'll get a final check sent to you at the end of the month. As of right now, you are no longer an employee of Hotel Armadale."

Lila sat silent for a moment, studying her boss. Under the fluorescent lights, his face looked slack-jawed and exhausted. There was a mustard stain on his tie. He had always been sloppy, as a man and as a cop. All he ever really cared about was covering his own ass. The priorities of a coward.

Good riddance, she thought, standing up. She slapped her ID and flashlight on the table.

"You'll land on your feet, kid." Danny's voice was a little strained from this attempt at positivity, but also relieved. She knew he'd been worried she would make a scene. But she wouldn't give him the pleasure of seeing her protest. It was pointless. Instead, she just nodded as she left his office and closed the door behind her.

The moment Lila walked out of the Armadale for the last time, a wall of humidity hit her, the sun mercilessly bright overhead. It was only 7:30 A.M., and already the temperature was unbearable. Two thousand eighteen was proving to be the hottest year on record—and the worst year of Lila's life.

Thoughts of her late mother's hospital bills, her overdue car payments, her rent, and her frozen credit cards descended on Lila like the oppressive weather, making it almost impossible to breathe. She was broke, she was in debt, and now she was unemployed.

She was crossing the parking lot toward her car, her mind listing one worry after another, when a rapid clicking noise interrupted her thoughts. She looked up and saw an old man on the other side of the street, sitting in a midnight-blue Bentley and pointing a long-lensed camera in her direction. She swiveled around to see what he was photographing, but there was nothing behind her except the empty parking lot. Was he taking pictures of her?

Just as she turned back to the man, the car pulled away and disappeared around the corner. Lila stood glued to the same spot, staring blankly at where the car had been. Its exhaust fumes still hung suspended in the morning air. There was something about that old man, about this specific moment in time, that seemed intensely familiar to Lila, almost as if this had happened before.

She shook herself out of her momentary daze and climbed into her already sunbaked car, which felt something like climbing into a furnace. Déjà vu, she thought with a shrug.

The sun had only been up for an hour, and Lila's day, as far as she was concerned, was already done.

CHAPTER 2

LILA LIVED IN a run-down two-story stucco apartment building overlooking a small patch of grass and palm trees called Ernesto Lecuona Park, in the heart of Little Havana. With its thin, dirty walls, cheap tiled floors, and cracked ceilings, her apartment had an undeniable charmlessness. No one would choose to live in a place like this. It was where unlucky people fell when they stopped reaching for the life they wanted.

Sweating from the heat of the day and profoundly exhausted, Lila undressed clumsily, leaving her clothes in a careless pile by the foot of the bed. The sharp smells of blood and vomit still clung to her hair. She wrapped herself in a robe and started a bath. Her robe was a thing of beauty, made of deep emerald silk delicately embroidered with white and purple lilies. It had been a gift from her mom, their last Christmas together. The card attached had read, "Something soft for my tough little cookie. Love, Mom."

Lila threw back two chalky aspirin and chased them down with a gulp of bourbon on the rocks. After everything that had just happened, she needed to clear her head.

A cop is only as good as her instincts. And for most of her

short but remarkable eight years on the Miami police force, Lila Day's instincts had been dead-on. She was famous among the force for her preternatural ability to know who was guilty, who was innocent, and how to tease out the truth. When cops and prosecutors asked her how she was able to solve tough cases before anyone else, she'd just shrug. In her mind, there was nothing to it. Her only confusion was why it took everybody else so long to figure things out.

When she was fresh out of the academy, Lila's first assignment had been patrolling Little Haiti, one of the toughest neighborhoods in Miami. All of her superiors and fellow rookies thought she'd quit within weeks. None of them understood why a twenty-one-year-old woman would choose to spend her life chasing after bad guys.

"A sweet thing like you," her sergeant had said to Lila her first day on patrol. "Those thugs'll be smacking their lips to get a taste."

Lila had been forced to put up with a lot of that kind of bullshit. That was one part of the job she didn't miss at all—the sneering, sleazy stuff the guys liked to pull. She always saw it as a test, and one she passed by simply ignoring them. She never thought much about her appearance, and hated when she saw women using their looks for some kind of advantage. That could only ever be a losing game. Men always told Lila that she was pretty. They also talked a lot of other shit, and she didn't pay that any mind either. What did it matter when there was a job to be done?

After just two years on the force, Lila made detective. Four years after that, she was assigned as lead investigator on the most high-profile case in the history of Miami: the Star Island massacre. There was an immediate outcry among the other detectives—she was too young, too inexperienced for a case that big. She was bound to fail.

And they were right.

Lila's hunt for the Star Island killer robbed her of her center of gravity. Suddenly the relentlessness that normally made her so good at her job was working against her. She couldn't solve the case, but neither could she move on and let it go.

When perfectionists fail, sometimes they shatter.

If instincts are what make a good cop, then self-doubt is what gets cops killed. And the endless hunt for the Star Island killer left Lila drowning in self-doubt. She had lost her trust in herself.

She sighed, dropped her robe, and stepped into the tub. She hadn't meant to think about the Star Island murders today. The case was her greatest failure as a cop, and now she'd failed herself again, as a lowly hotel security guard.

Just then, there was a violent knock at her front door. Lila froze, up to her ankles in bathwater. She looked at the clock. It was a little after eight in the morning. Who it was didn't matter. That was a knock Lila had no interest in answering. Ignoring it, she was just about to lie down in the bath, but the knocking grew louder and faster.

"What the hell?" Lila muttered. She got out of the tub and put her robe back on, hurrying toward the door to give that noisy bastard a piece of her mind. She glanced out her apartment window and was startled to see that the person knocking was none other than the old man she'd noticed earlier, the one who'd been taking pictures of her. He was wearing a black suit, a chauffeur's cap, and driving gloves. Lila looked to the street, and there was the midnight-blue Bentley, parked behind her car.

"Ms. Day? Ms. Day, please open the door," the old man said in a highly refined English accent. "Ms. Day, I come with an urgent request."

Lila was immune to most temptations, but she never could resist the almost gravitational pull of her curiosity. So now that a strange man with mysterious business had come literally knocking on her door, there was no way in hell she wasn't going to answer.

CHAPTER 3

MS. DAY, MY sincerest apologies. I know it is quite early," the old man said as Lila opened the door.

Despite the oppressive summer heat, he was dressed in a three-piece black wool suit. He carried himself in a stiff and disciplined manner. She watched as his eyes took note of her bare feet and the silk robe that covered her body yet concealed little of her shape. His face reddened slightly.

"I beg your forgiveness, but the inappropriateness of this meeting only reflects the urgent nature of my request. My name is Conrad Whittington. I'm in the employ of Mr. Theodore Hawkins. Do you remember Mr. Hawkins?"

"Of course," she answered, startled to hear the name.

"He would like to speak with you, immediately."

Conrad handed Lila his videophone. Lila recognized the face of the caller on-screen as that of tech billionaire Teddy Hawkins. She hadn't seen Teddy since she interviewed him several years ago, in connection with the Star Island case. Now he looked older than his thirty-five years, more tired and washed out.

"Detective Day," Teddy began. "We've met before."

"I remember," Lila said, curious.

To live in Miami was to know Teddy Hawkins, an MIT dropout turned tech billionaire who was once a fixture of the South Beach social scene. He had been famous, or, depending on who was telling the story, infamous, for the parties he used to throw at his Star Island estate. Everyone who was anyone in Miami had gathered around Teddy like moths to a flame. Until the Star Island massacre changed everything. The day after the murders, Teddy boarded up his Star Island mansion and never again set foot on the estate.

Lila had met Teddy once, when she interviewed him in March 2015, a few months after the murders. He hadn't been very willing to participate in the police investigation, but after Lila threatened to bring him down to the station, he agreed to cooperate. Teddy had never been a suspect in the murders—he was out of the country at the time—but he knew almost all of the victims socially, so Lila had hoped that he could be of some use. He wasn't.

And now here he was, on the phone, wanting to talk to her.

"I have a proposal for you," Teddy went on. "A job offer, if you will."

"A job offer?" she repeated dumbly. Conrad stood perfectly still on Lila's stoop.

"It's something we must discuss in person. I never talk business over the phone."

"Why didn't you just come yourself?" Lila asked, instantly on guard.

"Please, Detective Day, I'd prefer to have this conversation at my home, where we're guaranteed privacy. Conrad will drive you."

"And how do I know that I'll be safe?" Lila demanded. "After all, you had him follow me this morning. I saw him taking pictures of me outside the hotel."

"Those are standard precautions. You're in no danger. You have my word."

"Your word? Does that count for something?"

"I'd like to think it does." Teddy paused. Lila could see that he was searching for what to say. "From what I understand, as of this morning, you're out of a job. Is that correct?"

"How would you know that?" Lila snapped.

"I apologize. That's none of my business. I only ask for a few minutes of your time. Believe me when I say that this is something I know you'll find interesting."

"Fine," she said. "I need to change. Give me a minute."

Before Teddy could respond, she hung up and handed the phone back to Conrad.

"I'll be waiting for you in the car, miss," he said calmly, with a small, deferential bow.

Lila went back inside her apartment, grabbed the glass of now-watery bourbon that was sitting on the lip of the bathtub, and threw its contents down her throat. She let out a loud exhale. Seeing Teddy again had set her on edge. In her mind, he was inextricably linked to the Star Island killings. And that case was something she had wanted to forget.

She glanced in the mirror. She looked as exhausted as she felt. Since she'd turned thirty, Lila had noticed that her face was thinner and more angular, no longer round with the softness of girlhood. Dark shadows of fatigue had taken up permanent residence under her large hazel eyes.

She tied her long black hair up in a messy bun and splashed some cold water on her face, then threw on a white T-shirt and jeans. Christ, she missed her police uniform. But if she didn't have the protection of the uniform, the second best thing she could give herself was a gun. Lila quickly strapped on her ankle holster and selected her 9 mm Beretta, her favorite small gun for getting out of a pinch.

A few minutes later, Lila Day was in the backseat of the midnight-blue Bentley as it sped down the cramped and disintegrating streets of Little Havana. She blinked when opaque black scrims lowered over all the windows. She couldn't see anything.

"Conrad? What's going on?"

"Mr. Hawkins has requested that the location of his residence remain concealed."

Of course he had, Lila thought, rolling her eyes. As someone who'd had her fair share of real-life crime, she found it exasperating when people went looking for intrigue.

"I can still see out the front window," Lila pointed out to the back of the chauffeur's head.

"True, miss," Conrad said. Then he raised the solid divider between them.

With the privacy partition all the way up, Lila felt like she was riding in a black box. She didn't even know what direction they were going. She reached in her pocket for her cell phone, pulling up its GPS tracking to see the Maps app, but she couldn't get even a faint signal.

"Damn it," she said, throwing the phone down on the seat. Teddy must have installed a cell phone jammer in his car.

She leaned back on the dark leather seat and closed her eyes, preparing herself for the worst.

CHAPTER 4

By THE TIME Lila felt the car come to a definitive stop, she'd had at least an hour to work up a cold, almost breathless fury.

Conrad opened her door from the outside, and Lila stepped out to find herself in a vast and echoing garage that housed at least a dozen high-end cars. She couldn't help gasping; she'd always had a weakness for luxury cars.

"Lila," Teddy said as he walked across the room to greet her. His voice was low, and Lila found it infuriatingly calm. "Thank you for indulging my desire to meet face-to-face."

"You didn't give me much of a choice," Lila said sharply, all her anger returning to the surface.

While Teddy had once been known for his boyish handsomeness, his face was now a collection of furrows and dark shadows. He was still a good-looking man, that was undeniable—his features were as strong as Lila remembered—but there was a strained look about them now, a tightness to his square jaw and full lips that Lila hadn't seen before. He was pale, and his light brown hair had grown into an unkempt shag that was graying slightly around the temples. His round, heavily lashed brown eyes, once bright and playful, locked carefully on her.

For a moment, they regarded each other in an uncomfortable silence. "Why don't we go inside?" Teddy finally asked, walking across the enormous garage toward a large wooden door. Lila followed him, with Conrad trailing behind her. The weight of the gun strapped to her ankle was solid, reassuring.

"Quite a nice collection of cars you have here," Lila said as they passed a 1961 Ferrari GT and then a Mercedes-Benz SLR McLaren Stirling Moss. She ran her finger along it as she walked by.

"Oh, yes. Strange, I hardly drive any of them anymore," Teddy said distractedly as he climbed the stairs to the main house.

Money is always wasted on the rich, Lila thought.

The instant Teddy pushed the door open, Lila had to close her eyes against the blast of sunlight. She followed him into an enormous living room with a twenty-foot ceiling, wooden beams, and an entire glass wall overlooking a breathtaking view of the ocean.

"Please, sit with me," Teddy said, gesturing to two chairs covered in a supple leather the color of fresh cream.

Lila perched cautiously on a chair and looked outside. A perfectly green lawn was sliced in half by an infinity pool that stretched out toward the turquoise ocean.

"I was sad to hear that you lost your job," Teddy said.

Lila shrugged. "Well, that makes one of us. I wasn't too upset about it. Working hotel security isn't my calling, I guess."

"No, not that job. I mean, I was sorry that you left the police department. You were a good cop."

"Not good enough, clearly. But that's in the past now." Lila's tone was clipped. She hoped he hadn't brought her here to talk about the Star Island case, because she sure as hell didn't want to talk about it.

"Do you ever think about him?" Teddy asked, turning toward Lila.

"Who?"

"The Star Island killer, of course."

Lila stood up from her chair so fast she almost knocked it over. She didn't know what game he was playing, but she didn't need the mistakes of her past thrown in her face. "I should get going," she said, heading toward the door only to realize that she had no idea where she was and no way to get home.

"Not yet," Teddy said. "You haven't given me a chance to tell you why I've brought you here."

"Whatever it is, I'm not interested. And whatever you're searching for, you're not going to find it by keeping tabs on me. So call Conrad off, okay?"

"I watched you because I had to make sure you were the right person for the job," Teddy said, rising from his seat and walking slowly toward Lila. "Turns out you are."

"The right person for what job?"

"Catching the Star Island killer."

CHAPTER 5

IMPOSSIBLE." LILA'S VOICE was dangerously flat. "Trust me. I spent years of my life searching for the killer. And I got nowhere." The words stuck in her throat. Her failure to solve the case was a wound that wouldn't heal. And here was Teddy, picking at the scabs.

"Please, Detective," he implored. "Hear me out. If you aren't interested in my offer, I'll understand. Conrad will drive you home. You'll never hear from me again. Just five minutes, I promise."

Her curiosity getting the better of her as usual, Lila sat back down. But this time she curled her legs up in the chair, giving her quicker access to her gun, just in case.

"First," Teddy said, turning to face her, "how much do you know about the Janus Society?"

ON THAT FATEFUL New Year's Day when the Star Island killer struck, the world lost more than the twelve wealthy and influential individuals who were found dead in Chase Haverford's wine cellar. Though it was unknown at the time, the world had also been robbed of its greatest philanthropic organization—the Janus Society.

Founded in the infancy of the twentieth century, the Janus Society was an international charitable organization whose works were so admired that it had come to be known as the world's fairy godmother. Thanks to its donations, famines had been stopped, polio nearly eradicated, the ancient libraries of Timbuktu preserved, the Bolshoi Ballet saved from bankruptcy, oil spills contained, children educated, faltering economies salvaged, dying languages preserved, and on and on.

Every year on January 1, the society announced the recipient of its annual $100 million donation. Charities and environmental organizations worldwide often spent their New Year's Eve praying, hoping, that this would be their year. It was not unusual to hear of people waiting on their knees by the phone, begging for a call from the Janus Society. It had been named for a Roman god, the god of beginnings, and it provided countless opportunities for millions in need across the globe.

But the Janus Society had one extremely controversial feature: complete and utter secrecy. Not once in the hundred years the charity had been in operation was the identity of a single member exposed. Thus, people said, its donations were truly unbiased. No one could lobby the society to be picked, because no one had any idea who was even in the society, or where it was headquartered, or how many members it had.

So, when the Janus Society failed to announce the recipients of its annual donation on January 1, 2015, no one knew what to do or whom to call. It wasn't until the news of the Star Island massacre broke that people began putting two and two together. By the time that forensic accounting confirmed it, the media had been saying it for days: the Star Island twelve were the members of the Janus Society. And so the murders became the crime of the century.

I KNOW ENOUGH," Lila said in answer to Teddy's question, watching as he walked to the wall of windows overlooking the ocean. He slid open an enormous glass door, filling the air-conditioned room with a damp, ocean-scented breeze.

"Here's a question," Teddy said, changing the subject. "When you're in pursuit of a criminal, what's the most important yet most quickly depleted resource you have at your disposal?"

"Patience," Lila shot back. "I'm running quite low on it now, as a matter of fact."

"What I'm talking about," Teddy went on, ignoring her, "is time. When you're solving a case, time is of the essence, isn't it? The more time passes, the farther the murderers can run, the hazier the memories become."

"Yeah, something like that."

"Time goes on and people just want to forget about the past. Especially if it involves something like a mass murder."

After a long pause, Teddy sat back down in the chair next to Lila. "Exactly how long did you look for the Star Island killer?"

"A little over two years."

"And why did you stop?"

"Is there a point to all this?" Lila asked impatiently.

"There is," Teddy assured her. "Just tell me why you left the force."

"My chief pulled me off the case. But I'm guessing you already knew that."

Teddy nodded.

She continued, "He said I'd burned too many bridges. That I was doing more harm than good. After that, I knew it was time to go. I mean, what's the point if the bad guys get away with it?"

Silently, Conrad walked across the room and slid the door shut. The room instantly became ice cold once again.

"So you gave up?"

"I didn't have a choice. I wasn't getting anywhere. My chief was right. I'd pissed off too many people. No one likes it when a cop comes knocking on their door," Lila said. "But the rich seemed to take particular offense."

"It's not that we take particular offense," Teddy said with a smile. "It's just that we can usually buy people's silence. It's one of the few really valuable things that can be bought in this world."

Lila let out an exasperated sigh. "You said all you needed was five minutes. So tell me. Why am I here?"

"I've already told you. To catch the Star Island killer, once and for all."

"What makes you think this time will be any different?"

"This time," Teddy said with a hint of a smile on his lips, "you're going to solve the murder before it happens."

Lila let out a sudden snort of laughter. "And how exactly would I do that?" she asked in a mocking tone.

"Forget about that for now," Teddy replied. "Let's just say it's a given. What if you could go back to several months before the murders. Do you think you'd be able to catch the killer?"

For once, Lila was at a loss for words. What was he getting at?

"Do you?" he asked again, emphatically.

"Yes," she blurted out. "Of course I could. Knowing what

I know now, I'd be able to find that sick fuck in a matter of seconds."

At that, Teddy began to nod his head, a smile lighting up his face. "I knew you were the right person," he said.

"The right person?" Lila repeated, still uncertain what he was getting at.

"What I'm about to tell you may sound unbelievable." Teddy looked directly into her eyes, holding her gaze. "You're going to go back in time to find the Star Island killer."

"Oh, God." Lila closed her eyes and pressed her fingers against her temples. For a brief second, she'd let herself hope that Teddy had found some new lead, that he might actually have something for her. She scolded herself for her stupidity.

"Of course you don't believe me. I understand." Teddy stumbled over his words, talking quickly and anxiously. "But if you'll just let me prove it to you—"

"Listen," Lila interrupted. "I don't have time for this. I've had a long night. So if you'll excuse me." She stood up from her chair and walked toward the door to the garage.

"Of course." Teddy's expression was unreadable. "Conrad will drive you home."

Lila kept her eyes glued to the black partition as Teddy's car carried her back to reality. She kept replaying the scene in her head, the fact that Teddy thought he could actually send her back in time, the way his eyes had lit up with excitement as he described his plan to her. Well, she thought, the history books are full of rich people losing their minds. And now Teddy Hawkins was just one more eccentric billionaire gone over the edge.

But why was Teddy so fixated on the Star Island case? Maybe he'd lost friends in the massacre. Maybe he was worried for his own safety. Maybe—she cut off her speculation. Who cared anymore? If he wanted to take over the search for the Star Island killer, then good for him. Lila wanted nothing to do with it.

Let him walk into the labyrinth, she thought. She knew from experience that there was no coming out in one piece.

CHAPTER 6

LATER THAT EVENING, Lila was curled up on the threadbare couch in her apartment, staring blankly at the TV. She'd been in a state of agitated numbness all day, ever since her meeting with Teddy. Her thoughts were racing, but the rest of her felt lethargic and exhausted. She blamed Teddy. All the memories she'd tried to erase from her mind had been churned up by him and his ridiculous plan.

Suddenly, there was a loud knock at the door.

"Not again." She cursed, securing the tie of her silk robe around her waist as she quickly walked to the door. But no one was there. All she found was a large manila envelope sitting on the concrete landing.

Lila quickly grabbed the envelope and, shoving aside her slight hesitation (didn't danger always lurk in strange packages left on doorsteps?), tore it apart. Inside was a *Miami Herald* and a note that read:

> *Lila. You are holding in your hands proof that time travel exists. This is tomorrow's newspaper. I am writing to you from the future. Now do you believe?*
>
> *—Teddy*

"This guy is relentless," Lila said aloud as she inspected the newspaper. True enough, the date on the paper was tomorrow's date—July 21, 2018—but after all, Teddy Hawkins was a man with unlimited resources. How hard could it be to manufacture a fake newspaper?

Then she had a thought. The lottery results. As she flipped through the paper and found the numbers, Lila looked up at the clock. It was 11:15 P.M. Her heart racing, holding the night's Mega Money lottery numbers in her hand, she turned on the TV, switching channels until she found the one she wanted. A smiling woman in a red dress stood behind a Plexiglas cube full of airborne balls that bounced like kernels in a popcorn popper.

"Ladies and gentlemen, welcome to the Mega Money lottery drawing for tonight, July twentieth," said the woman. Her teeth were refrigerator white and her hair was teased into a hysterical meringue. "All right, then. Let's get to it."

One by one, five balls were sucked away from their furious tumbling and shot up a Plexiglas tube. "The numbers for tonight are: twelve . . . five . . . two . . . thirty. And the Mega ball number is . . . thirty-seven."

Lila looked down at the paper she was holding. There, in her hands, were the same numbers: 12-5-2-30-37.

"Impossible," she whispered.

Could Teddy have rigged the lottery? Maybe that was how he'd amassed such spectacular wealth, and now he was simply toying with her. Maybe this TV broadcast was closed-circuit, made only for her benefit as part of an elaborate hoax. Anything seemed more likely than the notion that, all by himself and without any media attention, Teddy Hawkins had built a time machine in his glass mansion by the sea.

She checked the lottery numbers online, just to make sure all the facts lined up. A mixture of shock and something closer to dread flooded through her when she saw that the numbers were exactly the same.

THE NEXT MORNING, the pink dawn light slanted into the living room as a mockingbird started to sing out in Lila's rundown corner of Miami. She still sat on her old couch, her bare feet up on the cluttered coffee table, the newspaper from the future spread across her lap. Sleep had been an impossibility. She'd spent the night reading through the paper, looking for anything—a clue, a mistake, a slipup in the forgery. But all she'd found were more questions.

Profound fatigue made her body feel almost weightless. Just as her eyes were starting to close at last, there was a loud knock at the door.

She looked at her watch: 6:18 A.M. There was no question in her mind as to who was doing the knocking. Rising slowly from the couch, Lila walked to the door and unlocked it. She turned back toward her bedroom, calling out over her shoulder, "Hi, Conrad. I just need a minute to get dressed. Then we can go."

In a little under an hour, Lila was back at Teddy's estate. Conrad led her behind the house to the pool.

"Mr. Hawkins is finishing his morning swim. It shouldn't be too long a wait."

Lila perched on the corner of a chaise longue, watching Teddy's form cut through the water, lap after lap, as if he was part sea creature. A tiny woman in a crisp white apron and with the kindly face of a Beatrix Potter squirrel brought over a

tray burdened with fresh fruit juices, coffee, and an entire bou-
langerie's worth of croissants, brioche, and other baked goods.

To her surprise, Lila realized she was starving and began to
greedily pile her plate full of pastries. She was just about to take
a large bite of a chocolate croissant when she heard Teddy's wet
footsteps *slap slap slap* on the warm concrete toward her. The
sun was hot enough to evaporate his footprints the second his
toes left the ground.

The early-morning light shone directly in her eyes. Using
her hand to shield her gaze, she saw Teddy smirking slightly
as he picked up a towel from a beach chair and wrapped it low
around his waist. Lila noted, almost clinically, how young and
strong his body was. The instant he caught her looking at him,
she cut her gaze away.

"So, do I have your attention?" Teddy sat down at the table,
pouring himself a glass of orange juice from a crystal pitcher.
Lila didn't appreciate his air of self-satisfaction.

"Okay," she conceded, "I'll bite. Getting the *Miami Herald*
delivered to my door five hours before it went to press is fairly
astonishing, even for someone of your means. So, let me ask
you, what kind of scheme are you running?"

"It's not a scheme at all. It's the work of science."

"The science of forgery, maybe. I just wish I'd gotten the
paper in time to actually buy a lottery ticket. I could've made
myself a millionaire last night."

"Trust me," Teddy said. "What I'm about to show you is
worth a hundred times any lottery winnings." He stood up and
began walking toward a small cabana behind the pool, in the
shadow of his grand estate. "Follow me," he added, beckoning
Lila over.

The inside of the cabana was covered in a kaleidoscope of Moroccan tiles and contained nothing more than a few pieces of weather-beaten wood furniture. Only a large David Hockney swimming pool painting decorated the walls.

"Have a seat," Teddy said. "I'll be a moment." He went into a changing room, closing the door behind him.

"Okay, what is it you're going to show me?" Lila called out.

"Something that will change your life." Teddy emerged wearing an all-white hooded hazmat suit.

"Nice outfit," Lila said with a laugh.

Teddy ignored her. "Please step in," he said, waving her into the small room.

Lila crossed the floor to step inside the windowless changing room. Teddy threw her a folded hazmat suit sealed in plastic wrap.

"Put this on," he instructed.

"Is this really necessary?"

"You can't proceed without one."

"As you wish," Lila shot back.

Once she'd pulled the paper-like fabric over her jeans and tank top, Teddy closed and bolted the door behind her. The moment the lock was thrown, the cabana was saturated in a bright white fluorescent light.

Teddy placed his palm on a silver screen on the wall that Lila hadn't noticed earlier. Red laser beams scanned the contours of his hand, and then the panel emitted three short, high-pitched beeps of acceptance. Without warning, a door in the floor gaped open, revealing a steep staircase that reached deep into the earth and disappeared into a cold, bluish light. The air from below was nearly arctic, raising goose bumps on Lila's arms.

Lila felt light-headed, like she'd stepped inside a science fiction movie, leaving the real world and its rules far behind. She watched in a daze as Teddy walked down a couple of the steel steps.

He paused halfway down and turned to look back up at Lila. His face appeared ghostly in the blue light. "Aren't you coming?" he asked. When she didn't answer, he tried again. "Do you trust me?"

"Not in the least," Lila replied drily.

"But you'll follow me anyway, won't you?" Teddy looked at her curiously. "Really, I've got to say, few things delight me more than a fearless woman." A boyish grin lit up his face. "Come on. I have a lot to show you and we don't have much time."

A sensible person would have walked away, Lila knew that. But she wasn't one of those people. And so she grabbed the railing and began, slowly, to descend the staircase.

CHAPTER 7

AFTER A COUPLE minutes of fumbling her way down the stairs, Lila saw Teddy come to a stop. She squinted in the dim light as things came into focus and saw that he was standing at a gigantic door set in a thick stone wall. He placed his hand on its illuminated panel until his handprint was recognized with a series of beeps. Teddy then spun the five-pronged spindle wheel at the door's center and turned back toward Lila. "Do you promise to tell no one about what you see here today?"

Lila nodded.

Teddy pulled the heavy door open, and Lila drew in a sharp breath at what lay inside.

Every inch of the floor, walls, and ceiling was covered in thin gold foil, with the exception of a twelve-foot-high, fifteen-foot-wide jade geodesic dome in the middle of the room. An oily smell hung in the air.

"Is this real?" Lila asked, her brain struggling to absorb the strange scene.

"As real as you and me." Teddy swept his hands close to the surface of the polished jade dome. The gold foil made everything in the room seem like it was glowing.

"As a child I always fantasized about traveling through time," he said quietly.

"How did you do it?" Lila was a trained interrogator. She wanted to believe Teddy, but if he was lying, she'd catch him in it. "The newspaper, I mean."

"Oh, that? Very simple. I met with you yesterday morning. You got the paper last night. This morning, the newspaper was delivered at six thirty. Then I came down here, put it in the machine, and sent it back in time."

"So, you beamed the paper to my front door?"

"I wish. I haven't developed the technology for that level of precision yet. I had a courier pick the paper up from where it landed and deliver it to your door."

"So when did you call the courier?"

Teddy shook his head. "I can tell you're dwelling on specifics. But I understand that this is tough to swallow, so I'll be as clear as possible. I knew I had to prove to you that I could send you back in time. That's when I thought of the newspaper idea. It seemed the easiest way. I knew I had to wait until today to send the paper back in time. But I called the courier yesterday evening to have them pick it up."

"So, last night you called a courier to pick up an envelope that you didn't send until today?" Lila asked. Her brain felt fizzy as she tried to wrap her mind around this contorted chronology.

"I understand that it seems impossible."

"You're right. It does." Lila fell silent as she walked around the dome. She reached out to touch the gleaming surface.

"Stop! Don't touch it!" Teddy shouted, his voice startling her. "Please be careful," he added in a softer tone. "This is an extremely controlled environment. Just one smudge on this surface could alter the machine in ways I can't predict."

Lila raised her hands to the sky, feeling like a criminal caught in the act.

"Perhaps it would be better if we went somewhere else to talk." Teddy looked around. "Conrad?"

Lila turned to see a panel of gold foil lowering, revealing a window. Conrad sat behind the glass in a long room lined in wall-to-wall computer screens. He was hunched over a formidable panel of flashing lights and switches.

"Yes, sir?" Conrad's voice came out over an invisible speaker.

"Open the control room door," Teddy commanded, and part of the wall immediately slid open.

Lila and Teddy joined Conrad in the control room, which looked out over the jade dome. Her head still reeling, Lila sat in a black leather office chair behind a dozen computer screens. Teddy wordlessly took the seat next to her. They both stared straight ahead at the gleaming dome.

"I'm sure you have questions for me," Teddy finally said.

"You bet your ass I do." Lila drummed her fingers anxiously on the control panel. "First off, how does it work?"

"How familiar are you with theoretical particle physics and quantum field theory?"

"You seem to know a lot about me. What do you think the answer to that question is?"

"I'd say you don't know much."

"You'd say right. So, in English, tell me how this thing works."

"I'm sure you know that everything is made up of tiny atoms, right?"

Lila gave Teddy a slow, unsure nod.

"So, even though this table is solid," Teddy knocked on

the desk in front of both of them, "it's actually made up of tiny molecules that are filled with holes and wrinkles. Loads of empty space. Well, time is the exact same way. It's not as solid as you think it is. Within the quantum foam of time, there are actually little crevices that are minuscule shortcuts through space and time. We call those wormholes."

Lila tried to give her full attention to Teddy, but her concentration was continually broken by Conrad, who was busy in the corner carefully loading stacks of hundred-dollar bills into a steel briefcase.

Teddy continued. "What I've been able to do is capture and enlarge these wormholes so that objects and people can travel through them. To put it as simply as I can, I've created a path through the fourth dimension."

On top of the money, Conrad placed a passport, and other documents and various papers.

"Are you still listening to me, Lila?" Teddy asked.

"Yes, wormhole. Quantum whatever. Sure. Why haven't you told the world yet? You could make billions."

Teddy shrugged. "I already have billions. Let's just say I'm not ready to share this technology with the world."

"You'd rather use it to send me back in time to stop a murderer?"

"No," Teddy interrupted, his voice low and urgent. "Not to stop the murders. You can't save those people, Lila."

"Excuse me?" she demanded, incredulous. "You expect me to travel back in time to witness a mass murder and do nothing to stop it?"

"If you stopped the murders, you would be violating several major laws of the universe. And there's no way to predict the outcome. It's too risky. There are rules to traveling through time, inviolable rules."

"Such as?" Lila asked with a slight sneer.

"Such as, you must do your utmost to avoid altering the course of time. That means you are forbidden from killing *anyone* or preventing *anyone* from being killed. You cannot and must not stop the Star Island massacre. If you did, you could be responsible for altering the present in unimaginable ways."

"Then what's the point of any of it?"

"Justice!" he exclaimed, his eyes glowing with determination. "What could be more powerful than bringing this murderer to justice?" Lila wondered again why Teddy was so invested in catching the Star Island killer.

"Tell me," she asked. "What's in it for you? Why are you as obsessed with this case as I am?"

"I have my reasons. That's all you need to know," he answered quietly.

"Okay, well, why bring me into this thing? Why don't you go instead?"

"To find the killer, you'll have to become part of that world. You'll have to infiltrate the Janus Society as deeply as you can. I was already part of that world. There's no way I could go back. That's very important, Lila, that you never let your past and future selves meet. Besides, you said it yourself—no one else is as obsessed with this case as you are. Not to mention that you're the best detective Miami's ever seen."

She disliked it when people tried to appeal to her vanity. "So you want me to time-travel to the past and then go undercover?"

"Precisely."

"And who am I going to be, exactly?"

"Your new identity will have to be someone of extreme wealth. That's important. None of the Janus Society members will trust you if you're not as rich as, or richer than, they are. They'll suspect you're after their money. I'll be giving you unlimited access to one of my accounts."

"I don't think I can pull off the whole high-society thing. They'll sniff me out in a minute," Lila said.

"Never underestimate the power of money. If you have enough of it, you'll be shocked at how quickly doors open up for you. And besides," he added, with a wicked grin, "this is Miami, after all, not Newport. Everyone is new money here."

Lila nodded, then thought of something else. "I can't let the members of the Janus Society know that I know they're in the club—they kept it a secret even from their own family members, their spouses, their children. How do you think I'll be able to gain access to the world's best-kept secret?"

"With this," Teddy said. He tossed a thumb drive into Lila's lap. "I've spent the last three years putting together that database, with detailed profiles of all the victims and potential suspects. I employed countless researchers. That's the most complete record in existence of the evidence you might need to solve the case."

For the second time that day, Lila was at a loss for words.

"I understand it's a lot to take in. But I want you to know that I am a man of endless resources and options. I speak with confidence when I say that you are the only person in the world who can do this."

Lila frowned, thinking suddenly of something. "You've sent

a paper through time, but have you sent a person back before? What's to say that I won't break up into a bunch of scattered molecules?"

"It's perfectly safe. I've done it, and so has Conrad."

Looking at both of these men, Lila somehow didn't find this news terribly reassuring. "Okay, let's say I do agree to this, and I'm not saying I will. What are the details?"

"You'll find an extensive outline of the plan on the thumb drive you have in your hand, under the filename Camilla Dayton. That will be your alias. You'll be arriving in late September 2014. You'll have three months to work undercover. And you'll return here, to the present, the day after the murders—January 1, 2015—at precisely 4:16 P.M."

"Why three months?"

"I don't feel comfortable sending you back for any more time than that. There are too many variables that are impossible to control." He looked at her intently. "Let's hope it's long enough."

"Will I lose those months of my life here?"

"Wormholes don't work the same in both directions. It'll be a few days here, not a few months. You'll arrive back here on . . . what day is it, Conrad?"

"July twenty-seventh, at 9:36 A.M., sir."

Lila thought about asking for clarification but decided against it. Whatever answer Teddy gave her would probably only leave her more confused.

"You can review everything tonight," Teddy was saying. "If you say no, that's fine. You'll never hear from me again. But I hope, out of courtesy, you would keep all of this to yourself. Conrad will take you home now. Please, think long and hard about my offer."

"I'll think about it. I promise you that much." Lila stood up, suddenly anxious to get home and review the thumb drive.

"That's all I ask," Teddy said, nodding to Conrad. "Please take Ms. Day home."

CHAPTER 8

LESS THAN TWENTY-FOUR hours later, Lila found herself sitting alone in the belly of a time machine, wondering frantically if she'd made the right decision. What had earlier seemed like a risk worth taking now appeared to be possibly the dumbest, most dangerous idea of her life.

Once again, she was wearing the white hazmat suit. Her hands were sweating, and her breath was quick and shallow in her chest. She tried to calm down by thinking of how she and Teddy had gone over everything: the plan, the cover story, what she would do once she was back in 2014.

This was her chance, Lila reminded herself. Her chance to finally bring a killer to justice, to solve the case that had ruined her life and start over fresh. That was what she tried to remember as she sat there praying she would emerge from Teddy's insane contraption alive.

The cockpit of the jade dome was a glorious combination of steel, quartz, and leather—like the inside of a high-end Swiss watch. Suddenly, the lights went out, leaving Lila in total darkness.

"Hello?" she cried. "Hello?" There was nothing. No light. No sound. Then a tremendous whirring noise erupted all around her. Lila immediately closed her eyes. It felt like an invisible pressure was pushing down upon her, pressing into her skull. Her ears popped painfully.

In the steel briefcase strapped underneath her seat, Lila had $20,000 in cash, a fake passport and New York driver's license, a checkbook and debit card linked to Teddy's bank account with a balance of $100 million, and, most important, Teddy's thumb drive.

She'd spent all night reviewing his countless files, but she'd seen only the tip of the iceberg. They were exhaustive and seemingly endless. He had somehow gotten his hands on the police files from her own investigation as well as those from the FBI, CIA, and Florida state police. It would take a year just to read it all.

So last night, Lila had paid the most attention to the file on Camilla Dayton, the new persona Teddy had created for her. He'd developed an extensive backstory for Camilla, along with suggestions of how Lila could insinuate herself into the world of the Janus Society members. His work was impressive and reassuring.

"We are T minus five from inflationary vacuum state," Conrad said, a mechanical precision to his voice. Lila opened her eyes to see that a screen had flickered to life before her. It showed Teddy in the control room, with Conrad at his side.

"Wait!" Lila shouted. All the whirring and the darkness and danger of this adventure suddenly felt much too real.

"Relax, Lila. I know you can do this," Teddy yelled. "The next time I see you, you'll have solved the Star Island murders. Remember that!"

"Four." Conrad continued the countdown. The sound of the whirring increased to a steady, high-pitched shriek.

"Three."

Panic flooded Lila, making time feel faster, and her body feel smaller and distorted.

"Two," Conrad said. The screen flickered off and the dome began to shake furiously.

"One." Everything was suddenly still and black, as though Lila had been dropped off a cliff. She opened her mouth and screamed as loud as she could, but there was no one to hear her. Her screams just evaporated into the surrounding darkness.

WHEN HER HEARTBEAT finally settled and her breath came back to her, Lila opened her eyes to find that she was lying on a dirty cement floor in a small cinder-block room with a red corrugated metal door. A single fluorescent tube lit up the room with a harsh, buzzing luminosity. The steel briefcase sat next to her.

She'd survived.

She scrambled to her feet and stripped off the hazmat suit. Clicking open the briefcase, Lila was relieved to see all its contents were, like her, miraculously intact.

It was just as Teddy had said it would be. He had described this room to a T. Why the wormhole emptied out into this bleak storage unit in North Miami was a mystery even to him. It was the one spatial link he'd managed to cut through the fabric of time.

Was she really in the past?

Lila rolled up the metal door, causing a racket that thundered around the empty storage facility, and peered down the long hallway. There wasn't a person in sight. She noted the number on the door: 2867. She would have to come back here by 4:16 P.M. on New Year's Day to return to the future. By then she would know who the Star Island killer was.

She headed toward the exit sign, walking in a combat crouch, her back pressed close to the wall, the briefcase in her hand.

When she stepped out of the storage building, the roar of the expressway and the crushing heat of the noon sun nearly flattened her. All of her senses felt heightened, sharper than normal. Luckily, Lila knew where she was—Miami's shittiest corner, by I-95 and Gratigny Parkway. About a ten-minute drive from the glamour and opulence of Star Island, but, from where she stood, it might as well have been a continent away.

Spotting a convenience store, she crossed the busy street and walked inside. As the automatic doors closed behind her, the air-conditioning hit her like an arctic blast. The effect was dizzying. A woman with pockmarked skin stood behind the counter.

"Excuse me. Can you call me a cab?" Lila asked.

"Use the pay phone," the woman said, scowling. She pointed to the corner of the store. "It's over there." Her rainbow-shaped eyebrows were drawn too high on her forehead, making her face look permanently surprised.

"I don't have any change."

"Then you gotta buy something."

Exasperated, Lila turned her back to the woman and opened her briefcase, sliding a hundred-dollar bill out from the stack.

She threw a paper on the counter and slapped the bill on top of it. "Will this work?" she snapped.

"You don't got anything smaller?" the woman whined.

"Nope."

Lila's annoyance with the woman instantly evaporated

when she saw the date on the *Miami Herald* she was buying. Thursday, September 25, 2014. *It's real,* Lila thought. *It's real.*

"Um, hello?" the convenience store clerk said, pulling Lila out of her daze. She looked up to find the woman impatiently waiting to hand over her change.

"Thanks," Lila said, still distracted. The woman, with a roll of her eyes, turned her attention to stacking chewing tobacco tins into a pyramid.

Using the pay phone, Lila called a taxi. "I need a cab at the corner of Gratigny and Northwest Twenty-Second. Going to the Ritz-Carlton. Yes, thank you."

She hung up the phone, then stepped outside to wait for the cab. Once again she moved from the arctic air-conditioning to the blisteringly hot, exhaust-filled streets. To live in Miami was to be too hot or too cold at almost all times. The fever and the chill. It was not a land of moderation.

The cab soon pulled up, and Lila found herself heading south toward Miami Beach with the windows down, letting the wind rake through her long black hair.

In her mind, one sentence repeated over and over. "My name is Camilla Dayton. My name is Camilla Dayton. My name is . . ."

CHAPTER 9

CHECKING INTO THE Ritz's five-thousand-dollar-a-night ocean-front suite with no luggage except a metal briefcase raised a few eyebrows behind the flower-laden check-in desk. But once Lila handed over the credit card in Camilla Dayton's name, which could easily shoulder the $50,000 hold that was placed on it, she might as well have been the Queen of England.

A young man with model good looks and heavy blond bangs appeared beside her as if by magic. "Just this way, Ms. Dayton."

Her room was breathtaking. Decorated like a Balinese paradise, it was all warm wood and white furniture, with a mesmerizing view. The sweet smell of tropical flowers gently scented the air.

"Do you have a hair salon on the premises?" Lila asked, after the boy had given her a brief tour.

"Of course. It's located on the second floor next to the south pool. Would you like me to get you an appointment?"

"Yes. Right away." Though Lila highly doubted she'd run into anyone she knew at the Ritz, she needed to look as different from herself as she could, as fast as she could.

"John Darling runs the salon. I'm sure you know of him."

Lila nodded her head, though she had absolutely no idea who he was. "He's impossible to book, but I can always pull some strings." The bellhop gave her a salacious wink. "For a friend."

Once he secured her a salon appointment, Lila tipped him a hundred dollars. After all, she knew it paid to have friends in low places.

John Darling turned out to be a muscular, taciturn man with arms covered in tattoos and long hair the color and texture of cornsilk. In a little under six hours—and with the help of no fewer than four other hairdressers—he turned Lila's long black mane into a sleek, shoulder-length blond bob.

"From feral to fab," John said, combing his fingers through her transformed hair. Lila regarded herself in the mirror and was shocked to see someone else look back. It was a jarring experience, seeing herself as just another South Beach blonde, the women she'd spent her whole life detesting.

Pleased to meet you, Camilla, she thought. The razored edge of the cut fell elegantly right above her prominent collarbones, and the side-swept bangs created a perfect frame for her face. She knew, objectively, that this was the kind of haircut most women dreamed of. But she couldn't think of it as anything more than a disguise.

When the salon receptionist told Lila how much she owed, Lila's first reaction was to slap her across the face. Spending roughly the amount she'd made on the force in a month for a cut and color was tantamount to larceny. But Lila choked back her impulsive reaction and simply smiled, placing the credit card on the counter between them.

It was time for the clothes.

Lila spent the remainder of the day at the mercy of the shopgirls of Miami's priciest boutiques. Tom Ford. Bulgari.

Gucci. Dior. Alexander McQueen. Christian Louboutin. And what seemed like a lifetime at the makeup counters in Barneys. These names meant nothing to her. Luckily, Teddy had written detailed instructions for her—where to go, who to ask for, what to say. In every store, just as she was instructed, Lila did the exact same thing. She would walk in, identify the most intimidating salesgirl in the shop, and then tell her, "I've just moved here from New York. I need an entire new wardrobe, and money is no object."

For Lila, it was almost a game to watch how the faces of the shopgirls transformed from indifference to delight once she made it clear that she had limitless money to spend. In an instant, there was champagne in her hand, a large private dressing room, and a steady stream of outfits for her to try on. Most of the clothes struck her as idiotic. And the cost was obscene. Three hundred and fifty dollars for a T-shirt. Fourteen hundred dollars for a skirt. After the first few items, she stopped looking at the price tags.

"Rich, gorgeous, and a perfect size two," one shopgirl cooed into Lila's ear as she zipped her into a particularly form-fitting strapless dress. "You must've made a deal with the devil."

Later that evening, once the bellboys had everything unpacked and put away in her hotel closets, Lila went to the minibar, grabbed a tiny bottle of Wild Turkey, and poured it over ice. She sank onto her terrace with a satisfied sigh, letting the sound of the ocean cascade over her. Then she picked up the phone and called the front desk.

"Yes, Ms. Dayton?"

"Please connect me to the Maserati dealership in Palm Beach." An enormous smile spread across her lips. She'd been saving the best part of her day for last.

Money wasn't important to Lila. Clothes, even less so. Shopping all day had felt like the worst form of punishment Teddy could inflict on her. But cars—luxury automobiles, that is—were a different story entirely. Lila could barely believe that finally, and in the most unlikely circumstance, she would be able to buy the car of her dreams.

"Connecting you now, Ms. Dayton." The phone rang. On the third ring, a man with a deep Italian accent picked up.

"Ferrari Maserati of Palm Beach, how can I help you?"

"Yes. Hello," Lila said. "I'm looking to purchase a 2014 Maserati GranTurismo MC convertible in black. Do you have one on the lot?"

"Yes, signorina, we do have that car. But not in black. We have it in a deep red color called Rosso Trionfale." The man rolled his *r*'s so comedically, Lila wondered if the accent was a put-on. "It's a beautiful color. The same as the Maserati Italian racing cars from the nineteen fifties. *Molto bello. Classico.* Much better than black. Would you like to come down for a test drive."

"The problem is I'm in Miami and don't have the time. Can I just give you my credit card number and you can bring the car and the papers to my hotel? It's been a long day, and I'd rather handle it this way."

There was a pause on the other end of the phone.

"Is this . . . *come si dice* . . . a punk?" the man asked in his heavy accent. "You want to buy a car over the phone? Signorina, this is not a pizza for delivery."

"Look, I just want to get the car. How much is it?"

"Let me pull up the information." Lila heard the sound of his fingers furiously hitting the computer keys as the man muttered something in Italian. "As is, the total cost of the GT convertible that we have on the floor is one hundred and thirteen thousand, five hundred and thirty-four dollars."

"That's fine. How soon will I have it?"

It took several more minutes, and the guarantee that she'd tip him five thousand dollars for his trouble, to convince the wary salesman to drive the car seventy miles south to Miami.

With that little treat making her feel a slight buzz of good fortune, Lila unpacked her newly purchased MacBook Air and brought it out to the veranda, along with more Wild Turkey mini bottles and Teddy's thumb drive. She sat in silence as she reviewed the files, beginning to chart out her next day. With a little over three months to complete her mission, she had no time to waste.

Three hours later, her immersion in the files was abruptly halted when her room phone rang. It was the front desk telling her that her car had arrived. She hurried down to the lobby. Even though she had a closet full of designer clothes, she was still wearing her old jeans and tank top. Everything else felt like a straitjacket. Tomorrow she'd dress the part. Tonight was for her.

Seeing that car sitting there waiting for her, all glossy and gorgeous, Lila felt that maybe, somehow, this would all turn out okay. She signed the papers, handed a check for an obscene amount of money to the flabbergasted Italian, and climbed into her new Maserati, almost pinching herself to make sure it wasn't a dream.

"Thanks, Teddy," she murmured, grinning widely.

Even in South Beach, the land where audacious beauty and absolute weirdness collide, where no one looks twice at a drag queen Rollerblading down the boardwalk in a mermaid costume, everyone who saw the beautiful blonde in the red Maserati gave her a second glance. But Lila was oblivious to their admiring stares. All that mattered to her was the feel of the car as it raced along the road.

Though she was in the past, never before had Lila felt so alive, so present, so *now*.

CHAPTER 10

WHEN LILA AWOKE the next morning, it took her a few confused seconds to remember where she was. The previous day had been as surreal as a dream, and now her mind was scrambling to make sense of it all.

She had slept fitfully amid the grandeur of her oceanfront suite. The bed felt too big, the mattress too soft. The sounds of the waves' rhythmic crashing and the wind-rustled palm fronds kept waking her up. But that white noise of the tropics was nothing compared to the riot of thoughts endlessly circling through her head. Her mind was buzzing with lists, ideas, plans, and theories about the Star Island massacre.

She had a second chance, and this time she wasn't going to blow it.

Now it was 10:00 A.M., and she was anxious to get a start on the day. Grabbing the laptop from the pillow beside her, Lila got up, put on a robe, and ordered a pot of black coffee from room service. As she passed by a mirror, she did a double take, startled at the sight of the stranger looking back at her. She ran her hand thoughtfully through her blond tresses, studying her reflection, and smiled. Not because of the hair—that would take some getting used to. But, for the first time in years, Lila was actually looking forward to the day ahead of her.

She hadn't felt this way since she left the force. Once again, she felt driven. She had a purpose.

After an extended battle with blush brushes, lipsticks, and mascara wands, Lila finally felt ready to face the world as Camilla Dayton. Her first target would be Effie Webster.

Of the twelve victims murdered by the Star Island killer that New Year's morning, only three were women. Vivienne Hunter, an aged widow who'd earned her fortune selling drugstore lipsticks and face creams to middle-class moms looking for glam on the cheap. Meredith Sloan, age thirty-five, who, along with her husband, had founded Miami's premier luxury real estate company and somehow gotten even richer after the floor fell out from under the economy in 2008. And Effie Webster, twenty-eight-year-old socialite, known for a weakness for South American soccer players and a penchant for trouble. Though she had once been South Beach's girl du jour, Effie had started cooling off in 2010. By 2014, she was approaching thirty and flirting with has-been status.

With his typical obsessive preparedness, Teddy had suggested multiple ways for Lila to insinuate herself into the Janus Society's social circle. Number one on the list was befriending Effie Webster. Unlike the other society members, Effie was around Lila's age, single, and fantastically social. Becoming a member of her entourage wouldn't be a total impossibility.

But Lila dreaded it. There were few things she found as tiresome as spoiled society girls, and Effie was goddess emeritus of all budding Miami socialites. And though she hated to admit it, Lila was worried Effie would see through her cover in a second. Teddy had said that money would open doors for her, but was it enough to stop Effie from sniffing Camilla Dayton out as a fake?

Lila left the Ritz around noon, got in her car, and drove parallel to the turquoise waters of the ocean along palm-tree-lined streets until she reached the stark white Art Deco masterpiece that was the Delano Hotel.

One of the sections of Teddy's thumb drive had been filled with meticulous agendas for all twelve victims during their last few months of life. The thoroughness of his investigative work astounded Lila. With the Miami police department's limited resources, she had only been able to scratch the surface of the information Teddy had uncovered and obsessively cataloged. Thanks to his work she knew what all twelve victims were doing that very day, Friday, September 26, 2014. Chase Haverford was in Rotterdam, finalizing the details of his new hotel. Vivienne Hunter was at the office of one of her South Beach dermatologists for her second minor cosmetic procedure that week. Theo von Fick, the German manufacturing baron, was holed up with his newest mistress, Loulou, in the South Beach condo he had just bought for her. The number one world-ranked tennis champion, Sam Logan, was in Beijing, playing at the China Open. The young Nigerian cement titan Adebayo "Johnny" Oluwa was in Lagos on business. Fernando Salazar, the Cuban-born political kingmaker, was hosting an anti-Castro convention in Miami with a few dozen fellow exiles. Retired TV morning show host Rusty Browder was deep-sea fishing off Key West with some old Sigma Chi buddies. Meredith Sloan was showing multimillion-dollar mansions to a Bulgarian émigré. Egyptian financier Khaled Fathallah was in Doha for the wedding of his youngest sister. Neville Crawley, the alcoholic heir apparent to his family's massive strip mall fortune, was doing what he did every day, hitting the links with a stiff gin and tonic in hand. Javier Martinez, the Argentine-born, internationally renowned art dealer, was flying back to Miami from an art fair in Berlin.

And Effie Webster, the most predictable and homebound member of the group, was lounging poolside at the Delano Hotel.

The moment Lila walked toward the Delano pool, she spotted Effie, sprawled out on a chaise longue, getting sprayed with Evian mist by a cabana boy. She was surrounded by a gaggle of bronzed and athletic men wearing the tiny Speedos that only those sculpted like Greek gods can get away with. Lila selected a spot by the pool so close to Effie that she could smell her suntan oil.

With her Hermès beach towel, Fendi swimsuit, and oversize Gucci glasses, Lila hoped that she came across as a South Beach ingenue, but inside, she was cringing. She hadn't ever been so naked in public, and kept nervously readjusting the tiny triangles of overpriced fabric covering her chest.

Glancing around, Lila noticed that everyone at the pool was sizing her up. She closed her eyes instinctively, letting the hot, bright sun kick up a light show of orange and red-colored splashes beneath her fluttering eyelids. Suddenly, there was shade. She opened her eyes to find a cabana boy standing over her, the large Evian mister in his hand.

"Care for a spritz, miss?" the boy said in a thick Cuban accent.

"Yes, thank you." Lila felt the delicate mist cool her skin as she kept her eye on her target.

Seeing Effie Webster in the flesh—alive, beautiful, and unaware of the horrors awaiting her—felt strange, like seeing a ghost, or a fictional character. Lila had spent so much time reviewing everything she could about Effie's death that she felt almost sick to her stomach at the thought of actually meeting her. Effie had very long, almost white-blond hair, which she was wearing in a casual topknot. Her dark blue eyes were deeply set into her oval face, and her delicate nose and chin were perfectly shaped by an expert surgeon's scalpel. Her famous figure, which was artfully displayed in a silver string bikini, was a combination of good genes and utter devotion to exercise and diet. No one could look quite that good without it being the number one priority and guiding principle of her life.

Lila watched as Effie flirted outrageously with the four gelled and waxed young men surrounding her. While one put tanning lotion on her back, she made eyes at another. The third guy was off getting her a drink from the bar, while the fourth sulked in the corner over her lack of interest.

There was almost a childlike quality to Effie, Lila quickly realized. She was slouched with boredom one minute, then squealing with excitement the next. A fit of giggling would be quickly followed by several minutes of sustained pouting. She switched from mood to mood with all the permanence of the sun's rays on the surface of the pool—and all the expertise of a master artist.

Lila could see that, behind it all, Effie was expertly calculating. She kept a close watch on who was watching her, constantly pushing and pulling to make sure everyone gave her their rapt attention. As the richest and best-known of all the models, cool kids, and young aristocrats who hung out at the Delano, Effie was at the center of this particular social circle.

Lila had to hand it to her, the girl clearly knew what she was doing.

Getting on Effie's radar would require strategy. Teddy had

suggested a straightforward introduction, but Lila knew a girl like Effie wouldn't take kindly to her walking over and saying hello. That would be the social equivalent of a cold call. She'd be setting herself up to be shot down. So, Lila came up with her own plan.

After Effie's murder, Lila had interviewed dozens of people connected in some way to the young socialite, and many had said the same thing—Effie was desperate to get back in the spotlight. She'd never recovered from the quick cancellation of her reality TV show, *Hedge Fun,* which followed her as she learned the ropes of her famous father's hedge-fund business. Ben Oliver, one of the biggest producers in all of reality TV, had produced the show. He'd been relieved when it was taken off the air.

"I mean, how compelling is it watching a dumb blonde cram for her Series 7 exam?" Oliver had asked Lila when she interviewed him. He mentioned that Effie and her agent had been stalking him since the show's cancellation, in hopes that he'd get her back on the small screen. Oliver hadn't answered their calls in months.

Lila stood up and approached Effie, who was lying on her back with her eyes closed and an empty glass in her hand.

"Effie Webster?" Lila said, in a voice full of fake surprise, as she reached the socialite's beach chair. She had to sidestep Effie's tiny swarm of male admirers, all of whom were trying to look totally relaxed while discreetly keeping their oiled-up muscles flexed.

Effie's blue eyes blinked sleepily open. "You're in my sun," she said, a dismissive curl to her upper lip. Lila felt a wave of annoyance rise up in her, but she managed a weak smile.

"My name's Camilla," Lila offered.

Effie said nothing, just stared at Lila with a blank, bored look on her face, as if she couldn't believe Lila had the audacity to breathe the same air.

"Did you not hear me?" Effie repeated. "I said, 'you're in my sun,' which is a nice way of saying, *move*."

Lila took a step back, her smile disappearing. "Sorry," she said. "I just wanted to tell you hi from Ben. He said I'd find you here."

At the mention of that name, Effie sat up slowly. "You don't mean Ben Oliver?" she asked, with false casualness.

"Yeah," Lila said, with a shrug of her shoulders.

"How do you know Ben? Are you in TV, too?"

"Oh, no, no." Lila laughed, as if nothing could be farther beneath her than a career in television. "But Ben and I go way back to Georgetown," she went on, using the biographical info she'd gleaned from researching Oliver last night. "When I told him I was coming to Miami, he said I had to connect with you."

"What did you say your name was?"

"Camilla." Lila paused. "Camilla Dayton." The sound of her new alias felt awkward as it came from her mouth.

"Join me," Effie said, gesturing to the chair next to her. "Stavros"—she scowled at the boy currently lounging in the chair—"can you get the fuck up?" The muscled boy in the Speedo lethargically rose to his feet and, without a glance backward, jumped into the crowded pool. Lila perched on the freshly vacant seat.

A man in an all-white waiter's uniform arrived with a tall drink on a silver tray. He carefully, deferentially, placed the sweating glass on the table between their two chairs. Without acknowledging him, Effie picked up the glass and sipped delicately from its thin straw.

"So, when did you get to Miami?" she asked.

"Yesterday," Lila said, finding it somehow amusing that Effie had gone from bitch to sweetheart in one second flat at the mention of the right name.

"Where from?"

Lila knew that, no matter what her answer, Effie would discover some way to find it wanting. "New York."

"Upper East Side, I suppose." Effie sighed as if nothing on the planet could be more tiresome.

"Is there something wrong with the Upper East Side?" Lila hoped she was right about her approach to Effie, that it was best not to come on too strong or try too hard. In a weird way, she was doing the same thing she'd done with the guys on the force—letting them come to her, rather than trying to win them over.

"Most of the girls I know who come here from New York are just a bunch of stuck-up bitches. Though I'm sure you're different," Effie said in a tone that made it clear she believed the opposite to be true. She lowered her comically large sunglasses over her eyes and reclined on the lounge chair.

"Yep," Lila said. "That sounds just about right. My husband, or I guess my soon-to-be-ex-husband, was very fond of their company. You can't swing a Birkin on Madison Avenue without hitting some bitch he's slept with."

Lila couldn't see Effie's expression behind the dark lenses of her sunglasses, but she kept going.

"That's why I came here. My lawyer told me I shouldn't leave the country while I'm filing for divorce, but I couldn't stay in New York." Lila paused, hoping Effie would join in.

"What did Ben say about me?" she asked, proving that she hadn't been listening to Lila at all.

Lila shrugged noncommittally. "Just to look out for you while I was here."

Effie bit her overly glossed lip, clearly thinking. Lila started to stand up. She was playing it cool, but her heart was racing. She'd never been good at the whole hard-to-get game. She just hoped to hell she was right in her judgment of Effie.

"Anyway, nice meeting you. Maybe we'll run into each other around town," Lila said, turning back to her chair.

She took a single step forward, then another one.

"Wait." Effie's voice came from behind her.

Lila turned around, trying to suppress the sly smile on her face. "Yeah?"

"Come sit," Effie said. "Let's have a drink."

"Sure," Lila said with feigned indifference, settling back into the lounge chair and lowering her Gucci sunglasses over her eyes.

CHAPTER 11

LILA'S FIRST WEEK as Camilla Dayton was an incredibly busy one. Though only eight of the twelve Janus Society members were in the country at the moment, she needed to set up the infrastructure of her surveillance for all of them—placing tracking devices on their cars, hacking into their phone and credit card records, and compiling background information on people each victim had encountered. Between sifting through all this new data, studying Teddy's database, and building her cover by circulating among the wealthy and powerful of Miami, she had no time to sleep.

But she never tired, even for a moment. On the contrary, her nerves were positively buzzing from the thrill of doing what she was born to do: hunting down a killer.

As she tracked the victims, learning the patterns of their days, it quickly became clear that Teddy's original plan remained the strongest one. Lila's best shot at gaining entry into the world of the Janus Society was through Effie Webster. So she set about becoming Effie's smiling shadow.

She started slowly. The day after they met at the Delano, she sent Effie a bouquet of flowers from Miami's top florist, with a card that read only "XXOO—Camilla." A few days later, she "accidentally" bumped into Effie at the Yves Saint Laurent boutique in Bal Harbour, where they each dropped a little under fifteen thousand dollars on flowing silk dresses that reminded Lila of something Stevie Nicks would wear. After their shopping spree, they split a bottle of Sancerre at the St. Regis hotel bar while Lila spilled her guts about the few ups and many downs of her fictitious divorce.

But Lila could sense that all Effie really wanted to hear about was her connection to Ben Oliver. So she thought she'd go ahead and bring it up herself.

"I tried to talk with Ben yesterday," Lila said as she topped off Effie's wineglass.

"Oh, yeah?" Effie asked with a studied indifference, though Lila could see a new brightness in her eyes.

"I wanted to thank him for putting me in touch with you, but his secretary told me he's out of the country for the next three months. Apparently he's in Guyana shooting the latest season of *Survivor*."

"Ugh, I wouldn't spend three months in Africa for all the money in the world!" Effie said with a shudder.

"I know," Lila agreed, fighting the temptation to point out that Effie had the wrong continent. "Here's to Ben." She raised her wineglass and touched it to Effie's with a clink.

"To Ben," Effie murmured, then downed the rest of her glass in a single gulp.

"Anyway," Lila went on, redirecting the conversation toward the only subjects she knew would hold Effie's attention—clothes and herself—"I'm so glad you talked me into that dress today."

"Absolutely." Effie's face was a bit flushed. Lila hoped the wine was taking effect. "I think I'll wear mine to the club tomorrow," Effie added, reaching for the last of the wine in the bottle.

Lila knew that by "the club," Effie meant the Fisher Island Club, Miami's most exclusive country club. Every person in the Janus Society was a member there. Lila was dying to explore it, but she could only go as the guest of a member.

"That sounds fun," Lila said casually. "I'd love to see the club sometime."

"Fun doesn't begin to describe it," Effie countered. "The club is where everyone hangs out. My family have been members since the beginning of time, practically, so I know everyone worth knowing," she said. "Why don't you come with me? If you're going to be in Miami, you really have to join."

"Great," Lila said quickly.

They decided that Lila would come to Effie's house on Star Island around noon on Saturday, and they would go to the club on Effie's boat. Effie also decided that they both "simply must" wear the silk georgette dresses they'd just bought at Yves Saint Laurent.

Effie was making it clear that if Lila was going to have the good fortune to be in her entourage, she'd have to play second fiddle. But that was fine with Lila. If Effie wanted the spotlight, she was more than welcome to it.

The next day, at noon sharp, Lila pulled her Maserati up to Effie's gargantuan, perfectly manicured Spanish Colonial mansion. It struck her with renewed force that in a few short months, this whole world of privilege would be shattered. Effie and the eleven other members of the Janus Society would be murdered at Chase Haverford's mansion, just a stone's throw from this very house.

Effie opened the door looking bleary-eyed and hungover. She greeted Lila's smile with a blank face.

Lila pulled out her cell phone. "Your place is exactly what I want mine to look like," she gushed. "Can I take some pictures to show my designer?"

Effie enthusiastically agreed, her sour mood instantaneously lifted. With iPhone in hand, Lila followed Effie through the sprawling multitude of rooms, snapping dozens of shots as she oohed and aahed in reply to Effie's various stories about the house.

Then they cut across the green oceanfront lawn toward the dock, where Effie kept her boat. A strong tropical breeze had been tossing everything to and fro since morning, and the ocean was choppy. A gust of wind suddenly hit both women at once, blowing their light-as-a-feather dresses over their heads. To Lila's surprise, she heard herself shrieking and giggling along with Effie. *Get it together,* she admonished herself as she stepped onto Effie's red-and-yellow-striped Pantera speedboat.

There was no bridge to Fisher Island, so club members had to get there by ferry (the default method for trophy wives and their unruly children), helicopter (the favored mode of transport of the tycoons), or private boat. Effie preferred the last option.

"Hold on," Effie warned, flashing Lila a wild grin. "I like to drive fast."

A sudden wall of g-force threw Lila back in her seat as the boat roared into the open water. The boat's nose smashed into each wave's crest, then slammed back. Lila clutched the side with both hands as she bounced in her seat, each slam onto the water smashing her tailbone.

"You New York girls aren't that hardy on the sea, are you?" Effie said, pointing at Lila's white-knuckled grip. "Better stand up, or you'll break your ass."

The ride was ten minutes of sheer terror for Lila. Effie didn't see a wave she didn't want to smash straight into. Lila couldn't believe that while she, a seasoned cop, was in a state of panic, Effie was utterly placid.

This girl just may be crazy, Lila thought.

Finally, the boat pulled up to one of the many docks on Fisher Island, and Lila gave a silent prayer of thanks that they'd arrived safe and sound.

"Come on, Manhattan," Effie said, tossing the tie line to one of the boys standing at attention on the dock. "Let me show you how we do things here in the Sunshine State."

The Fisher Island Club was breathtaking. The Spanish Colonial roof had been tiled by an artisan imported from Madrid. Each blade of grass on the entire island was manicured with ferocious precision. There were four staff for every member, and it showed. Two doormen dressed in matching white linen shirts opened the wooden front doors as Effie and Lila breezed through.

The doormen bowed deeply for Effie. The Websters were charter members and therefore expected to be treated deferentially by all those lucky enough to wobble around in their wake. The family's revered status in the South Beach social scene was proof positive of Teddy's claim that becoming a senior member of any of Miami's institutions takes less time, and more money, than you'd think.

Lila looked around the first floor of the club and saw the entire South Beach social scene, in all its splendor, laid out before her. Everyone within sight bore the marks of extreme wealth and the relaxed, self-important insouciance that it buys. The room was a sea of tanned skin, straight white teeth, and hair that screamed effort-filled effortlessness. It was like a summer camp for billionaires.

"That's Scott and Meredith Sloan at the bar," Effie said, pointing to a rather dashing couple visibly scowling at each other. "It looks like they're already fighting. By the end of the night, they'll practically be scratching each other's eyes out. Come on, I want to introduce you to them." Lila was curious to see how Meredith Sloan and Effie would interact, whether anything they said or did would hint at the fact that they shared membership in the Janus Society.

Meredith had a severe sort of beauty, with her long caramel-colored hair and the hollow look of a woman who existed purely on liquids and willpower. Her husband was turned toward her, with his back to the room. As Lila and Effie walked up to the couple, Lila noticed that Scott had Meredith's tiny wrist in his hand.

"Don't make a goddamned scene again, dear," Lila heard Meredith hiss. "If you want to get colorful, wait until we get home." Meredith, seeing that Effie was approaching, switched her face from withering to welcoming with a swiftness Lila had only ever seen from Effie herself.

"Darling Effie!" Meredith cried, wresting her wrist from her husband. "How are you?"

"I'm perfection, and so glad you're both here because I wanted to introduce you to my very good friend, Camilla Dayton. She's fresh off the boat from New York. Camilla, this is Meredith and Scott Sloan."

The wave of sadness that had hit Lila when she first saw Effie revisited her now. Meredith Sloan, yet another of the Star

Island killer's victims, would be dead within months. And here she was, drinking, laughing, battling with her husband, as if the life before her stretched on indefinitely.

Studying Effie and Meredith as they smiled at each other, Lila looked carefully for anything out of the ordinary between them, any subtle hint that there was much more uniting them than the Fisher Island social scene, but their body language betrayed nothing. Both appeared to be experts at keeping secrets.

"Are you staying in Miami long?" Scott asked as he swayed slightly from side to side. He was a heavyset man with fine, thinning hair. Lila could smell the booze on his breath.

"Actually, I'm thinking of moving here."

Addressing Lila, Effie said, "Now, Camilla, these two are the Miami power couple when it comes to real estate. They'll get you all set up with a gorgeous place in an instant. Am I right?"

"It's a buyer's market," Scott said. He fumbled in the interior pocket of his seersucker jacket and pulled out a business card, handing it to Lila.

"Here," he said. "Call our office to set up an appointment. We can take you to see some properties right away."

"Actually," Meredith interjected, "the house next to Effie on Star Island just went on the market. I listed the property a few days ago."

Lila knew that the more time she could spend on Star Island, the better for her investigation. She nodded.

"Effie will tell you, Star Island is marvelous," Meredith said, already in sell mode.

"Ladies," Scott said with an over-the-top bow, "it would seem my wife's drink is empty. Chivalry requires that I fetch her another." He grabbed Meredith's hand. As he was bending to put his wet, drunken lips on her skin, she snatched her hand away.

"I've had quite enough to drink. And so have you, darling," she said with a false sweetness that struck Lila as more terrifying than a display of blatant hostility.

"Ah, my ever faithful wife," Scott said. He stumbled out onto the veranda overlooking the ocean and headed for the poolside bar.

"Forgive my husband," Meredith said, turning her attention to Lila. "He's been . . . overserved today. But he's right. Do call us. We can take you around to look at places as soon as tomorrow. Now, if you'll excuse me."

As Meredith left, Effie rolled her eyes. "Does that make you nostalgic for your own blissful marriage?" she asked.

"And how," Lila said, following the unhappy couple with her eyes, her mind busily sifting through this new information. She hadn't known how fractured the Sloans' marriage was. "Always check out the husband first," they used to say on the force. And in about a third of the murders she'd seen during her time as a detective, the perp had ended up being the person who shared the victim's bed.

Scott Sloan was officially a person of interest.

Lila had questioned Scott several times in the weeks following the Star Island massacre. She remembered that he'd seemed extremely distraught at Meredith's death, yet she was surprised that, given how upset he'd appeared to be, he never once shed a tear. She had a gut feeling that it was all an act.

Her suspicions were as good as confirmed when, about six months after he came off the suspects list, he got remarried to a nineteen-year-old Ukrainian model named Oksana Peterenko.

Not the typical behavior of a man lamenting the loss of his one true love.

When she questioned him, he had vowed that he had no idea his wife was a member of the Janus Society, nor did he have any idea why someone would've wanted to kill her. So much of what he said had struck Lila as bald-faced lies, yet she'd never been able to back up her hunch with any sort of proof.

As she stood watching him weave his way through the club with Meredith in tow, Lila began to think of all the ways Scott might benefit from his wife's death. But what about the eleven other lives? Were they just collateral damage?

As Scott and Meredith cut across the lawn and down to the beach, Lila made a snap decision.

"I'm famished," she said. "Should I go get us some food?"

Effie looked at her quizzically. To Effie, who existed exclusively on vodka, Red Bull, and an occasional can of Ensure, the thought of eating was preposterous.

"Do people still eat in New York?" she asked glibly. "No matter. I think you can find something in the clubhouse. Nothing for me, thanks. Find me later, 'kay?"

In an instant, Effie had turned her back on Lila and was air-kissing a tall man with a waxed mustache.

Lila quickly walked into the clubhouse, then ducked out another door, and headed toward the beach, down the steps, and onto the sand, where she ditched the strappy sandals that had been torturing her feet. Several young children were making sand castles with their nannies. A group of toned women were doing sun salutations in the afternoon's burning light. She saw Scott walk away from the crowds, Meredith following closely behind him. Keeping her distance, Lila trailed them. The couple walked behind a large cluster of palm trees and escaped Lila's gaze. As she got a bit closer, she heard them shouting.

"Get the hell away from me," Scott yelled. Meredith said something in response, but the crash of the ocean waves and her lowered tone made it impossible to hear. Lila stood very still, her ears straining, her feet burning on the hot sand.

"I don't even know who you are anymore. It's nothing but secrets with you," Scott said.

Meredith gave another inaudible reply.

"Trust you? How dare you ask me that? Trust between us died when you picked them over me." The roar of Scott's voice grew louder until, too late, Lila realized he was walking back toward her. He abruptly turned the corner and rushed past Lila, once again running away from his wife. Luckily, he was in too much of a drunken rage to realize that Lila was there, but his sober wife was much more observant. The moment she laid eyes on the young woman just standing there on the beach, a wicked smile spread across her face.

"Enjoying the show, Camilla?"

"Excuse me?" Lila asked.

"Playing dumb only works on the boys. I know better," Meredith said over her shoulder, as she walked back toward the clubhouse.

Needing to put her burning feet in the water and to absorb what she'd just heard, Lila went into the ocean up to her ankles, holding up her designer dress to avoid ruining it.

Them over me, Scott had said.

From the sound of it, Scott did know about the Janus Society. Lila was right. He had lied to her during the investigation. She had never understood how a husband, no matter how distant, could be unaware of such large sums of money being donated every year. And, more important, why was the society such a secret in the first place? During all the years she spent hunting the Star Island killer, that was the one question she could never come close to answering. She was convinced that the moment she figured out the mystery at the core of the society, she would figure out who the killer was.

If Scott had lied to her about the Janus Society, what else had he lied about? Certainly his so-called devastation after Meredith's death. Given what Lila had overheard, he seemed nothing like a man who would mourn his wife. This was a man who wanted his wife gone. By the time Lila returned, Effie was halfway into her second Red Bull vodka, and flirting with a handsome Australian bartender. Her blue eyes were unfocused and shining. When she saw Lila, she slipped an arm around her waist. "I'm broiling up here. Let's go sit by the pool. I'll be the tour guide and you'll be the tourist."

When they reached the pool area, Effie let out a shriek at the sight of a man lying in what she loudly claimed was "her" spot.

"Goddamn Russian!" she cried. "How many times have I told you to keep the fuck out of my chair?" The man opened his eyes, slowly blinking. He had a fleshy face with disproportionately full lips and incredibly bushy eyebrows sarcastically hanging above his sunken eyes. He was one of the most unattractive men Lila had ever laid eyes on.

"Is this not a free country?" the man said in a thick accent.

"Does any of this look free to you? Now, get up," Effie commanded.

The Russian slapped his big, muscular thighs, relishing his role as an obstacle between a drunken socialite and something she wanted. "Climb up here, stomach first. I'm strong just like any good chair. Part wood also." He looked at Lila, then winked. "Same offer for you. I don't play favorites."

"As sweet as that sounds, I'll pass," Lila said, rolling her eyes.

"All you American girls don't know a good time when you see it," the man said, standing up from the chair. It was now covered in small, curly black hairs from his back. "You can stop buzzing around me. I go now." As he stood, a young blond woman appeared out of nowhere holding a black robe, which she placed around his shoulders.

"My name is Alexei Dortzovich," he said to Lila, placing his hand on the small of her back. "You are new here?"

"Just in from New York," Lila answered. "My name's Camilla."

At this information, Alexei shrugged his shoulders. He didn't seem to care what her name was. "People around here will tell you I'm a bad man," Alexei said as he leaned into Lila. His fingers trailed up the side of her body and curled around her upper arm, brushing against her breast as he whispered, "But what they don't know is that I'm much worse than they think." Then he and his tiny blond shadow walked away.

"What a lovely man," Lila said to Effie, shaking off the feeling of his hand on her body.

"It's awful, the Russians are taking over Miami. And I thought the Cubans were bad."

Once the chaise longue was swept free of body hair and covered with fresh towels, Effie and Lila took off the dresses that were covering their bikinis and lay back in the hot sun. Alexei was now on the other side of the pool, having what looked like an intense conversation with Fernando Salazar, the so-called Cuban Kissinger and member of the Janus Society.

Just as Lila was about to make another excuse so that she could listen in on their conversation, the two men nodded at each other, then parted ways.

Effie saw Lila looking at Alexei. "Just a warning," she said. "That guy is not someone you want to cross, at all."

"Why?" Lila asked, excited to finally be getting some valuable information out of Effie.

"People say he's Russian mob for sure."

"You believe them?"

"Seems likely. He's always got armed guards. He's as rich as a sultan. Supposedly he's some oil tycoon, but who knows?"

"And what about that guy he was just talking to?" Lila pointed at Salazar, hoping that now, unlike with Meredith, Effie might reveal something about the Janus Society.

"Ugh. He's, like, the king of the Cubans. My dad told me he fought in the day of the pigs, or whatever?"

"The Bay of Pigs?"

"That's it," Effie said, putting her finger to the tip of her surgically perfected nose.

"Do you know him?" Lila pressed. She hoped that Effie was drunk enough to let something slip.

Effie shot her a devilish smile. "Of course," she said. "Isn't it clear to you by now that I know absolutely everyone?" Effie flagged a passing waitress for another vodka drink and a bottle of Evian, and Lila knew the moment had passed.

As the afternoon went on, Effie worked away at her drink, inundating Lila with the gossip on every man, woman, and child that passed by. "Oh, that guy? He spent five years in prison for insider trading. See that woman over there? She travels to Brazil so some quack can inject her butt with this weird stuff that's totally illegal in this country. That girl got kicked out of school for cutting herself; rumor is that she and her brother, who's over there, are doing it. And that guy, the cute one, I fucked him. Smallest dick I've ever seen. Such a shame. He's so hot."

The whole nonstop monologue detailing the scandals, incest, embezzlements, crimes, and punishments of Miami's high society had Lila's head swimming. She wished she could take out a notepad and write everything down—she marveled that Effie's brain managed to keep track of it all. The problem, Lila realized as Effie launched into yet another sordid story, wouldn't be finding the villain among the innocent victims. The real difficulty would be locating any innocence in this city at all.

"How do you know so much about everyone?" Lila asked, when Effie finally came up for air.

Effie smiled, looking incredibly pleased with herself. "Secrets are the key to everything. Other people chase after money and sex and power. But not me. I learned a long time ago that knowing everyone's dirty little secret is as good as gold."

The club was packed with Janus Society members. Chase Haverford, the hotel magnate and host on the night of the massacre, was at the bar by the pool, shouting obscenities into his phone. Javier Martinez spent the afternoon drinking mojitos and ogling the cabana boys while playing game upon game of dominoes with his young Dominican lover. Javier's vast fortune was always a source of gossip within the Miami social scene. He was an antiques and art dealer, but he was far too wealthy for that to be his only source of income. Lila knew there were constant whispers that he was mixed up in the black market, but nothing had ever been proven, even after his death.

When Lila walked by the tennis courts on her way to get

sunscreen from the ladies' locker room for Effie, she spotted Sam Logan, the tennis star, giving an impromptu lesson to a woman wearing a miniskirt that looked to be a child's size. And then Neville Crawley, "of the Newport Crawleys," quickly passed by, heading from his yacht to the golf course. Despite the day's crushing humidity, he was wearing a blue blazer with gold buttons.

Lila used her cell phone to take pictures of each and every Janus Society member present. Most of the time, to hide the fact that she was acting like a paparazzo, she pretended to be taking a selfie, positioning herself in front of the camera and pouting while really training the lens on her chosen subject. No one even batted an eye at a beautiful girl taking endless pictures of herself. Extreme vanity, in this world, was a given.

When she got back to the chair with SPF 50 for Effie, Lila saw yet another Janus Society member, Vivienne Hunter, stepping inside a private cabana, her head wrapped in an Hermès scarf. She was pale as snow, the majority of her face obscured by large sunglasses. Her lips were thickly painted a deep red and penciled outside of her natural lip line, giving her an "I'm ready for my close-up, Mr. DeMille" kind of vibe.

"Ugh, I know," Effie said, following Lila's gaze. "That woman is about as happy in the sun as a vampire. Why does she even bother coming here? I mean, really, move to Transylvania with the rest of the living dead."

"And I can assume you know her?" Lila asked. Effie knew Vivienne well enough to die with her.

"That old bat? What's there to know except that she's made a fortune selling cheap lipsticks. But now she looks like an animatronic wax figure. Something out of Madame Tussauds."

The crime scene photos that Lila had studied for years came

screaming into her mind. She saw Vivienne Hunter dead, a sapphire necklace hanging from her white neck, her slightly parted scarlet lips echoing the gaping crimson gunshot wound in the center of her forehead. Lila shivered.

The sun began to set, turning the light around them into a hallucinatory mix of purples and pinks. A cooling breeze came off the ocean. The club staff began putting amber-colored tea light vases on all the tables. Lila glanced over at Effie, who looked quite bedraggled now that she was sobering up.

"Want to head back?" Lila asked. Effie nodded, threw on her dress, and began walking to the docks. Lila followed close behind, wondering if she should try to drive the boat home.

As they were both about to climb aboard Effie's terror express, a wooden sailboat pulled up to the dock. Suddenly something heavy and wet clunked Lila on the head.

"Ouch!" she exclaimed, ducking forward in a protective crouch. Effie shrieked. A thick rope fell splat at Lila's feet.

"Just wrap it on the cleat," a voice shouted to her.

"What?" Lila asked, rubbing the back of her head. Who on earth would hit her in the head with a wet rope, then instruct her to do something with it?

She looked up to see a young, tanned man flashing an amused smile at her and Effie. He looked so familiar, but Lila couldn't remember where she'd seen him before.

"Christ," Effie shouted. "You got my dress wet!" Effie's clothes, like her moods, were not to be trifled with.

With a disgusted look on her face, Effie bent down, picked up the wet rope, and weakly tossed it. It fell limply a foot away from their feet. "Tie up your own boat, Dylan."

Lila grabbed her cell phone and quickly took a picture of Dylan for her files, thinking he wouldn't notice. But he did. In an instant, he arranged himself in a heroic pose for the camera, putting his foot on the lip of the boat and his fists on his hips. *Who does this guy think he is?* Lila thought, irritated that she'd been caught.

With a startling agility, Dylan walked along the thin lip of his boat's deck, one bare foot placed directly in front of the other like a tightrope walker. Then he hopped onto the dock and scooped up the rope.

"Not much of a sailor, are you?" he asked Lila as he wound the rope around the metal cleat bolted into the dock. He was strikingly handsome, with warm brown eyes and a lightning-quick smile. But all Lila saw was another South Beach pretty boy.

"She's from New York," Effie offered by way of explanation, climbing into her boat.

"Then what's your excuse, Effie?" Dylan asked. Keeping his gaze trained on Lila, he said, "And does your friend have a name?"

"Lila," Lila answered. Then she paused, catching herself. "I mean Camilla. Camilla Dayton."

"You sure about that now?" Dylan laughed.

She looked at him stone-faced, causing his smile to quickly disappear.

"Did I hurt you?" he asked quietly.

Effie revved her soul-clatteringly loud twin engines. She was growing impatient. "Come on, Camilla!"

Dylan continued staring at Lila in a way that made her feel incredibly uncomfortable.

"I've got to go," she said to him.

"What Effie wants, Effie gets. I learned that years ago. The hard way. Anyway, I'm Dylan Rhodes," he said, extending his hand. Lila shook it, taking note of his tan, muscular forearms, the thick brown hair falling just so into his eyes. "Maybe we'll run into each other at another, less rushed time."

"Camilla, now!" Effie barked.

"Sure. Nice meeting you," Lila said, pulling her hand away and turning back toward Effie.

That night, as Lila was logging her observations for the day and downloading her pictures, she lingered over her final shot—the one of Dylan Rhodes, posed as the conquering hero. She couldn't help smiling at the sight of it.

"Idiot," Lila said aloud in the solitude of her hotel room.

But she kept looking at the picture.

CHAPTER 12

ON SUNDAY MORNING, from the veranda of her hotel room, Lila called the number listed on the business card Scott Sloan had given her. She didn't want to waste any time. Based on what she'd overheard yesterday, she believed that Scott knew about the existence of the Janus Society. And if he knew of its existence, then he might have had a reason to kill its members, including his wife.

"Hello, Scott Sloan's office," a woman with a syrupy Southern accent answered.

"Scott, please," Lila said.

"He's unavailable at the moment. But I could transfer you to his wife, Meredith's line?"

There was nothing inherently suspicious in that, Lila knew, but she couldn't help wondering where Scott had gone without Meredith. Didn't they share all their clients?

"No," Lila snapped, acting on impulse. "This is Andrea Baxter," she said, grabbing the first name that popped into her head. "We had an appointment and I've been waiting for forty-five goddamned minutes." In Lila's experience, the old saying about catching more flies with honey than vinegar was 100 percent bullshit.

"Oh, my stars," the secretary said. "That's impossible. He wouldn't have scheduled you now. He's unavailable between eight forty-five and ten thirty every morning." Unavailable, Lila thought. That was the second time Scott's assistant had used that word. Where was he?

"Well, I'm standing here like an idiot at three Indian Creek," Lila said, really laying it on thick. She could hear the woman on the other end of the phone begin to breathe audibly. "How fast can he get here? Because if I don't see him in ten minutes, he's losing a huge commission."

"I'll try him, but he's at the Four Seasons now, so it would take over an hour to reach you," the assistant babbled. "What did you say your name was? I'm sure we can reschedule if you'll give me a—"

But Lila had already hung up the phone, hopped into her Maserati, and was speeding south along Collins Avenue toward the Four Seasons. It might be nothing, but she knew from experience that it was best to pursue every lead. And right now, Scott Sloan was definitely a suspect.

By the time she walked into the lobby it was 9:20. His secretary had said he'd be here until 10:30, which meant there wasn't much time. Scott was somewhere in the hotel, but Lila had no idea where. The solicitous man at the front desk confirmed that he wasn't a guest, and Lila didn't find him during her brief survey of the pool and the hotel restaurants.

Lila stopped for a moment, giving her mind a chance to process everything. The assistant had said he was unavailable for almost two hours every morning and then let it slip that he was at this hotel. What could he be doing? Maybe the gym?

Sure enough, after signing a fake name at the registry for the hotel's subterranean fitness club and searching its many nooks and crannies, Lila spotted Scott in a small room off the long hallway. She peeked through the tiny window of the door to see him standing on a yoga mat, balancing on one leg with his arms stretched into the air, swaying side to side to keep his balance. Next to him was a young woman with blond hair down to her waist, wearing tiny white shorts and a tank top with the Om symbol on it.

"Yoga?" Lila wondered aloud. Boozy, country-club Scott didn't strike her as the yoga type.

Lila quickly ducked to make sure that neither of them saw her spying through the window. She turned to leave but glanced back one last time—just in time to see Scott quickly kiss the yoga instructor on the mouth. From the way the woman kissed him back, Lila knew it wasn't the first kiss they'd shared. Now things were beginning to make more sense.

Smiling, Lila turned and walked back to the club reception desk to book a private session with the "darling yoga girl with the long blond hair." It turned out the girl, whose name was Willow Morris, had an opening in a couple hours. Lila happily booked it, then headed to the spa gift shop. Camilla Dayton would be needing some yoga pants.

"My name's Camilla," Lila said as she stepped into the yoga studio at noon. Willow, instead of shaking Lila's outstretched hand, put her own palms together, closed her doe eyes, and gave her a small bow.

"Namaste," Willow said.

Lila was struck by the girl's wide-eyed, cheerful face. It was the kind of face that missionaries wear as they walk up to strangers asking them if they know Jesus Christ is their Lord and Savior—the face of a true believer. Lila smiled, already faltering. She'd handled a broad range of characters in her day—ex-cons, drug dealers, corrupt politicians—but sincerity and earnestness were her kryptonite, and she didn't know how to face them.

Amid burning incense, sitar music, and flickering candles, Lila grudgingly began her first-ever yoga class. She quickly found that she was about as limber as a cement block. And if Willow told her to "relax and breathe" one more time, she might just deck her. Lila wasn't a yoga expert, but she'd been breathing on her own for thirty years, and it had been working just fine so far.

While they were moving through a series of what Lila could only think of as sadistic contortions, Willow asked Lila about herself, which gave Lila the opportunity, between groans, to tell the now-familiar story of her escape from New York, the philandering ex-husband, the agony of loss. Willow stood nodding in sympathy, a slight frown on her face.

"Everything," she said, "contains both meaning and the opposite of meaning, which is no meaning." Lila felt her body quivering with the effort it took to keep her balance while also suppressing an eye roll. Instead, she simply nodded.

"Breathe your ex-husband *out*!" Willow shouted as Lila struggled to mimic her posture. "Breathe your freedom *in*!"

After the ninety-minute lesson was over, Lila casually asked Willow out for a drink—saying that, being new to the city and all, she'd love to pick her brain about Miami.

"There's a place right down the beach that does a killer guava smoothie. Guava is really good for detoxifying your organs," Willow offered, bending in a way that made Lila wonder if she had any organs at all.

As they walked together, Lila returned to her tale of the philandering husband back in New York. In order to get Willow to spill about Scott, she figured she needed to do much more spilling herself.

"What breaks my heart the most is that he lied to me." Lila breathed in sharply, hoping Willow would get the sense that tears were about to flow. "And what I hate most of all is that I should've known. Before I was his wife, I was his mistress. I mean, how dumb am I?" Lila looked at Willow to see if she was getting anywhere.

Willow's head was turned away from Lila, toward the ocean, her face sporting her usual serene smile.

"If a man cheated on another woman with me, why did I think he wouldn't cheat on me with another woman?"

Willow took Lila's hand in hers; her eyes looked like those of a baby seal about to be clubbed. "There are no patterns in the now. You trusted, and opened your heart. That's all that truly matters."

"Tell that to my divorce lawyer," Lila said with a sigh.

After a short walk, they arrived at a little palm-frond shack just feet from the ocean's edge. A young Japanese guy wearing only a crocheted Rastafarian hat and surf shorts was behind the bar. Bhangra music blasted from an old speaker atop a defunct vending machine. The bartender nodded to Willow, who nodded back.

"Hey, Kiyoshi," Willow said. "Can you whip us up two of those guava smoothies when you get a chance?"

Lila knew it was early in the day to drink, but she also knew she wouldn't get any information out of this girl through the power of antioxidants alone. She needed to get Willow drunk, and she needed it now.

"Um . . . ," she said, fumbling with the straps of her new Lu-lulemon top. "I hate to admit it, but after dredging up all those memories, I could really use a drink." Willow paused, looking at Lila, and Lila worried she'd gone too far. But then, to her relief, Willow loudly slammed her hand on the bar.

"You're right! A drink is what we both need. Kiyoshi always has a bottle of something behind that bar of his. Am I right, my man?" she asked.

Kiyoshi's face was as stoic and unreadable as an owl's. "Cuban moonshine," he said, pulling an unlabeled bottle out from behind a pile of coconuts. He then poured a bit into the blender. Lila knew that wouldn't be good enough.

"Why don't you grab us a table?" she suggested to Willow. Once the young woman had walked away, Lila slipped Kiyoshi a hundred-dollar bill with the instructions to "make those drinks as stiff as a corpse."

She watched with delight as he poured half the bottle into the blender.

That should do it, Lila thought.

About halfway through the smoothie, the Cuban moonshine started to work its magic. Lila continued to talk so incessantly about her fake ex-husband and his fake mistress that she was beginning to believe she really had been wronged.

"And you should see the slut he's with now. She's barely out of high school. He's using our money to produce her album."

"What if they're really in love?" Willow said slowly. She was drunk. *Lightweight,* Lila thought, with a feeling of smug superiority. "I mean . . ." Willow paused, lowering her face to the straw to take another sip. "People fall in love and people fall out of love."

Lila waited, sensing that Willow was on the edge of confessing. In the ocean, a group of surfers battled loudly for a wave. The shack started to fill up with sunburned tourists and marijuana-soaked locals. Kiyoshi put Fela Kuti on the sound system.

"The man I love is married," Willow said finally. "That doesn't make me a bad person, does it?"

"I guess that depends." Lila had to strike a delicate balance. In order to get more out of Willow, she needed to make her feel bad about her actions, but not so bad that she would clam up.

"I mean, it started as nothing. He's a client of mine. And all I remember about our first few sessions is how much sadness he had in his body. You couldn't not feel it. I mean, his aura was literally black, you know?" She finished her drink and signaled Kiyoshi for another. Lila made eye contact with the bartender, nodding to make sure the second drink was as strong as the first.

"So we start talking," Willow said, taking a deep sip of her second drink. "Turns out, his wife is having this big affair and their marriage is essentially over. Well, love is my religion." She placed her two tiny hands over her heart and made a small sound that sounded like the cooing of a dove. "I don't know how it happened. I was trying to heal his broken heart and somehow we fell in love." *And a few months from now,* Lila thought, *Meredith Sloan will be dead and Scott Sloan will be married to a Ukrainian lingerie model. Ain't love grand?*

"If she's having an affair, why doesn't he just leave her?" Lila asked.

"They run a big business together. If he leaves his wife for me, he's worried that he'll lose everything in the divorce. But his wife's lover is really high-profile, so we know that it's bound to become common knowledge soon enough." Willow let out a long, pitiful sigh. "The only way the marriage will end is if she leaves him first."

"Will she?" Lila prodded gently.

"Who knows? All I know is that they're so unhappy." Willow leaned in toward Lila's face. She smelled like coconut oil and baby powder. "I couldn't live the way they do, with so much anger and hate."

"I've been there," Lila said. "And it isn't pretty. That much misery can make people do crazy things. Once I found out about my husband's affairs, I had these long, intricate daydreams about him stepping off a curb and being plowed down by a truck."

Willow's face lit up with the delight that comes from a shared understanding. "Yep," she said, nodding, "Scott has those. Oh, does he ever!"

"He fantasizes about killing his wife?"

"When you put it that way, it sounds really bad. I know it's a karmic nightmare to wish another person ill, but it helps him release his anger. And he has so much anger." Willow sighed. "I mean, it's not like he would ever actually do it. He's absolutely terrified of his wife. She's a real nightmare. At least, that's what he tells me."

It seemed to Lila that bashing her boyfriend's wife was something Willow had been aching to do.

"She sounds awful," Lila offered, desperate to keep Willow talking. "Actually, I don't think the world would miss her too much if she was hit by a truck."

At this, Willow let out a big laugh. Then, as if shocked by her own reaction, she became stern-faced. "That's the last thing he wants, trust me."

"Relax, I was just making a bad joke," Lila said, putting

her hand on top of Willow's. She knew that keeping the mood light was imperative to keeping the conversation going. "Obviously, I know you don't want her to die."

"Oh, I know." Willow snatched her hand from under Lila's and gave it a tiny flick, followed by a nervous giggle. "The whole thing is so ugly, I sometimes wonder how I became a part of any of it. All I meant was that, if she dies, he gets nothing. Her family made sure of that."

"Her family?" Lila asked. If what Willow was saying was true, this news changed everything.

Willow nodded. "She comes from serious money. If she dies, he gets zero. It's all in their crazy prenup. Leave it to her to control him even from the grave," she added, a little bitterly. Lila liked drunk Willow. She had a bit of a tough streak.

So, Lila thought, as Willow rambled on. *If Meredith dies, Scott gets nothing. If that's true, it wouldn't be remotely in his interest to kill her.*

"Anyway," Willow was saying, "Scott and I have been trying to get news of his wife's affair out in the public, to force the divorce. Both of us have sent anonymous tips to the South Beach gossip columns several times."

"And?"

"Nothing." Willow pouted. "We think the papers don't want to risk a lawsuit. So it seems pretty hopeless at the moment," she said with her face in a frown and her body in a slouch. Then, shaking off her temporary blues, Willow straightened her back and looked thoughtfully out toward the ocean. "But I know it will all work out in the end."

"I'm sure you're right," Lila said, knowing perfectly well that it wouldn't. "Oh, I meant to ask," she added with a studied casualness, "have you ever heard of the Janus Society?"

"Janus Society? Is that the new club on Ocean Drive?"

"Never mind. Forget I asked. Let's go back," Lila said, pulling Willow to her feet. On the way out, she put another hundred on the bar for Kiyoshi. She always rewarded the barkeeps with generous pours.

LATER THAT EVENING, Lila was back at her hotel room, once again on her laptop. She was hoping that somewhere in the thousands of pages of files, Teddy had included a copy of the prenuptial agreement between Scott and Meredith Sloan. After a quick search, Lila located it in Meredith's file.

Decoding the legalese wasn't easy, but after rereading the document a couple of times, Lila found the telltale clause buried in the twenty-six pages: "Prospective Husband and Prospective Wife waive the right to share in each other's estates upon their death."

With that one line, Scott Sloan lost his main motivation for the murder of his wife. Really, given that most of their money came from Meredith's family, Scott had everything to lose from her death.

Lila couldn't remember what had happened to Scott after he'd remarried. She quickly searched through the files for any financial information on Scott Sloan after 2014. What she discovered shocked her. Though he was still living the moneyed life, it was all an act. Without Meredith's money, he was drowning in debt. Even the millions he made selling his half of the real estate business to her family did little to help him out of a $25 million hole.

Scott was a first-class asshole, that much was clear. But he was not the Star Island killer. Lila crossed her first suspect off the list.

CHAPTER 13

"THERE ARE EIGHT bedrooms—not including the master suite, of course—a grand reception room, home entertainment center, personal gym, and double boat dock," Meredith Sloan was saying as she walked Effie and Lila around the empty house on Star Island Drive. "They're asking twenty-five million," she said. "But in this soft market, we can give them an opening offer of twenty."

Lila absorbed this information with a thoughtful nod. Meredith had agreed to show her around some of South Beach's most opulent homes, and Lila felt she had to at least pretend she was interested in purchasing one of them. Currently they were touring the Mediterranean-style monstrosity that just so happened to be next door to Effie.

Effie, who was along for the ride, didn't feel the need to pretend to be interested in anything. "God, Camilla, I really want you to move in here so we can be close, but this place is a dump," she said, looking around in horror. "Does it even have staff quarters?" she asked Meredith.

"Yes, there are ample staff quarters on the ground floor and a coach house for guests," Meredith said quickly. "It's really the complete package. Everything a young lady looking to settle down needs."

"Of course, if you bought this place, you'd have to completely renovate. The southwestern thing is so passé." Effie sniffed as she took in the turquoise walls and the cowhide furniture with a visible shudder. "It's like living in a Georgia O'Keeffe painting." She gestured pointedly at a cow skull hanging over the adobe fireplace.

Lila looked around. Her shabby Little Havana apartment was smaller than the foyer of this house. The fact that it was seen as at all reasonable for one person to live in a ten-thousand-square-foot house all by herself, as Effie did, struck her as sheer lunacy.

"Can I see the pool?" Lila asked sweetly. She needed some fresh air.

As they stood by the palm-tree-lined heated pool, Effie leaned toward Lila and whispered, "This place is a total shithole. Let's get out of here."

"Totally," Lila said, smiling. Only Effie Webster would be able to call this mansion a shithole, but Lila needed an excuse to leave. The two women grinned at each other.

"Thanks, Meredith," Effie said, giving her two air kisses on her sunken cheeks. "We'll let you know."

"I'll be in touch," Lila said to Meredith.

"I have other listings I can show you," Meredith said, clearly anxious not to lose Lila as a client. "Maybe later in the week?"

"Okay!" Lila and Effie both called out over their shoulders as they turned to walk back to Effie's place.

"God," Effie said in disbelief, "you live next to people for years and you never know what unbelievably bad taste they have. It's like everyone is a stranger!" She burst into laughter. "I mean, did you see their collection of taxidermied armadillos? I should've taken pictures. No one's going to believe me."

"That was grotesque," Lila said, then let out an exasperated sigh. "I'll never find a place as beautiful as yours."

"That's true," Effie said, never shy to take a compliment.

"If I do buy that place," Lila continued, "I'd have to gut it. I'd need to be over here every day to oversee the renovations."

"Of course!" Effie exclaimed. "Never trust anyone in construction. They're criminals."

"But it'll be such a hassle. The drive to and from the hotel every day will be brutal . . . ," Lila said leadingly. "And I hate the idea of buying somewhere that I haven't lived before. I'd really be buying that place for the location, you know? Is it crazy to commit to somewhere that I've never spent more than a day?"

Effie stopped abruptly in her tracks. "I just had a brilliant idea! You should just move into my guesthouse while you figure out where you'll buy."

That was exactly what Lila was hoping she'd say. Nothing could be better for her investigation than living with one of the victims. Her access would be 24/7.

"That's very generous, Effie," Lila said carefully, "but it's too much to ask of you."

"How much is that room at the Ritz costing you each night?"

"Five thousand dollars," she said. Even though it felt like pretend cash, and Teddy had given her $100 million of disposable money, it made Lila absolutely ill to pay that much each night for a place to lay her head.

"That's crazy when I have this huge empty guesthouse. And we're together almost every day anyway. Come on," Effie said in a singsong voice. "It'll be fun. We'll be roommates! Besides, if it doesn't work out, you can always get your hotel room back."

Roommates. Lila had never actually lived with another woman before. And what Effie said was true—they did spend most of their time together. They walked back into Effie's mansion through the sliding glass doors that led directly to the kitchen.

"Okay," Lila said slowly. "Roommates." She smiled as Effie danced around her colossal kitchen in search of celebratory champagne. Never in a million years would she have guessed that she, Lila Day, would be roommates with a girl who was a socialite, and kind of a bitch.

"Great!" Effie squealed as she opened a bottle of Veuve with a loud pop. "It's settled. You'll move in tomorrow. It'll be easier to find a house on Star Island when you're already here. And if you do buy the house next door, you'll be close to supervise its necessary demolition." Effie poured them two glasses of bubbly and raised hers with a wink. "Here's to us."

"Thank you, Effie!" Suddenly, Lila threw her arms around Effie, feeling a genuine warmth toward this bouncing, silly, fragile creature. "You're the best!" she said, realizing that, in a strange way, she actually meant it.

Lila and Effie decided to celebrate their new roommate status with a day at the Fisher Island Club. They were on the way there, with Effie at the wheel of her speedboat of terror, when Effie grinned wickedly at Lila. "I know what's going to happen today," she shouted over the churning water and roaring twin engines.

"What?" Lila asked, as she gripped the sides of the boat. Over the last two weeks, she'd become more accustomed to certain things, but Effie's nautical style was not one of them.

"Today we're going to find you a man! It's been long enough

of Ms. Mopey Divorcée. Plus, you acting like a nun is making me feel too slutty. The men of Miami are waiting for you! All you have to do is say the word."

"Okay," Lila agreed, though she had zero interest in actually dating any of the men Effie knew. But this way, she thought, she could get Effie to introduce her to more of the men of South Beach. One of them might know something relevant to the murders.

"Yay! Let the manhunt begin!" Effie exclaimed as she pulled up to the dock of the club.

When they stepped inside the clubhouse's grand dining room overlooking the ocean, the room was absolutely packed. A gorgeous man wearing a cream linen suit stood atop the bar, holding a bottle of Cristal in one hand and a large saber in the other. Lila gasped when she realized who it was.

Teddy Hawkins.

"Champagne!" Teddy cried to a rapt audience. "In victory one deserves it! In defeat one needs it!" With that, he swept the saber across the top of the champagne bottle, slicing the lip of the neck right off and sending the cork flying through the air. Everyone in the room erupted into a cheer.

Suddenly, the dining hall was flooded with waiters, all carrying trays of champagne in crystal flutes.

"Who is that?" Lila asked Effie.

"Teddy Hawkins. You know, the tech guy."

"Oh, right. I've seen him on TV, but never in person."

"Well, I'll introduce you. He's a good friend," Effie boasted.

Lila couldn't take her eyes off Teddy. The man before her now was radiant and strong—vibrating with life, pouring champagne, laughing. He was the very opposite of the driven and tormented man who'd sent her back in time. Future Teddy was fixated on the Star Island massacre with a frightening intensity. This Teddy came across as some sort of rock star.

Spotting Meredith Sloan standing alone at the bar, holding champagne flutes in both hands, Effie grabbed Lila's hand and quickly walked over to her. The women all greeted each other in South Beach fashion, by touching cheeks while pursing their lips in an air kiss. Effie, who was an expert at this greeting, always kept her eyes open, already scanning the room to see who she would say hello to next.

"You're here," Meredith said, in that tone of hers that was warm on the top and cold underneath. "Have you thought any more about the house?" Even when there was a lilt in her voice, her eyes remained steely. Lila sensed that there was an impenetrable toughness at the core of Meredith Sloan.

"I have," Lila said vaguely.

"What's all this fuss about?" Effie interrupted, gesturing to the boisterous celebration going on around them.

"Well, my darling Teddy just took his company public," Meredith said.

The three women turned to look toward Teddy, who was standing in a sea of middle-aged white men in suits, a veritable Brooks Brothers army that looked as if it were trying to consume him.

"As of the opening of the markets this morning," Meredith continued, "that man over there is a billionaire."

"How do you know Teddy?" Lila asked Meredith. She did call him darling, after all.

"Everybody knows Teddy," Effie said.

"We've known each other our whole lives." Meredith smiled, looking quite pleased with herself. "Our families used to winter together in Miami and summer on Cape Cod."

"I know!" Effie squealed to Lila with sudden delight. "We'll introduce the two of you!" She hooked her arm under Lila's and dragged her toward Teddy. "Maybe you'll really hit it off. He's a nice guy," she whispered into Lila's ear.

Teddy had only warned Lila against meeting herself from the past, but she couldn't help worrying at the thought of meeting him. What if something she did or said somehow changed who he was, causing him to never build a time machine and thus never send her back in time? Then what?

"Teddy! Congratulations!" Effie exclaimed. "Meredith told us the exciting news about your company."

Lila was trying to hide behind Effie's slender frame, keeping her eye on the rest of the room. *Is it crazy to wonder if he'll recognize me?* she thought.

"Let me introduce you to my friend Camilla Dayton. She's staying with me until Meredith can find her a house."

"Pleasure to meet you," Lila said, searching Teddy's bright eyes for any signs of recognition. There were none.

"The pleasure is mine, I assure you." He reached out and shook Lila's hand, his grip firm and solid. "Drinking champagne in the company of beautiful women is more pleasure than any man deserves."

Meredith walked up to the three of them holding two flutes of champagne, and looking at Teddy with impatience. Lila got the feeling that Meredith didn't appreciate her old friend Teddy giving his attentions to two younger women.

Teddy smiled at her. "Meredith, is one of those champagne flutes for me or are you drinking for two tonight?"

"For you, my dear," Meredith said, returning his good-natured smile as she handed him the champagne.

Lila suddenly spotted Dylan in the far corner of the room. She took a few steps toward him to get a better look. He was talking with the Nigerian cement titan Johnny Oluwa, one of the Janus Society members.

But her view of Dylan was quickly blotted out by Effie's face. "So," she loudly whispered, "what do you think of Teddy?" Effie and Lila both looked back toward Teddy, who was caught in some serious-looking conversation with Meredith as the room made merry around them.

"He seems great, Ef, but I'm not sure he's my type," Lila said. "I mean, look." She pointed. "I've never seen a man less interested in me."

"Actually, weird. From this angle he seems kind of into Meredith." Effie paused, then scoffed. "Yeah, Meredith wishes."

At that moment, Meredith walked away from Teddy toward the pool. After he'd spent a few minutes standing by himself, his victorious smile somewhat dampened into a tight-lipped curl, Teddy followed her.

"Do you know the guy in the corner?" Lila said, pointing to Dylan and Johnny.

Effie rolled her eyes. "Yes, Camilla, I told you. I know everyone. The white guy you met before. And the black guy's name is Johnny. He's from Africa."

"Where in Africa?" Lila asked, hoping that Effie knew more than she was letting on.

"Does it matter?"

"And how do they know each other?"

"Dylan's like me, he knows everyone. But I'm pretty sure they went to the same high school. It was for international students. Why? Are you interested in him?" Effie looked closely at Lila. "He is good-looking. But, trust me, you wouldn't be the first woman who tried and failed to land Dylan Rhodes."

Lila wondered, given how close Dylan seemed to be with

a vast number of the society members, why she hadn't come across him when she investigated every man, woman, and child connected to the Star Island twelve.

"Who says I'm trying to land anybody?" Lila laughed, taking a few pictures of Dylan and the rest of the party. "How do you know him, though?"

"God, enough with the questions!" Effie sighed. "He's rich and handsome and famously single. Isn't that all the information you really need?" She gave Lila a gentle poke in the ribs with her elbow, wiggling her eyebrows salaciously.

Lila couldn't help but laugh at Effie's playfulness. Maybe she needed to be around lighthearted people more often.

"Listen, can you get me another champagne?" Effie asked. "I've got to visit the powder room." She handed Lila her empty glass and crossed the floor, saying emphatic hellos to no less than a dozen people on the way. The last person Effie greeted before she disappeared was Chase Haverford, the man in whose home the Star Island twelve would soon die.

Lila made her way to the bar, which had grown overcrowded with people clamoring for drinks. The smell of crushed mint filled the air as the bartenders hustled to make mojitos in bulk. Lila thought she heard someone saying her name and turned to find Dylan standing next to her, extending a full glass of champagne toward her.

"Hey, sailor," he said with a smile as Lila took the glass from his hands. She felt a reddish heat crawl up her neck. "How's the head?"

"Head?"

"From where the rope hit. On the dock?"

"Recovering," Lila said in an affectless tone. "Don't worry. I won't sue."

"It looks like South Beach is treating you well. You seem like a native already."

"That's all thanks to Effie," Lila said. "Just today she invited me to stay at her guesthouse while I'm looking for a place of my own."

Dylan shot her a quizzical look. "That doesn't sound like the Effie I know." Lila let out a little laugh, thinking that was what was called for, but from his puzzled expression, she could tell he wasn't joking.

"That's not very nice," Lila replied, feeling strangely protective of Effie.

"But neither is Effie. Trust me on this one, okay?" He looked around to make sure Effie wasn't in earshot. "Just be careful that all this so-called generosity of hers doesn't come with a hefty price tag. Knowing Effie, it will."

"Well, she had only nice things to say about you." Lila sniffed.

"If she's not bad-mouthing me, then I am certain she's up to no good. And speak of the devil," Dylan said, pointing his head to where Effie was crossing the room toward them. Her face was drained of color, her eyes raw and red as if she'd been crying.

"Listen, Camilla, I was hoping that I could call you sometime. Maybe take you out to dinner?"

As Lila was figuring out what to say, Effie sidled up next to her, wrapping her hands around Lila's arm.

"Hi, Dylan," she said quickly. "Listen, Camilla, we need to go right now."

Lila looked at her friend. She was shaking ever so slightly. "What's wrong, Effie?"

"Wrong? Why do you think anything's wrong? I just need

to go right now." Effie pulled Lila's arm toward the door. "I have a terrible headache. Let's go."

Both women looked at Dylan. "You understand, don't you, Dylan?" Effie murmured.

"More than you know," Dylan replied, with a sort of melancholy sternness that Lila didn't understand.

CHAPTER 14

LILA'S CELL PHONE vibrated on the passenger seat as her car raced down the Overseas Highway toward Key Largo. As she sliced through the tropical throng of the Everglades, she checked to see who was calling. Meredith Sloan. Again. Fourth time since last night. Lila had made an offer on the Star Island house next to Effie's a week ago, just to keep up appearances—an incredibly low one that she knew Meredith would have no choice but to refuse—and now Meredith was calling nonstop with so-called updates on the other bidders. Lila silenced her phone and tossed it into the backseat.

Today there was no Camilla Dayton. Today, Lila Day would exist wholly in her own skin. No pretending. No hiding.

It had been more than a month since she'd traveled to the past, and every day she'd devoted herself to finding the Star Island killer. But today was different. It was November 2. The anniversary of her mother's death, which Lila considered to be the anniversary of her greatest failure.

On November 2, 2015, Theresa Day died from a blood cancer she had battled for years. She died completely alone in her bed, without her two daughters by her side. Lila's only sister, Ava, had been gone for years—she'd fled the country, accused of a crime that Lila was convinced she didn't commit. As far as Lila knew, Ava had no idea their mom was even sick.

As for Lila, the day of her mother's death, she was at the police station working on the Star Island case, too absorbed by her job to know how serious her mom's condition had become. Too stupid to understand how much her mother needed her.

Every November 2 since, Lila had driven down to Key Largo, where her family spent their Christmas vacations when she was a child. They would rent a run-down cottage right on the ocean, collect seashells during the day, and play board games at night. Now, every year on the anniversary of her mother's death, Lila came back to this spot to be alone. It was where she felt closest to her mother's spirit. It was where she'd scattered her mother's ashes.

This day had another layer of strangeness to add to its agonies. Right now, even as Lila was memorializing her mother's death, her mom was still alive. She wouldn't be dead for another year, and there was nothing that Lila could do to stop it.

The thought turned Lila's stomach. She wanted to track down her past self and give her a good talking-to, save herself from all the mistakes she was making at that very moment. She wanted to find that Lila and make her understand that her mom wouldn't be around much longer. She wanted her to pay more attention to the things that mattered.

But she couldn't find her past self. All of her mistakes would need to unfold just as they did before Lila traveled back to 2014. They needed to unfold into this big mess of a life.

She parked her car at Pennekamp Park and walked toward Far Beach. It was a warm day, but the beach was practically empty. Lila sat down, took off her shoes, and dug her toes deep into the cool, fine sand. She closed her eyes and started to let her mind drift.

"Camilla? Is that you?"

Lila bolted upright. She must've fallen asleep because, as she looked around, she realized that the sun was beginning to set and there was a chill coming into the air. She rapidly blinked her eyes, and there, standing above her, was Dylan Rhodes.

"Dylan?" she mumbled, as she tried to get her bearings. "What's going on? How did you get here?"

"Sailing." He pointed to a sailboat docked a couple hundred feet out in Largo Sound. "Just coming back from the Bahamas."

"But why are you here, I mean, on this beach?" Lila, still pulling herself out of a deep sleep, was confused and profoundly irritated. She was here to mourn her mother, and this square-jawed Mr. Wonderful was not part of the plan.

"I dropped anchor and kayaked in." Lila looked over to see a red kayak pulled up on the beach. "This is one of the best spots in the country. But I didn't think anyone knew about it." He plopped down next to Lila, sitting a bit too close for her comfort.

"Neither did I. That's what I like about it. You can be alone here," Lila said in a tone so snippy that there was no way Dylan wouldn't pick up on her annoyance.

She felt his eyes on her. There was something about the intense way he looked at her that made Lila uncomfortable.

She gave him a sideways glare. "What?" she asked.

"Sorry," he said, switching the direction of his gaze to the ocean. "I didn't mean to stare. It's just that you look so different than the other times I've seen you."

A thin current of panic shot through her. Lila was wearing the worn-out jeans and tank top she'd had on the day she arrived from the future. Her hair was up, and her face didn't have a stitch of makeup. Was she exposing the real her, risking her cover?

"Actually," he said, "I like you better like this. All that other stuff is just gilding the lily, so to speak."

Lila rolled her eyes, ignoring his attempt at flirting.

"So," he went on, unfazed. "Where's your new roomie?"

"I haven't the faintest idea," she replied. "We're separate people, you know."

"Not from what I've seen," Dylan said, giving her that teasing smile of his. Lila hated how everything he said sounded like some kind of mix of a jab and a joke.

"Meaning what?"

"Meaning the last time I saw you two, you were practically attached at the hip. It's like she's making you into a mini-Effie. And, trust me, one Effie in the world is quite enough."

Lila was getting tired of Dylan's constant need to slag Effie. Granted, Effie wasn't going to win any humanitarian-of-the-year awards, but Lila was coming to think of her as a friend.

She stood up.

"You leaving?" he asked, scrambling to his feet.

"Looks that way." She turned to walk back toward her car.

"Hey," he called after her. She turned to see his smile was gone. "I'm sorry. I didn't mean to lay into Effie again. It's just I think you're different"—he paused—"better than her."

"Why do you think you know me?"

"I just do. I know who you are."

"Oh, really," Lila said with a tight laugh. His arrogant

presumption was startling. "Then you know why I'm here, I assume?"

"No, I don't," Dylan admitted.

"Then let me enlighten you. Three years ago, today, my mom died." The words were hot in her throat. "And this is where I scattered her ashes. So I came to be with her, and now you're here." She felt the tears spring to her eyes, her voice beginning to crack. "And a bad day just got worse, thanks to you."

It was the first time since she'd traveled back to 2014 that Lila had dropped her facade in front of another person. Even though she was flooded with pain, it felt good to be herself again, if only for a moment.

She quickly blinked her eyes, trying desperately not to cry. But from the look on Dylan's face, she knew her words had struck a blow. A blow that was undeservedly strong.

"I'm sorry, Camilla. I didn't know."

"Exactly. You didn't," she spit, though she knew her anger was misplaced. The harder she tried to suppress the tears, the more acutely she felt them coming. She turned her back on Dylan, not wanting him to see her like this. But she couldn't help the anguished sob that burst out of her mouth. Tears streamed down her face.

"Please, just go," she said, in a defeated voice. But instead, she felt him come up beside her.

"Come with me," he said. "I want to show you something."

Lila shook her head, unable to speak. The surge of grief had left her feeling depleted and exhausted.

"Trust me," Dylan said. Lila looked up into his clear, brown eyes, so genuine in that moment.

"Okay," she whispered.

Together they walked along the beach in silence. Lila tried to stop crying, but now that she'd opened the floodgates, she seemed unable to stop. As he led her along a sandy path that cut through the dense tropical forest, Lila began to feel her resistance toward Dylan soften slightly. She had always been alone on this day, and it was nice to have someone beside her for once.

Though the path continued straight, Dylan turned right, taking her through a dense thicket of palm trees until, breath-takingly, dark jungle opened up onto a small, secluded beach.

"How'd you know this was here?" Lila asked, amazed that she'd never found this magical place before.

"My dad found it. He used to bring me here. See that spot?" Dylan pointed to a rocky inlet full of still, turquoise water. "That's where he taught me to swim. Then when it was low tide we'd spend the day walking so far out that I thought we were in the middle of the ocean floor."

They both stood still, lost in their own memories.

"He's gone now, too," Dylan said.

Lila kept looking forward. She understood now. He knew what it was to lose someone.

"What happened?" she asked softly.

"He got sick. The details aren't important. But he was my world. Taught me everything. Gave me everything. When I lost him, I thought it would break me. But it didn't. I'm still here." He paused. "And so are you."

Lila nodded. In her pocket, her cell phone rang, destroying the serenity of the moment. She glanced at the screen.

It was Meredith.

"Christ," Lila said. "Meredith Sloan for the fifth time today. She's relentless."

"She's a piece of work, that one," Dylan agreed, with a smile.

"I find her absolutely terrifying." Lila laughed. She felt light, almost giddy, as if her tears, her anger, her moment of honesty had lifted a heavy weight off her chest.

"It's nice to see you smiling," Dylan said softly, stepping toward her.

"Listen, I should head back. The sun's almost down and I—"

"Me too," he interrupted. Letting her know she didn't need to give him an excuse.

Before they stepped back onto the beach, Lila turned to him, suddenly and impulsively, grabbing his hand. "I'm sorry about your dad. And thanks—for being here, today."

"My pleasure," Dylan said. "Do you think . . ." He paused, his eyes fixed on her.

"Do I think what?"

"That I can call you sometime?"

Before she could think twice about it, Lila just nodded. She took his phone and quickly put in her number. What could possibly come of it? She would only be here two more months.

Dylan grinned and turned to start pushing his kayak back in the water.

"So," he called out over his shoulder. "Why's Meredith hounding you?"

"House stuff. I put in a bid for a house on Star Island. The one next to Effie's." Lila saw a look of disappointment flicker across Dylan's face.

"You don't approve?" she asked.

"I don't know," he answered. "You just don't strike me as the Star Island type."

"What makes you think you know me at all?"

"You can't fool everyone all the time," he said with a smile as he jumped smoothly into the kayak.

Then, as he started to paddle back to his boat, he called to her over his shoulder. "And just remember, our world isn't as perfect as you may think it is."

Of course it's not, she thought sadly. *Of course it's not.*

CHAPTER 15

WEEKS PASSED. LILA'S work on the case was progressing, but not as fast as she'd have liked. She hated to admit it, but she was starting to worry. For every suspect she eliminated, she accumulated a dozen more questions. Most frustrating of all was the fact that she hadn't gotten any closer to figuring out the mystery at the heart of the Janus Society. Even with endless information at her fingertips, even spending time with the society members themselves, she felt like a rat in a maze, hitting one dead end after another.

So here she was, spending yet another Friday afternoon sitting by the pool at Effie's Star Island house while Effie pounded back shots of tequila. In six days it would be Thanksgiving. Time was running out. As the sun retreated toward the horizon, Lila wondered for the thousandth time whether focusing on Effie had been a mistake. Was she wasting her time?

Ever since the night at Fisher Island when Effie had become so upset, she'd been acting strange and secretive. She'd also been drunk and high more often than normal, which, given Effie's appetite for altered states, was slightly alarming to Lila.

"So," Effie continued, now rolling a joint on the cover of an

Italian *Vogue* she had balanced on her thighs, "if Meredith says there's another offer on the house, you have to match it, right?"

The sun had become magenta, and the evening sky was darkening with purple clouds. Sunsets gave Lila a pure physical pleasure, like diving into the ocean on a hot summer's day.

"First thing tomorrow, Ef," Lila promised. "I just don't want to get into a back-and-forth with her tonight." Though the whole farce of bidding on the house was a good way to keep Meredith around, Lila had absolutely no intention of spending that kind of actual money while here. It didn't seem right.

"Speaking of exhausting. I'm going to your old stomping grounds to be with my dad and stepmonster for Thanksgiving." Effie rolled her eyes, so Lila rolled hers while Effie watched. Effie required active listening from those she deemed lucky enough to hear her stories. By this point, Lila knew when to gasp, clap, roll her eyes, nod, frown, and smile.

"I'll be forced to breathe the same air as Coleen Mathewson Webster, a.k.a. my stepmother, and her three little horrific children. They're about as pleasant as a tornado, and slightly more destructive. My dad will be at the office the whole time while Coleen bosses everyone around, including me. It's excruciating. Meanwhile, my real mom is in an ashram somewhere in Costa Rica sleeping on a tatami mat and trying to embrace the now with a guy named Swami Gerry. What a joke."

"Thanksgiving just as the Puritans intended," Lila said, which got a meager smile out of Effie.

"Hey," Effie said as she lit the joint. "Aren't you going somewhere for Thanksgiving?"

"Me?"

"I know you said your mom and dad aren't around anymore, but you've got to have someone else, right? Or are you my little lost orphan?" Effie put on a big faux pout, the facial equivalent of the emoticons she included in so many of her texts.

Lila thought of her own Thanksgiving in 2014. The tiny house with the paper-thin walls in a dying part of Fort Myers. Her mother, looking thin and tired but assuring Lila she was fine. Lila should've known better. That was the last Thanksgiving she ever had with her mom.

She let out a big sigh. "I mean, I've got the fat aunts and the bitchy cousins just like anyone else. It's just that, being in the middle of a divorce and all, I don't want to have to go into everything with them. You know?" Lila figured it was as good an excuse as any. Luckily Effie seemed to eat it up.

"I'm with you there." Effie nodded. "Some people like to be around family when they're down. But my family attacks the weak like a pack of wild animals."

The two women sat gloomily on chaise longues as evening began to engulf the air.

Lila jumped when her cell phone vibrated. Assuming it was Meredith, she was about to silence the phone. But she didn't recognize the number.

"Who is it?" Effie asked, hungry for some distraction from her sour state.

"I don't know."

"Well, answer it, for Christ's sake!" As a woman who was constantly on her phone, talking, texting, tweeting, and documenting her every move, thought, and half-baked opinion, Effie believed that if the phone was making a ring, beep, or chirp, it had to be tended to like a baby bird.

When Lila answered, she was startled to hear Dylan's voice.

"Who is it?" Effie mouthed.

"Dylan," Lila silently mouthed back. Effie scrunched her

face to convey confusion. Lila shrugged a bewildered look right back at her. She hadn't told Effie about the afternoon she'd spent with Dylan at Key Largo. She had tried not to think of it at all. Or if she had, she'd convinced herself that the chemistry she had felt was imagined.

"I'm sorry it took me so long to call. I've been . . . out of the country," Dylan said. "But I was hoping I could convince you to join me for dinner tonight."

"Ummm . . ." Lila stalled, trying to figure out what to say. Part of her wanted to see him, part of her knew it was a bad idea, and part of her was reminded that she had plans tonight. According to Teddy's information, Rusty Browder was attending a fund-raising event for the University of Miami. She was planning on crashing it, hoping to get some one-on-one time with yet another member of the Janus Society.

"Thanks so much, but I'm busy tonight." As Lila said these words, Effie began to vigorously shake her head no. "I'm—"

Effie got up and ripped the phone out of Lila's hand.

"Hi, Dylan. It's Effie. Camilla would love to join you for dinner tonight." She smiled wolfishly at Lila. "Great. How soon can you be here? Perfect. Ciao!" With smug satisfaction, Effie handed the phone back to Lila.

"He'll be here in ten minutes."

"Ten minutes!"

"Oh, relax. Just throw on a dress, tie your hair in a bun, and put on some lipstick. It's not like a man is going to object if you're a little slapdash. Plus, I have my own plans tonight. And I don't think my date would appreciate you tagging along."

As Lila was getting ready in her room, she found herself becoming nervous and excited, like a teenager before prom. "You're a cop, goddamnit," she scolded her reflection. But the woman in the mirror, with her golden hair braided and pinned (thanks to Effie's quick handiwork), the flowing couture dress that revealed her long, bare neck and bronzed shoulders, and the Jimmy Choo heels, was as far from a cop—and as far from herself—as she could get.

Ten minutes later, Dylan pulled up in a silver vintage convertible Mercedes. A perfect car. But as she watched him get out and walk to her, Lila tried to quell any excitement she might feel. *This is just part of the mission,* she forcibly reminded herself. She was here to get intel, and that was it.

Dylan kissed her on the cheek. He smelled like woodsmoke and cedar shavings, a scent that was so anti-Miami, Lila wondered if he had a cologne called Lumberjack.

"Camilla," he said. "You look like a dream come true."

He took her to The Villa by Barton G., housed in the South Beach mansion where Gianni Versace had lived and then died—shot dead as he was coming home from his morning walk along Ocean Drive. No murder had brought Miami that much attention until the Star Island massacre seventeen years later.

They sat under an awning by the gold-lined pool. Dylan ordered cocktails and then leaned forward, getting closer to Lila than she liked.

"It's funny seeing you here tonight, all dolled up," he said as the waiter set down their elegant appetizers. "You're so much different than the day I ran into you at Key Largo."

"I wasn't myself that day."

"See, I was thinking the exact opposite. You seemed much more yourself to me."

Lila remained uncomfortably silent. The way Dylan looked at her made her nervous. He seemed to see through her, which was the last thing she wanted.

"Are you liking the food?" he asked, noticing Lila push her truffled asparagus salad around the hand-painted china.

"The food's great." That wasn't a lie, the food was delicious, but Lila wanted to make sure this dinner counted. She needed to see what Dylan knew about the Janus Society.

"I saw you talking to Johnny Oluwa the other day at the club. Effie said you two went to school together?"

Dylan gave a faint smile. "Does that mean you're asking Effie about me? I'll take that as a good sign."

He hadn't answered her question. Just as she was about to ask it again, she heard a thickly accented voice cry, *"Ay Dios mio!"*

Lila turned and immediately recognized Javier Martinez. One of the Janus Society members, the walking dead. He was standing by their table with a horrified look on his face.

"Dylan, it seems this woman is immune to your ample charms."

"I'm not sure you're really helping me out any, Javier," Dylan said with a smile. He stood up, and the two men embraced warmly.

"Javier, let me introduce you to the lovely Camilla Dayton. Camilla has just moved here from Manhattan."

"I thought I knew all the stylish women in the city. How did you slip under the radar?"

"It's a pleasure to meet you," Lila said, feeling relieved. The whole evening she had been chastising herself for wasting her night with Dylan when she should have stuck with her original plan, but now Javier was here. This was her chance. Javier curled his hand gently around her fingers, bowed deeply, and kissed her hand.

"Javier here is the city's top guy when it comes to art," Dylan said.

"Not just art, my dear Dylan. I collect all things beautiful. I'm like a magpie. Always bringing shiny things back to my nest."

"Then you're just the man I need," Lila exclaimed.

"No, darling, the man you need is right there." Javier pointed at Dylan. "He's the man we all need, actually."

"For decorating, I mean." Lila smiled. "I'm buying a place soon and I'm desperate for help filling it up with some beautiful things."

"Well, that's music to my ears, sunshine to my eyes!" Javier exclaimed. He tucked his hand into his perfectly tailored suit coat and produced a business card. "Come by my gallery tomorrow, if you can. I'm free in the afternoon."

"I'll be there. Is two good?"

"Glorious. Now, I must go back to my dining companion," Javier said, waving his hand toward a strong-featured, darkly tanned man, the spitting image of a young Picasso. The man was looking around peevishly. "My amour is allergic to solitude. If I'm gone for more than five minutes, he'll find someone else to entertain him. So, I'll let you two get back to having no fun whatsoever."

"He's a charmer," Lila said, watching Javier drift back to his pouting boyfriend. "So, how do you two know each other?"

"From around." Dylan sighed. He was becoming annoyed, Lila could tell.

Before she could continue, the sommelier stopped by with a bottle of Krug Grande Cuvée. "Compliments of Señor Martinez."

"From around where specifically?" Lila asked as the waiter poured. She was anxious to get something valuable out of Dylan.

Dylan took a large gulp of the champagne, then raised the glass to Javier across the mosaic patio. The two men silently nodded at each other. "I'll answer this last question, but then we've got to talk about something other than my social connections." He paused and gave Lila a stern look until she nodded her acquiescence to his demand. "Javier is one of the world's top yacht racers. But, of course, if I may be so bold, so am I. We were both on the same team, years ago, for the America's Cup."

"Did you win?" Lila asked, taking a large sip of champagne.

"Not quite. Our boat flipped over off the coast of Auckland. It got absolutely destroyed. Total humiliation. We all had to be scooped out of the ocean by a rescue boat with the world's cameras trained right on us." He smiled ruefully. "That was the last time someone trusted either of us with a four-million-dollar boat."

As the meal progressed, the champagne began working on both of them, ironing out their wrinkles and relaxing their limbs. Smiles came more easily to both of their faces. Whenever Lila the detective came out, Dylan expertly sidestepped her direct questions. And Lila started to forget that she wasn't supposed to enjoy herself.

"Do you ever sail?" Dylan asked.

"Never."

"We'll have to do something about that, and soon. Miami is at its most beautiful when you see it from the ocean." Just then, Chase Haverford walked into the restaurant. The moment Dylan saw him, he got up from his seat. "Camilla, will you excuse me for one second?" She watched as he walked over to the waiter and then disappeared into the Rococo mansion.

After Lila had been sitting by herself for a few minutes, sipping champagne, her phone rang. It was Dylan.

"Come meet me out front," he said, before quickly hanging up.

Walking down the mansion steps where Versace had been murdered in cold blood, Lila spotted Dylan waiting for her with a take-out bag under his arm, his car at the ready. As she descended the stairs, he moved toward her, grabbing her hand. "I had to get out of there," he murmured, his fingers trailing along her bare arm. "And it seemed like you wanted to leave, too." Lila felt dizzy from his touch, and from the champagne. As Dylan climbed into the car and put his warm hand gently on hers, she felt her defenses against him weakening. She didn't pull away from his touch, but she didn't acknowledge it either.

They sped down Ocean Drive in silence. The gentle warmth of the air felt neither hot nor cold on her skin. It was perfect, like there was no boundary between her and the night. They were floating together.

Dylan stopped the car at Lummus Park. They got out and strolled down to the ocean, Dylan carrying the bag. The sound of the wildly crashing waves was the only noise punctuating the placid night. Farther down the beach someone had made a bonfire.

"Let's climb up there." Dylan pointed to a lifeguard's stand painted to look like the American flag.

"Okay," Lila said, smiling at the spontaneity of it.

When they were perched at the top of the lifeguard stand, Dylan reached into the bag and pulled out a take-out box, placing it on Lila's lap.

"I thought we'd have dessert by the ocean," he said. "I love the food at those ritzy restaurants, but sometimes I can't stand the atmosphere. I hope you don't mind."

Nothing could've pleased Lila more. She closed her eyes and took a deep breath, letting the briny sea air fill her lungs.

"This is perfect," she said, reclining on the wooden slats with a long, contented sigh.

They sat together, shoulder to shoulder facing the ocean, and carefully ate their pristine desserts forkful by tiny forkful. As Lila bit into a gold-dusted beignet, the taste of rich chocolate and cinnamon flooded her mouth.

Just then, Dylan leaned over to kiss her. A jolt shot through her, along with an immediate impulse to pull away. But she didn't. He put his hand in her hair, his full lips pressed on hers. His mouth tasted of ripe strawberries. Her head was telling her to act smart, to end it now, to focus. But instead her arms wrapped around him as she pulled his body closer.

CHAPTER 16

THE JAVIER MARTINEZ Gallery was in a run-down industrial section of North Miami, sandwiched between a boarded-up auto repair shop and a vacant lot, not very far from Teddy Hawkins's storage-space/time-portal. As Lila parked her treasured car in the empty street full of abandoned businesses, she wondered why a man as old-school refined as Javier would choose this seedy spot for his gallery.

It was an exceptionally hot day for late November, so Lila was relieved when she entered Javier's ice-cold and cavernous gallery. Filling the entirety of the room were hundreds of pink fluorescent tubes placed at various angles along the walls. The windowless space echoed with that particularly unpleasant buzz that fluorescent lighting gives off. The card affixed to the wall read:

JACK MOLINA
"HORIZONTAL OF PERSONAL ECSTASY #1"
FLUORESCENT TUBING
$30,000

Feeling about as comfortable around conceptual art as Pat Robertson in a drag bar, Lila took an involuntary step back.

"Camilla! Darling!" Javier cried. He hurried toward her, dressed in an orange-and-white-checked shirt and lime-green polka-dot bow tie, and grabbed the sides of her shoulders, placing a quick kiss on each of her cheeks. "What do you think of this piece?" he asked. "The artist, a personal friend, created it specifically for this room."

"I feel like I'm being microwaved," Lila blurted out.

Javier let out an enormous laugh. "So do I," he said in a conspiratorial whisper. "I tell the gallery girls who work here to limit their time in this room. I'm convinced too much exposure will make them infertile! But come. Let's get out of this assault. I'll show you the rest of my gallery."

Lila followed as Javier led her into a smaller room. It was dominated by two enormous canvases, covered in thick layers of rich-hued paint that dripped down in kaleidoscopic fields of color.

"This is incredible!" Lila said, surprised to feel genuinely excited by these paintings.

"Gerhard Richter. He's a genius." Javier held his hands close to the surface of one of the paintings, as if to feel its energy field. "It saddens me that I only have two. These will go for around ten million each."

"No shit," Lila muttered, then cursed internally. Camilla Dayton wouldn't bat an eyelash at such a sum. She looked at Javier to see if he'd noticed her slip, but he was only smiling at her.

"No shit," he agreed. "Most of the people who can afford art this masterful don't deserve it. With the rare exception, such as yourself, my darling. This is why artists trust me with their paintings. I make sure they go to the right people. It's more like an adoption agency than an art gallery. Not every asshole who can afford a Gerhard Richter will get to have one, if I have anything to do with it."

Javier led Lila into yet another room, this one filled with samurai swords and ornate horned fighting helmets. He picked up a silver blade with a red bamboo handle, which was mounted on the wall. "This one's from the Edo period. That's about four hundred years ago." He swung the heavy sword over his head and then cut it through the air with great effortlessness and agility. "Wall Street types just love this samurai shit. I think half the CEOs in the Fortune five hundred have one of these in their offices. So predictable."

"How'd you get so comfortable with a sword?" Lila asked. Racer of yachts, dealer of art, wielder of weapons. What else, Lila wondered, fell into Javier's realm of expertise? How close an eye should she keep on this jack-of-all-trades?

"I had a young man's dreams of acting. When I was at university in Buenos Aires, I tried out for every play, but all I ever got to do was some sword fighting. I was never the hero or the lover. Always the soldier." Javier lunged with his sword into an invisible opponent, then placed the weapon in his imaginary sheath and took a deep, grand bow. Lila clapped.

"You may have missed your calling," she said.

"Hardly, my dear. In essence, a salesman is an actor. I merely play a different part depending on who the person is and what I want from them. It's quite simple."

"And what part are you playing for me?"

"Today, for you, I'm playing a very special part, one quite close to my heart: Javier Martinez. For you, I play myself. And you'll play the wealthy divorcée."

He put the samurai sword back on the wall.

As they toured the remaining rooms of the vast gallery, Lila talked about the Star Island house she was supposedly purchasing, and Javier suggested how to decorate it. If Javier had his way, all of Teddy's money would go toward art.

Finally, after she'd seen everything, Lila turned toward the door. Now that she and Javier had a connection, she'd be able to spend time with him, maybe find out who his enemies were.

"Well, Javier, thanks for showing me around. I—"

"Now, what time is it?" Javier said, looking at his watch and cutting Lila off midsentence. "It's almost three o'clock, and I'm starving. Camilla, will you join me for lunch? I know of the most fabulous place in Miami to eat, and, let me tell you, it's somewhere Effie would never, ever take you."

"Perfect," Lila said. No time like the present to spend more time with Javier. He led the way out of the gallery and into the chauffeured black Escalade idling by the front door. As Lila settled into the backseat with Javier, she took note of the custom details. The outside of the car was definitely armored, and Lila suspected that the heavily tinted glass was bulletproof. Whatever Javier was into, it went far beyond the art world if he thought he needed this type of protection.

"*¿Adónde, señor?*" the driver asked.

"*El Pub, por favor.*"

After a short drive, they pulled up to a small, humble restaurant right on Calle Ocho, in the heart of Little Havana. Several groups of white-haired Cuban men sat with curious tourists at the outdoor tables, talking and eating their lunch. The place was bookended by two six-foot fiberglass roosters painted in the red, white, and blue of the Cuban flag.

The young waitress standing behind El Pub's linoleum

counter broke into a huge smile when Javier walked into the restaurant. He took a seat on a stool and patted the adjacent stool for Lila to join him.

"Looking at you, I'd say you exist on birdseed," Javier admonished, giving Lila a thorough once-over. "All skin and bones like you girls want to look, but this is a Cuban restaurant. There's no birdseed on the menu, so I'll order for you if it's okay."

Five minutes later, Lila was tucking into the best *ropa vieja* she'd ever tasted, and Javier was gobbling down a cubano sandwich. Yesterday they had both eaten at the most expensive restaurant in the city. But Lila was much happier here, spending less on her whole lunch than the price of one pre-dinner cocktail at The Villa.

"Thank you for sending that champagne over last night," Lila said.

"Please." Javier delicately patted the sides of his mouth with the corner of his napkin. "I did it for Dylan. The man looked like he was drowning, with you practically pouting into your foie gras. Rich, handsome, and charming isn't your thing?"

Lila's mind raced back to the kiss she and Dylan had shared. Her face turned crimson, and her eyes dropped to the counter. "Actually, the night ended better than it started."

"It couldn't have gotten much worse." Javier let out an exasperated sigh. "I haven't had an easy road, darling, trust me on that. But I thank Christ every day that I'm not attracted to women. Your kind are . . ."

Javier abruptly stopped speaking as the door to the restaurant opened and Carlos Mas Canosa walked in, followed by two bodyguards in black suits and sunglasses. Lila suppressed the gasp that almost escaped from her lips. Before the Star

Island killer monopolized the Miami Police Department's time and money, Mas Canosa had been their number one target—a known head of the Juárez cartel, murderer of hundreds of drug war soldiers, kingpins, and civilians. Everyone called him El Chapo, or "Shorty," because even in his heeled cowboy boots he was barely five feet, three inches.

No one made eye contact with El Chapo as he walked across the dining room, then into the men's room at the back of the restaurant. His two bodyguards stood at attention at the entrance to the restroom.

"Keep enjoying your food. I want you to fatten up a little bit," Javier said, twisting around to give the restaurant a quick scan. "Miami men aren't like those walking haircuts on Wall Street that I'm sure you're used to dating—they like their women a bit curvier. Now, excuse me. I'll be back momentarily." He turned and headed toward the back of the restaurant, where El Chapo had disappeared seconds before.

Sitting there alone at the linoleum counter as the sweet young waitress refilled her barely touched coffee, Lila wondered what, exactly, was going on. Was El Chapo the Star Island killer? Was it a drug deal gone bad? What was the connection between Javier and El Chapo?

With the hope of overhearing something from the women's room, Lila got up and headed in that direction. But as she was about to open the bathroom door, she felt a steely grip on her left shoulder. It was one of El Chapo's bodyguards.

"Pardon me, señorita," said the giant man with a shaved head and a jowly face like a bulldog's. "Bathroom's closed."

"I just need to quickly wash my hands," Lila said.

"You'll have to wait. Out of order."

Not wanting to continue a debate with a refrigerator-sized

man, Lila returned to her spot at the counter. The previously lively restaurant had taken on a funereal tone.

"Does that guy come in here a lot?" Lila asked the waitress, whose big brown eyes had widened into frightened saucers. The waitress looked at her but then quickly looked away, not answering, not nodding, nothing. El Chapo's favorite way of dealing with his enemies, and those who spoke out of turn, like overly chatty waitresses, was beheading. Rumor was his men played soccer with the heads of rival cartel members.

Ten minutes later, El Chapo came out of the washroom, followed by his two bodyguards. When all three of them exited El Pub, the entirety of the restaurant exhaled. A minute later, Javier glided back to his seat and returned to his now cold cubano sandwich.

"Who was that man?" Lila asked, playing the wealthy divorcée from out of town.

"What man?" Javier said, blinking at her blankly.

"The tiny guy with the bodyguards?" His blank look went unchanged. Lila's tone got louder, "Javier, the man you were just in the washroom with for the last ten minutes?"

"I don't know what you're implying, dear Camilla," Javier said with the self-righteous tone of the unjustly offended, "but the days when men like me were forced to hide away in washrooms for clandestine assignations are long, long gone."

"That's not what I was saying, Javier. And you know it." Two red-faced tourists squeezed through the door with Miami guidebooks in their hands and cameras around their necks. Javier looked at them like they were carriers of a plague.

"I've got to get out of here. It's getting a bit too midwestern for my sensibilities. Well, my darling, did you enjoy your field trip to the wrong side of the tracks?" Javier asked.

"I know more about places like this than you'd think, Javier," Lila snapped, irritated at the thought that something important had happened and she'd somehow missed it. Little did Javier know that her own apartment was just a few blocks from this very spot. "I haven't always been wealthy."

"Of course!" Javier exclaimed. "I knew there was something different about you, a toughness that sets you apart. Now I know why. You started with nothing."

Lila thought suddenly of her childhood. Her dad hadn't been in the picture, so she, her sister, and her mom had learned to live on her mother's meager paycheck. Though they had little, Lila's mom was a wild and artistic dreamer. She would spin tales for her two little girls about a better life than the one they were living: a sophisticated life full of glamour and art and luxury. A life very similar to the one Lila was leading now, as Camilla Dayton. Thoughts of her mother brought tears to Lila's eyes. Javier reached his hand out to hers, patting it affectionately.

"Remembering one's childhood is always an exercise in melancholy, dear Camilla. Don't feel shy about being sad."

A contemplative silence fell over Javier. He watched Lila in a way that made her feel he was sizing her up somehow. Then he broke into a smile. Whatever question had come to his mind had now been settled.

"I've got a quick errand to run. But maybe you should come with me. It's close by. I don't get over here that often. Do you have the time?"

Of course Lila would come along. That mysterious meeting with El Chapo had just made Javier Martinez, the charming and unassuming art dealer, much more interesting.

During their twenty-minute drive north on I-95, Lila and

Javier mostly talked about art. Javier went on and on about how he found Claes Oldenburg to be grotesque and spent another five minutes detailing his obsession with Richard Serra. Lila smiled and nodded when she knew it was conversational to do so, but she wasn't listening. He was talking bullshit, just filling up the empty air, and they both knew it. She needed to figure out Javier's role in all of this. What was he up to, and how was it connected to the Star Island killer?

When the car made a left on Ali Baba Avenue, Lila realized they were in Opa-Locka, a bizarre, forgotten town founded by an aviation Hall of Famer who'd designed the place with a Thousand and One Nights theme, as if it was his own personal amusement park. Though some of the Moorish architecture remained, like the crescent moons sitting atop the white-domed roofs, now it was just another shitty Florida city, populated with one-level cement homes with bars on their windows and foreclosure signs on their dirt lawns.

The car pulled to a stop in front of a small pink stucco house with two large Dobermans in the front yard.

"Would you believe that inside this horrendous little house is the world's sole connection for ancient Mayan sculptures?"

No, Lila thought. The house's windows were covered on the outside by steel bars and on the inside with flattened cardboard boxes. *No, I wouldn't believe for one second that the occupant of this house is in any way connected to the art world.*

Lila, Javier, and Javier's driver got out of the car. The driver removed a large metal briefcase, which he kept close at his side. As he handed it to Javier, Lila noticed that the briefcase had a biometric fingerprint lock. Whatever was in that case had to be extremely valuable.

The moment the three of them set off in the direction of the house, the two dogs began barking and jumping, putting their paws on the top of the chain-link fence. The front door of the house swung open to reveal a tall, reed-thin man with a black mustache and a thick scar wrapped around his neck.

"*Mi amigo. ¡Callesen estos perros del diablo si no quieres que ellos ahogan en mis balas!*" Javier shouted over the cacophony of barking, snarling dogs. *Shut up those devil dogs if you don't want them to choke on my bullets,* he'd said. Then, as gentle as the morning sun, Javier turned to Lila. "You don't speak Spanish, do you?"

Lila shook her head no, though the answer was, of course, yes. To be a detective in Miami and not have at least a pretty good handle on Spanish was to just be bad at your job.

The mustachioed man called something to the dogs, who both sat down immediately and ceased their barking.

"These people don't speak a word of English, so just wait for me in the kitchen. I'll only be a couple quick minutes, then I'll show you some of his best sculptures."

Javier shook hands with the thin man, whispering something into his ear. The man gave Lila a slow once-over, then smiled, nodded, and slapped Javier on the back in approval. Javier walked a couple steps ahead of Lila, then turned to give her a devilish look. He had the face of a little boy about to set off a firecracker, full of bad intentions.

"Isn't my job fun?" he said.

The inside of the tiny house was anything but fun. It smelled of stale marijuana smoke and an indescribable musty scent that Lila figured was the by-product of the enormous iguana sleeping in the terrarium that took up half of the living room.

Javier and the man retreated into a back room, closing the door behind them. The driver stood by the door, and Lila went, as Javier instructed, down the hallway to the kitchen. A young woman stood at the stove, and a tiny toddler in a dirty T-shirt was in a high chair, picking at Cheerios spread out in front of him. The woman nodded at Lila and gestured to the small kitchen table, where Lila took a seat.

Lila wondered what Javier, an incredibly rich man and member of the Janus Society, was up to in a shithole like this. If this guy was in fact a black market smuggler of archaeological remains, he could get up to twenty years for doing what he was doing. But it seemed like something more was going on here.

She had less than six weeks left to figure everything out before Javier and the rest of the society would be dead. Lila decided that tomorrow, she would set up some surveillance on this run-down house. The bigger question was why Javier, a near-perfect stranger, had brought her along on what was clearly an incriminating errand. Was this some sort of test? And if so, would she pass?

A few minutes later, Javier rushed into the kitchen with the thin man following behind. He no longer had the briefcase and was looking slightly flushed, a thin sheen of perspiration on his forehead. Upon seeing the baby, he let out a yawp of delight before sweeping the child up into his arms.

"*¡Pero que precioso bebe!*" he said as he tossed the delighted baby up into the air. "What a beautiful baby boy," he repeated in English. Then, in an instant, he turned to Lila and planted a big kiss on her lips. Lila was shocked.

"You and I should have us one of these," he said to her.

Lila blinked at him, unable to say anything. *Who is this guy?* she wondered.

"Come on, Camilla." Javier grabbed her hand as she stood up from the chair. "Let's get back to the city. We'll have to wait on seeing the sculptures. He didn't have what I thought he would."

During the drive back to his North Miami gallery, while Lila was trying to make sense of it all, Javier chattered on endlessly. About his plans for Art Basel Miami Beach, which was coming up in December. About the forthcoming gallery expansion and how he was trying to get Cindy Sherman to let him exhibit her newest works.

"You should buy a Cindy Sherman," he said and then gasped when Lila told him she didn't know who that was. His energy was positively electric. He was a bundle of fidgets and smiles. Whatever shady dealings he had conducted, they had been to his liking.

The car pulled off the highway, heading down the empty streets of Miami's abandoned warehouse sector. "So what was in that case?" Lila asked.

"Money. Bribery money specifically. Mexican customs officials need a lot of, let's say, convincing to let Mayan artifacts go across the border."

"Is it illegal?"

"Don't act like such an innocent. I know you're smarter than that. Most of the things you see in a museum got there by way of war and plunder. The art world is just as dirty as any other business."

"But why did you bring me?" she asked.

"Oh, yes, I do suppose I owe you an explanation. That man you met today is old-school Mexican, which means he didn't take too kindly to the rumors he heard about me. Specifically my appetite for cabana boys. So I told him you were my girlfriend."

"That explains the kiss," Lila said, finally understanding.

"Yes, the kiss. Be sure not to tell Dylan," he said in a teasing voice. "The last thing I need is to be challenged to a duel."

The SUV pulled into a small alley behind the Javier Martinez Gallery. Javier got out of the car, and Lila followed him into the back entrance. He placed his hand on a scanner, then entered a ten-digit code into the key pad before inserting a key in a lock. Lila made a note of the two cameras that were mounted by the door. Saying that this place was heavily secured would be putting it mildly.

After the massacre, Lila's team of forensic accountants had gone over the businesses of Javier and all his known associates with a fine-tooth comb. Everything came up clean. But after what she'd seen today, Lila felt more certain than ever that the rumors about the suspicious nature of his wealth were true.

"Let's sit for a minute in my office," Javier said. "I want to show you a catalog of Cindy Sherman. She's so hot right now. Her prints are very expensive, but I know they'll only appreciate in value."

He walked across the room to a large bookshelf, standing with his back to her. "I know it's somewhere around here," he muttered.

Lila checked the room for cameras. There were none. People like Javier tended to keep their most personal spaces camera- and bug-free, so as not to incriminate themselves if the information got into the wrong hands. She eyed his computer. In preparation for a moment like this, Lila had been carrying a device no bigger than a thumb drive that could make an exact clone of a hard drive in two minutes. Teddy had included it in the suitcase he'd sent back in time, and now she finally had a chance to use it. Whatever Javier was up to, she had a feeling that there'd be at least some record of it on his computer.

Javier quickly found the Cindy Sherman catalog, handed it to Lila, then settled behind his elegant antique desk. As she flipped through the color-saturated photos, one of the gallery girls poked her head in the door.

"Mr. Martinez?" The girl wore a black sheath dress, a bun on the top of her head, and bright red lipstick. She looked to Lila like a child playing dress-up. "There's a man who has a question about the de Kooning."

Javier sighed and leaned back in his chair. "Thank you, Allison. I'll be there in a moment." The gallery girl left, and Javier wearily rose to his feet. After his buzzing frenetic energy, he seemed to be hitting a low. "Never once in my life has a walk-in bought a painting. Yet I'm expected to spend time with every idiot who sniffs around this place. Give me a moment."

Lila stayed seated, wanting to seem engrossed in the catalog she was perusing, as Javier headed to the gallery's main room. He turned back toward her. "Camilla, darling, are you coming?"

"Actually, I really love these photographs. Can I stick around? Talk about getting one of these for me?"

A flash of concern washed over Javier's face, but then his countenance relaxed. "Fine. Of course. I'll have Allison bring you in a glass of something cool, and we'll talk details in a moment."

Javier closed the office door, and Lila held her breath as she listened for his footsteps retreating down the hall. With her drive at the ready, she leaped up and bent under the desk to insert it into the computer tower.

Right then, the door opened. Lila held her breath. She was caught with her head under the desk. She popped back up, locking eyes with the young girl, who had a glass of perspiring white wine in her hand.

"Ms. Dayton?" Allison said with a confused look in her eyes.

"Thank you, dear," Lila said coolly, taking the glass from the girl. "I love this desk of Javier's. I was just looking to see if it was an original." Lila took a few steps back, pretending to admire the desk. "It really is an extraordinary piece."

"Yes! It is lovely," Allison said. "It's ebonized walnut, from the Louis XVI period. Quite rare. Shall I tell Javier you're interested?"

"I'll tell him myself."

With that the girl nodded and left the room. Lila looked at the drive, which was flashing blue, meaning it was done downloading. She removed it from the computer and tucked it into her bra for safekeeping just as Javier walked back into his office.

"What a monumental waste of time. De Kooning! That man couldn't afford a ticket to a museum, let alone a four-point-two-million-dollar masterpiece." Javier collapsed into his chair with a disgusted exhale. "So, my dear," he said, regaining his composure. "See anything that catches your fancy?"

He paused and looked her dead in the eye. "Aside from my desk, of course."

CHAPTER 17

THE FOLLOWING WEEK Effie took off for Thanksgiving in New York City.

"I'll spend some time with my family. But other than that it'll be just another shopping and spa-ing trip, my dear. I usually do it every month, but you've been such a welcome distraction that I haven't found it necessary. But my roots! *Quelle horreur!* They're ridiculous now."

Effie pointed, with her face twisted into a repulsed grimace, toward her hairline, which showed a barely perceptible difference in color between her light golden locks and her slightly less golden roots. "I can't trust any of these South Beach queens with my hair. You and I know there's only one person who can do the right blond, and that's Oscar. You do go to Oscar Blandi, right?" she asked, glancing back at Lila, who merely nodded. "Besides, you don't need me anymore. Now you can rely on Mr. Rhodes's company. Have fun!"

Lila had told Effie about her date with Dylan, and the long kiss that ended the night. Recounting the details over drinks by the pool, Lila had allowed herself, for the first time, to enjoy the feeling. For one moment, everything felt normal. She was just a girl telling her friend about a boy.

But the truth was so much more complicated than that.

And so Lila waved good-bye to Effie, thankful for a break from her host's oversight. For the last few days, Effie had been acting withdrawn and taciturn. She was constantly retreating behind closed doors to make surreptitious, whispered phone calls, which Lila had "happened" upon, forcing Effie to skitter away. Lila suspected that this trip was more than just family time and spa-ing.

However, now that Effie was out of town, Lila could momentarily shed the skin of Camilla Dayton and hunker down on her laptop to go over the information from Javier's hard drive. She needed to devote her days to the investigation, not Effie's social calendar.

She spent the next few days sitting under an umbrella by the pool, makeup off and hair undone, combing through the mountains of files from Javier's computer.

On her third morning, just as frustration was beginning to consume her over finding nothing, she heard someone call her name from far away.

Lila glanced up to see Dylan's boat pulling up to Effie's dock. She closed her laptop with a smile and hurried across the lawn to greet him.

He tied up his boat and walked toward her. The moment they met, he threw his arms around her.

"You've been hiding from me," he whispered into her ear. "So I thought I'd drop by. Perhaps take you on a sail?"

She shook her head no, but when she looked into his expectant face, she heard herself say, "Yes."

She dashed into the guesthouse, hid her laptop, and put on a bathing suit. As she reemerged, she heard the roar of engines. Looking toward the dock, she saw an enormous red, white, and blue speedboat idling next to Dylan's sailboat. Alexei Dortzo-vich, the Russian billionaire she'd met at the club, was at the helm. He and Dylan were talking. About what, she couldn't hear over the deafening engine noise.

She walked quickly across the lawn, but before she could set foot on the dock, Alexei's speedboat roared away.

As Lila boarded the sailboat, she noticed that Dylan's face looked flushed, as if he'd just been in an argument.

"Who was that guy?" she asked.

"You haven't had the displeasure of meeting Alexei Dortzo-vich yet?" Dylan replied. There was an angry edge to his voice.

"Just once," Lila said, "at the club one afternoon. What were you guys talking about?"

"Nothing." He set about the complicated task of getting the sailboat away from the dock and out into the sea.

Lila decided to drop the subject for now. Instead, she picked up the bottle of champagne chilling in a silver wine cooler. "Should I open this?" she asked, which finally got a smile out of Dylan.

"No, let me. Here, you grab the wheel. Just keep us heading straight."

She should have kept her eye on the horizon, but she couldn't help but watch Dylan as he moved along the deck, grabbing two champagne flutes, popping the cork, and pouring them each a glass. She wanted to laugh out loud. She never thought real life could look like this.

"So, why didn't you return my call?" Dylan asked as the boat sliced through the waters. He had taken back the steering wheel after Lila proved more interested in watching him than watching the waves.

"I've got a lot on my plate right now," she said, taking a large sip of champagne.

"Camilla," Dylan said softly. "I like being with you, and I hope you feel the same."

She nodded yes. It was undeniable. Something about him made Lila feel that she could finally exhale, live, be her real self.

"Good," he said. His face lit up into a smile, one she couldn't help but return.

Dylan grabbed Lila's hand and pulled her to him, swinging her around so that her hands were on the steering wheel and he was standing behind her. She leaned back against him, and he pressed his lips into the top of her head. Then Dylan moved his hand down her side to the soft of her belly. She turned to face him and they kissed. As their kiss grew deeper, her thoughts fluttered away like a flock of birds scattering suddenly into the air.

For that moment, there was only him.

"So," she asked, as their cheeks were pressed together, "where are you taking me?"

"Just a little barrier island way out in Biscayne Bay. It's one of my favorite places in the world. And we should have it all to ourselves."

The sailboat gracefully cut across the water, and the skyline of Miami receded into the distance as they approached an island that looked like nothing more than a few palm trees hovering above the turquoise waters.

Lila marveled at Dylan's movements as he guided the boat in the right direction. Each gesture, step, and movement was full of ease.

"How long have you been sailing?" she asked.

"Forever. This is my granddad's boat." He ran his hand along the steering wheel with tender care. "I've always loved this boat. But after he died, it was neglected. A few years ago, my brother and I decided to fix it up ourselves. Took us three years, but now she's a thing of beauty. Speaking of beauty," he asked with a wicked grin, "do you have your bathing suit on under that dress?"

To answer his question, Lila slipped the thin straps of her dress off her shoulders and let the whole thing fall to the ground, revealing a small black-and-white polka-dot bikini.

"I'll take that as a yes then." Dylan laughed and threw a large anchor overboard. "You don't mind swimming to the island from here, do you?"

"I'm game."

Dylan took in the sails. Then he threw some sort of large trunk overboard and jumped in after it. Lila dove headfirst into the water.

"What's in the trunk?" she asked as they swam to the shore, Dylan dragging the object behind him.

"Lunch, of course."

THE AFTERNOON WAS perfect. They spent the day swimming, snorkeling, eating, laughing, and drinking the two bottles of champagne Dylan had packed on ice at the bottom of the cooler. There was not a soul around to share in the fine white sand and the warm azure waters lapping at the shore. It was just the two of them, alone in paradise.

On the trip back to Star Island, they stayed curled against each other the whole time. As Dylan steered, Lila stood behind him, her arms wrapped around his chest, her head pressed on his back, watching the setting sun slowly transform the sky into a rainbow of bruised purples and reds.

"When can I see you again?" Dylan asked as Lila climbed off the boat and onto the dock. He had his hand in hers to steady her as she jumped onto the land's reassuring embrace, but now he wouldn't let it go. She leaned in to kiss him once more.

"Thanksgiving is Thursday. . . . So, after that, I guess."

"Saturday?" He was still holding her hand. She didn't want him to let go either, but her mind was already turning away from Dylan and back toward thoughts of the case.

"Saturday," Lila said as she kissed his hand and then let it go.

After an afternoon of swimming and sailing, Lila's legs felt unsteady on the stable earth. *That's what love is like,* she thought as she walked toward the guesthouse. *You become so accustomed to its exciting textures and rhythms that solid ground begins to feel unnatural.*

Lila noticed that the lights in Effie's master suite were all on. She stepped forward, curious. Was her host already back from New York? *Wait, did I just say love?*

She shook off thoughts of Dylan and entered the house, climbing quietly up the grand staircase.

Effie's bedroom door was open. Lila called out her name. Upon hearing nothing, she stuck her head inside. No Effie. She was about to head back to the guesthouse when she heard muffled shouting from inside the bathroom.

"Effie?"

Still no response. She paused, quieting her senses so that she could hear even the smallest noise, a skill she'd honed during her years as a cop. Then she heard the muffled voice again. It sounded like Effie was crying.

She crept closer to the bathroom door to listen.

"How can you say that," Lila heard Effie cry, "and say you love me at the same time?" The crying turned hysterical. "No!" Effie shouted. "I don't care what the others think."

Never once in all their late-night talks about love and men had Effie even come close to giving Lila the impression that she had a special somebody. There were men in Effie's life—an endless rotation of attractive men going through the revolving door of her bedroom—but what Lila overheard was an Effie that she didn't know existed. Just as she was turning to sneak back out of Effie's room, the bathroom door opened.

Lila froze in her tracks. Effie stood in the doorway, her eyes red and a startled look on her face. Both women stared at each other.

"You're back!" Lila said. "So soon?"

"What are you doing here?" Effie asked peevishly, but Lila saw that her eyes were darting nervously around the room.

"I thought you were spending Thanksgiving in New York."

"Plans changed. My family was driving me bonkers." She scowled at Lila. "So I see you've made yourself quite at home in my absence. Thought you'd take over my room when I was gone?"

"No, Ef. Don't be crazy. I just saw your light on, so I came to see if you were home."

"And now you've got your answer."

Lila didn't understand why Effie seemed so angry.

"Plus, I wanted to ask if I could borrow a dress," Lila lied. If there was one tangent she had found that could distract Effie from a bad mood, it was clothes.

Effie frowned, then ducked back into the bathroom. "Take whatever you want," she said as she began to draw a bath. "You always do."

Before Lila could ask her what she meant, Effie closed the door on her.

CHAPTER 18

DESPITE THE HIGH of her day sailing with Dylan and her low of fighting with Effie, all Lila really wanted to do was get back to searching Javier's files. She couldn't believe that a man with his fingers in so many black markets had no dirt on him. Finally back in the comfort and safety of the guesthouse, Lila could return to reviewing his files.

Once again, she plowed through the usual stuff. Invoices. Texts for various gallery openings. E-mails to and from artists. Then she stumbled upon something alarming. A subset of files were under military-grade data encryption. Whatever Javier had saved there was something he wanted to keep very, very secret.

Lila didn't bat an eye at the heavy encryption. When she was still a cop, she'd been part of an investigative team that went after Shadow, the notorious ringleader of an international hacking collective. He'd been convicted of more than a hundred counts of identity fraud, grand larceny, and conspiracy in 2015. But this was still 2014, and Shadow was a free man. She knew that, for a fee, he'd crack this encryption.

It would be easy, but expensive. Of course, Lila didn't care about the money. She remembered from the investigation how to get in touch with him. She typed his e-mail address, xXxXXxshaDOWxxXxX@gmail.com, into her computer with the message "i walk through the Va11ey of the shadow of d3ath" and hit Send. Seconds later, he e-mailed back. The terms were quickly established, she wired the money, and he downloaded the files. Hours later the encryption was cracked.

It surprised Lila how little she cared about giving money to a known criminal. Perhaps the laissez-faire attitude of Miami was infecting her. Then again, it probably helped that she knew she'd be throwing him in jail soon enough.

As she reviewed the files, Lila quickly understood why Javier was so anxious to hide this information. She was staring at concrete proof that Miami's elite art dealer was also a world-class arms dealer.

It all made sense. The mystery. The money. The secrets.

"So that's the source of all his wealth," Lila muttered as she pored over page after page of documents detailing the acquisition and shipment of assault rifles, machine guns, and large quantities of ammunition. The destinations for these weapons of minor destruction read like a UN conflict list: Sierra Leone. Honduras. The Ivory Coast. Bogotá. The Congo. Syria. Places of human suffering, mayhem, revolution, and repression, where arms trafficking was internationally prohibited. There was an incredible number of records detailing wire transfers from global bank accounts to one in the Cayman Islands, which Lila presumed was Javier's.

But there was one file that didn't fit with the others. In it were a number of documents with detailed information about a man named Frederic Sandoval. It was an entire dossier on his movements. Where he was. What he was doing. Lila looked at countless surveillance photos showing a long-faced man who appeared to be around sixty, with thinning hair and stooped posture. Javier had been compiling this information for several months.

Why is Javier so interested in this guy? Lila wondered.

She turned to the exhaustive database compiled by Teddy and typed in Frederic Sandoval. There was nothing. Nothing under Fred. Nothing under Sandoval. She then typed the name into an online search. There were plenty of Fred Sandovals in the digital universe, with their Facebook pages and LinkedIn profiles, but none of them resembled the man exhaustively watched by Javier.

Never since she'd left the Miami PD had Lila wished she was still a cop as much as at that moment. If she was on the force, she could have access to background checks, credit card activity, and anything else she'd need to uncover a possible connection between Sandoval and Javier. But that was all in the past. She wasn't a cop anymore.

Wait, Lila thought, shaking her head. *This* was still the past. She was still a cop.

And suddenly she knew how she would find out who Frederic Sandoval was.

CHAPTER 19

PRETENDING TO BE someone else is a difficult task, but Lila discovered that pretending to be herself was even harder.

She needed to figure out how Sandoval and Martinez were connected, and she knew the best way was to access the Miami Police Department's criminal records database. And the only way to do that was by becoming her old self, Detective Lila Day, so that she could sneak into the police station.

Teddy had warned her against the dangers of meeting herself in the past. Which was why the night of Thanksgiving would be perfect for this particular undercover stint. On Thanksgiving, she knew that past-Lila would be sitting at her mother's cheap dining room table and wolfing down a meal her mom had spent all day cooking. And not only would her past self be out of the station on Thanksgiving—so would almost everybody else.

Lila had spent the morning in Miami gathering the wig and clothes she needed to transform back into herself, covering up the blond glamour of Camilla Dayton with the black-haired, fashion-challenged Detective Lila Day.

It was 10 P.M. when she had the cab drop her off at the Burger King a block from the station, a place she used to frequently grab a fast lunch from when she was on the force. She knew the layout well. She entered the restaurant by the side door, glancing briefly at the gray-faced staff standing bored behind the counter and the customers hunched over grease-stained paper wrappers, then went directly to the bathroom. In the handicap stall, she shed her high-priced clothes and put on the black wig and the sensible black pantsuit that had been her chosen uniform since the moment she was promoted to detective.

Looking at herself in the fluorescent lights of the Burger King bathroom gave Lila a pleasant shock. "There you are," she said to her reflection, feeling a sense of comfort in seeing a familiar person look back at her after two months of inhabiting what often felt like the body and mind of a stranger. The only problem was her hair. It was off, badly off, so she twisted it up in a sloppy bun secured to the top of her head.

Doing her best impersonation of herself, she climbed the stairs to the police station and boldly opened the door like she belonged there. Sitting behind the front desk was Sergeant Corey Kreps. Kreps was a veteran cop of thirty years who always managed to land the shit assignments, thanks to his habit of starting and ending each shift blind drunk on Jameson's, though he told everyone he had a desk job due to his "bum back."

"Who'd you have to piss off to be working Thanksgiving night, sweetheart?" Kreps asked her, his way of saying hello. She could smell the whiskey on his breath from ten feet away.

"Same person you pissed off, seeing as you've been sitting

here all night," Lila said, thinking her voice sounded strange in her ears. But from the way Kreps smiled at her, she knew she had passed the test.

"Go shit in your hat, Detective," the sergeant said before turning his attentions back to the sports section.

"Same to you, Kreps." With that, Lila walked past the front desk, through the lobby, and into the bowels of the station.

As she went down the familiar halls and into the dank little office shared by all of Central Miami's homicide detectives, a sense of homecoming overwhelmed her. Who knew that the odor of sweat and stale coffee could smell so sweet?

The Homicide office was empty, just as she'd thought it would be. She sat down at her desk, running her hand along the familiar collection of objects. The framed picture of her family at Disney World back in 1993, when she was five; the piles of notebooks; the handcuffs; the stained coffee mug; the stack of reports in various stages of completion.

All of her senses on alert, Lila logged in to the computer on her desk. She pulled up the city's criminal database and typed into the search field: Frederic Sandoval. Unlike Google, which spit out a handful of civilian Sandovals with proper jobs and active social media profiles, this database immediately delivered to her the Sandoval she was looking for. Staring at her from the mug shot was the balding, long-faced man that Javier had been stalking.

On February 5, 2001, Sandoval was arrested for breaking and entering. He was convicted and sentenced for grand larceny, serving fourteen months at the Everglades Correctional Institution. Then, in 2005, Sandoval was convicted on racketeering and drug charges. He was sentenced to three years in a state prison but was out in eighteen months for good behavior.

Sandoval was the primary suspect in the March 2012 shooting of known drug trafficker Buddy Fenton, but he was never brought up on charges. Lila knew what that meant. Since that attempted murder in the first degree was his third conviction, Sandoval would have faced a lifetime prison sentence without any hope for parole. Instead of facing those years, he turned snitch, and the police dropped the charges.

Lila sat there in the dark, furiously scanning the files devoted to the Fenton shooting. She reviewed all the forensic evidence and pictures of the crime scene showing Fenton slouched against a wall, a bullet through his forehead.

She gasped audibly when she saw it. The gun linked to the shooting was a Colt 45—the same gun used by the Star Island killer.

It was a common gun, of course, but she couldn't help thinking the connection was meaningful. The questions swirled in Lila's head: Did Sandoval have some dirt on Javier that he was going to use to secure his own freedom? Did Javier know this was happening, and was he planning on assassinating Sandoval to protect himself? Was the Star Island massacre nothing more than Sandoval preempting his own murder by killing Javier, with the eleven other victims just in the wrong place at the wrong time?

She decided to print off the pages of the Fenton case to look them over back on Star Island. But just as the first page was being spit out by the printer, she heard footsteps echoing loudly down the hall. The hairs on the back of her neck prickled. Something was wrong. No one should be here now. Quickly, she got up from the desk and hurried over to the window of the Homicide office, which overlooked the hall. What she saw made her heart stop.

The person walking in her direction was her.

Crouching low to the floor, Lila rushed toward her old desk, opened the bottom drawer, and removed a black metal lockbox. She entered the combination, and the lock clicked. She removed the revolver she stored there for safekeeping and tucked it in the front of her suit pants. If she was going to confront Frederic Sandoval, she'd need to come in heavy.

The footsteps grew louder. She rushed over to the printer and grabbed the page that she'd managed to print off, ducking beneath a desk adjacent to the door just as the footsteps stopped.

"Okay," she heard her past self mutter. "What the hell?"

Her heart beating so loud she thought it would burst, Lila turned and fled out of the side entrance, which opened into an empty alley.

Her breathing was heavy. She pressed her back against the station wall, bending forward, desperate to slow her mind and her pulse. A chill ran down her spine.

She remembered this night with icy clarity—the night her gun was stolen. It was a mystery that had haunted Lila for years. The police had launched a minor investigation to locate the firearm (a missing police weapon was always a big deal), but nothing had ever been discovered; only Lila's fingerprints were ever found on the lockbox and only she knew the combination.

She had stolen the gun, she knew that now. Years later, plus one trip back in time, the mystery of the missing revolver had been solved.

She walked back to the Burger King in a daze of confusion and shed her disguise on top of her disguise in the handicap stall, returning to only one layer of deceit. Once she was Camilla Dayton again, she looked at the printed page she'd managed to grab before fleeing the station. On it was Sandoval's last known address.

Tomorrow she'd pay him a visit.

CHAPTER 20

ON SATURDAY MORNING, Lila heard someone tapping on the sliding glass door of the guesthouse. She looked at her phone. It was a little before nine. She peeked around the corner to see Effie standing there, holding a silver tray with a French press and two croissants.

Lila paused. She'd been avoiding Effie ever since their strange fight in her bedroom.

She glanced quickly around the room. The gun was locked away, as were the notebooks full of her observations on the investigation. She went to the door and opened it for Effie, who stood there beaming like Little Miss Mary Sunshine.

"I thought I'd surprise you with a little breakfast," Effie said as she walked into the living room, putting the tray down on the coffee table.

Something had to be up. Effie was never awake this early, plus Lila suspected that Effie had never before carried a tray in her life.

"How nice." Lila hoped her smile didn't look as disingenuous as it felt.

"It's my way of saying sorry." Effie put the tray down and sighed back into a large white armchair. The entire guesthouse was outfitted with white furniture, like one of the showroom apartments architects build to advertise a new condo complex. Lila perched on the snow-white couch across from Effie, slightly holding her breath. She gave Effie a questioning, curious look.

"What's there to be sorry for, Ef?" When Lila wasn't sure what to do, she played dumb. It was a pretty woman's habit and she hated to use it, but it tended to work with Effie.

"Oh, you know. I didn't mean to bark at you the other night. I just always go crazy around Thanksgiving. The whole trip was totally exhausting." Effie reached for a croissant, broke off a small piece, and put it back on the plate. In all their meals together, Lila had never seen her take more than a couple small bites of anything set before her.

"It's okay," Lila said.

Effie rushed over to the couch, plopped down next to Lila, and threw her arms around her. "So you forgive me?"

"Of course," Lila said, playfully wrestling out of Effie's embrace. After a moment, she decided to go ahead and ask, "Is everything okay? Who were you on the phone with the other night?" Lila wondered why Effie was being so secretive about it.

"Oh, it was nothing," Effie said.

"You sounded upset."

"And you sound like the nagging mother I never had and never wanted."

"Fine," Lila said. "I'll mind my own business. And don't worry. I've been on the phone with Meredith Sloan about the house. I'm putting in a new offer tomorrow. I'll be out of your hair in no time."

While living at Effie Webster's had given her invaluable

access to the rest of the Star Island twelve, Lila had been wondering if now was a good time to move on.

"No! Please don't move out just yet," Effie protested. "I know I've been distant, but I need you right now." Her eyes were wide and pleading.

The force and urgency in Effie's voice surprised Lila. Whatever was going on had spooked Effie, that was for sure. She was scared, but about what?

"Effie. You know I'm always here for you if you need me." This Lila said from the heart.

"Then it's settled!" Effie exclaimed. "You're mine for a while longer." She poured herself a cup of coffee, but her hands were so shaky that some fell into the delicate saucer under the china cup. Then she grabbed the broken-off bite of croissant, spread a little strawberry jam on it, and put it back down on the plate, as if she were feeding herself via osmosis through her fingertips.

"Now, time to get dressed!" she squealed, jumping up and resting the coffee cup precariously on the couch's arm, causing the china to rattle. As Lila rose, she saw that Effie's cup had left a brown ring on the white upholstery. Effie saw Lila looking at the spot.

"Oh, don't fuss over that. I'm sure it'll come out, no problem." It was then that Lila realized Effie had never been forced to learn the lessons that come from cleaning up after your own mess. People had walked behind Effie her whole life, sweeping away what she had carelessly smashed.

For a moment, Lila hated spoiled, selfish Effie.

"Come on, you old hen," Effie said, seeing the sternness that had taken over Lila's face. "I'll fix it." She took a white linen napkin from the silver tray and gallantly placed it over the stain, like a knight laying his cloak over a muddy puddle. "There. Just like magic."

She seized Lila's arm and walked her quickly toward the bathroom.

"Go freshen up. It's Saturday. And you know what that means. We're heading to the club."

"Actually, Effie, I wasn't sure what the plan was, so I told Dylan we could do something." It was a partial lie. She was meeting Dylan later in the day for lunch, but she had planned on scoping out Frederic Sandoval's house in the morning. She had zero interest in spending the day with Effie at the club.

"Are you kidding?"

The two women stopped and stared at each other. Effie's mood swings had Lila feeling unsure which way was up, and she was tired of it. After a moment, Effie turned away from Lila and walked back into the living room.

"I wouldn't get too attached to Dylan if I were you," she called over her shoulder.

Lila stepped out of the bathroom toward Effie. "What do you mean?"

"Just that he doesn't always play well with others. You know, he's one of those guys who never wants anyone to slow him down," Effie said.

Lila shrugged. It sounded like what people said about her. "Don't worry about me, Effie," she said. "I can handle myself, just like you."

Effie went back to the main house in a major sulk. While Lila got dressed, she mulled over what was going on with her friend. She didn't know what to think. Effie had seemed so open, so transparent when they first met, but that had radically changed. Now it seemed she was all secrets, hidden agendas, and bad feelings. And now Effie was hiding an affair from Lila—a serious and heartbreaking affair, by the sound of it. But why? Lila shook her head. It was probably nothing more than typical Effie drama. And Lila had more important things to do than worry about a socialite's love life.

WEARING HER BLOND hair up in a messy ponytail and a low-key outfit of jeans and a black sweater, Lila got in her car and headed toward Sandoval's last known address. In a twenty-minute drive, she went from the opulence of Star Island to the wasteland of Liberty City. Once upon a time she'd thought that the wealthy, with their islands, their bridges, their yachts, and their country clubs, operated completely unaware that they lived a stone's throw from soul-crushing poverty. But now Lila realized that the rich were only too aware of the poor. That awareness was precisely why they lived on those islands with their bridges.

Lila pulled up across the street from what she hoped was still Sandoval's house and paused for a moment, taking in the surroundings. The house was on a run-down residential block full of postage-stamp front yards with patches of browned grass and the occasional withering palm tree. Two young girls rode up and down the street on pink bikes as an old woman watched them from a broken-down couch on the front porch. There was no sign of life around Sandoval's house.

Lila drove around the corner, parked, and walked to the house, her gun tucked securely in her jeans.

The calm afternoon was suddenly interrupted by the sound of a man's anguished cry erupting from inside Sandoval's house. Lila immediately and instinctively started to sprint forward, reaching for her revolver, ready to fire. Her racing pulse made her temples throb, but her hands were steady.

"Police," she said, out of habit.

The man wailed again. She heard the rustling sound of someone else moving inside.

"Police!" she shouted again. There was no answer.

Lila kicked the door in and stumbled inside. Sandoval was lying on the floor, his hands clutching his chest, his face a purplish red.

His eyes bulged with desperation when he saw her.

"My heart," he gasped.

Lila couldn't believe it. She had walked in on him having a heart attack. Quickly, she picked up Sandoval's house phone and dialed 911. She knew she couldn't speak. Every call was recorded. If she communicated with the emergency operator, she would have the police searching for a woman who shouldn't exist.

Lila placed the receiver next to Sandoval's mouth.

"Tell them to send an ambulance," she whispered to the dying man. But he couldn't summon the words, only groans of pain and terror.

Lila felt his pulse. It was as fast as a hummingbird's. He wouldn't last long.

"Don't die! Don't die!" she repeated in barely a whisper as she began to administer CPR. She needed this man to live, so she could learn why Javier Martinez was tracking him. She needed to find the Star Island killer.

Suddenly Sandoval's body spasmed under her hands. She continued CPR even as she felt all the life drain out of him. She reached to feel his pulse again, but she already knew it was pointless. He was gone, his mouth frozen in a grimace.

Lila sank to the floor as a wave of exhaustion crashed over her. Sandoval had been her only real lead in the case, and now he was dead, and she knew nothing about his involvement with Javier or any of the others. She was back to square one.

She took a deep breath and glanced quickly around the desolate little house. She knew that a patrol car would follow up on that 911 call in the next few minutes, and she couldn't risk being at the scene. There was no chance that she'd be able to search the house for other possible clues without running the risk of being caught by the police.

Lila grabbed a baseball cap from the kitchen table, pulled it low over her face, and ran out through the back door, keeping her gaze down the whole time. She jumped in her car and peeled off toward the highway. On the drive south, Lila tried to piece together what had just happened.

Frederic Sandoval wasn't the killer, that was for sure. He'd be six feet under on the night of the Star Island massacre. And whatever else he had known was now gone with him. He was just one more dead end. A bubble of rage burst inside her. Why did every lead go nowhere? What if she'd come all the way back in time only to end up exactly where she'd started?

Her phone rang. It was Dylan. Lila looked at the clock.

"Fuck!" she said aloud. She was supposed to have been at his place half an hour ago.

"You like making me wait, don't you," he said playfully, when she pressed Accept.

"It's not that. It's just . . ." Lila couldn't focus. "I need to cancel lunch."

"Why?"

She could hear the disappointment in his voice. It made her ever angrier at herself. She felt like she couldn't do anything right.

"Nothing . . . bad day . . . I wouldn't be good company." Her mind was still back at Sandoval's house. Maybe she could go there once the paramedics and police had cleared out. Then she'd be able to carry out a thorough search, though it would be after law enforcement had already gone through the place.

"Listen," Dylan said. "Where are you right now?"

"Ninety-five. I just passed exit two," she said.

"I live fifteen minutes away. Come over. I can still make you lunch. You can tell me what's wrong, and we'll figure it out. Trust me, whatever the problem is, it can wait. A little break will make things seem clearer."

"I don't think it's a good idea."

"You need to eat."

Actually, Lila couldn't remember the last time she'd had a sit-down meal. Maybe Dylan was right. Maybe what she needed more than anything was to get some space and perspective on the case.

The morning had been a heartbreaking bust. The rational part of Lila knew she should be by herself and try to focus, to get a grip on a case that had slipped out of her hands yet again. But the rational part of her wasn't in charge at the moment. She wanted to see Dylan, and she wasn't going to justify anything to herself right now.

"Text me your address," she said. "I'll be there in ten." Lila pressed her foot down on the gas, letting the car unleash its full power.

At least out here, with her car ripping down the highway, Lila could remember what it felt like to be in control.

CHAPTER 21

SITTING RIGHT ON the water, with the sparkling decadence of Miami just across the bay, Dylan's house had a surprisingly intimate feel. With teak ceilings and coral rock throughout, it was Polynesian splendor mixed with the coziness of an Aspen ski lodge.

When Dylan saw Lila, her clothes rumpled and her face red from heat and frustration, he took her in his arms.

"I'm glad you came," he said, pulling her closer.

In his embrace, Lila felt the balled fist that was in her stomach begin to relax.

"Here," he said, taking her hand, "I'll show you around. Then we'll get good and drunk so you can shake off the morning."

The house was peppered with tokens from Dylan's travels around the world. Tribal masks from Ghana, one collected for each year he went on safari there. Textiles from Peru, where he and his brother had hiked the Inca Trail. A collection of ancient stoneware vases from when he'd lived in Japan for a few years. The rug underfoot had come from a Moroccan souk. Each item carried a story that Lila found intoxicating.

"You travel a lot with your brother?" she asked as she felt Dylan's eyes on her.

"Yep," he said as he led the way down the hall, pulling her behind him.

"So, your brother lives here?" She felt awkward. She wondered if coming here had been a mistake.

"He's out of the country right now. But he's planning on settling in Miami soon. We're talking about starting a business, rehabbing old sailboats."

Lila nodded.

Dylan burst into laughter. "God, you're not very good at this, are you?"

"What?"

"Human conversation! You're being so formal." His infectious smile made her smile as well. Suddenly, she felt lighter. "You know, I *have* kissed you," he went on, teasing. "Don't you remember?"

Lila's cheeks instantly burned. "Yes," she said, still smiling, "of course I remember."

"Oh, good. For a second I worried I made that bit up."

He grabbed her by the shoulders and walked her into his kitchen. "Sit here," he instructed, pointing to a stool by the counter. "And drink this, please. You're in need of serious help." He handed her a glass of wine.

"Do I seem that tense?"

"Oh, no. You're as light as a lead balloon," Dylan joked. "But now you can relax. All you have to do is watch me cook, and as long as I don't burn the place down, that should be a fairly low-key activity."

Lila settled back with her wine, sipping it slowly. She did watch Dylan. In fact, she couldn't keep her eyes off him. All the physical elegance and efficiency he showed when he sailed was on display in the kitchen as well. She felt giddy just being close to him. Every time he brushed past her on the way to the stove, she shivered.

"Try this," he said, holding out a spoonful of sauce. Lila opened her mouth, then closed her eyes as she sampled his cooking. It tasted of fresh herbs, lemon rind, and a dash of something she couldn't place.

"So, what do you think?" he asked, searching her eyes, his face close to hers. She broke his gaze by looking down at the floor. She was trying with all of her might to conceal how intoxicated she was at this very moment—with him, his cooking, the wine, the house, the aromas of the food wafting toward her. It was too much.

A feeble "Yummy" was all she managed to say. He looked at her quizzically as he went back to the stove, carefully minding his many bubbling pots and simmering pans.

"So, wanna tell me what happened to you today?" Dylan asked.

"Not at all," she said.

"Ah, a woman of mystery. I like that." He walked back toward her, refilled her glass, and then he kissed her on the lips. The taste of his mouth, the feel of his lips, and the effects of the wine pulled Lila's mind out of its whirring machinations. She wrapped her arms around him and kissed him deeply, the anger and disappointments of the day channeling rapidly into her desire for him.

They dined on his terrace under a ring of palm trees, with the Miami skyline serving as their view. The food was exquisite. Dylan and Lila sat shoulder to shoulder, holding hands under the table while they ate.

Lila couldn't remember the last time she'd felt this happy. She knew she was flirting with disaster, but she didn't care. Whatever happened, this moment was worth it.

After they finished their meals, they took the bottle of wine and walked over to the pool. They sat next to each other on the lip, dipping their toes into the warm water.

"Thanks for all this," Lila said. "You made a horrible day wonderful. I would never have thought it was possible, but you managed."

She slipped her hand under his shirt to feel his skin and his warmth. They kissed again.

When his hand gently moved up her thigh to between her legs, a brief, feeble protest arose in her mind. *This is too far. This is much, much too far, too fast.* But Lila's mind was no match for her heart. She wanted him desperately. She needed to feel the weight of him on top of her, the sensation of his skin on hers.

After they made love, Dylan rose from the bed, taking Lila's hand in his. "Come with me," he said, tenderly. Together, naked, satisfied but not satiated, they walked down the stairs and outside. The sun was just beginning to set. The ocean breeze on her naked skin, Dylan's hand in hers, made her feel weightless and free.

Her usual shyness had no place in this moment. *Let people look at us,* she thought. *We are perfect. We are beautiful.*

Wordlessly, Dylan dove into the pool, and she followed after him. There they stayed until the darkness of night enveloped them. Swimming, kissing, sliding in and out of each other's embrace under a canopy of stars, brimming with the sweet stupidity brought on by passion's earliest expression. Buried in the past, in a sea of lies, Lila felt that she had accidentally stumbled upon something pure, something beautiful. Was this what falling in love felt like?

As she fell asleep in his arms, Lila drowsily let herself wonder if she and Dylan could have a future together. Not a present. But a future.

CHAPTER 22

LOVE'S DISTRACTIONS DIDN'T last that long for Lila. After spending the night holed up with Dylan, she was anxious to get back to the case, though emerging from the little cocoon the two of them had created required most of her willpower. But she knew time was growing short, and the killer still eluded her.

She drove straight from Dylan's back north to Liberty City. Frederic Sandoval's house was seemingly undisturbed, except for a small memorial of lit candles and flowers that had been placed on the cement stoop. Lila walked around to the back of the house, jimmied the lock, and stealthily entered his kitchen.

Moving with the ease of a practiced professional, she searched methodically and quickly for papers, correspondence, clues. But all she found were old half-filled prescription bottles, a carton of Camels, a bag of worthless lottery tickets, and a sink of unwashed dishes. The sad detritus of a small life.

Then, under Sandoval's bed, she found boxes and boxes of photo albums filled with pictures, newspaper articles, and magazine profiles of Pedro Bolivar, the Colombian tennis star.

Bolivar was ranked number two in the world, after Sam Logan, the world champion and victim of the Star Island killer. The scrapbooks were extensive, dating from when Bolivar was a boy to the present. Was Sandoval somehow connected to Logan? And where did Javier fit into all of this?

She had to figure it out. Lila grabbed the albums and went back to her car.

Intent on spending the next few days reviewing every bit of information she had compiled, including Teddy's database, Lila pulled into the Star Island estate and was relieved to see Effie's car gone from the driveway. It was Sunday night, which meant that she was probably well into her third pisco sour at the Regent Cocktail Club, where she was sleeping with a model/bartender aptly named Adonis.

When she got to the guesthouse, Lila closed all the blinds and went to the safe, where she exchanged her gun for Teddy's thumb drive and her computer. She poured herself a big glass of Wild Turkey and tried to relax, in the hope of stumbling upon a revelation. But her mind kept on spinning in circles. The Janus Society. Javier's arms smuggling and his surveillance of Sandoval. Sandoval's death. And Sandoval's obsession with Sam Logan's major tennis rival.

None of it made any sense.

With everything that she knew, and with everything she'd given to this case, how could the killer still be outwitting her?

She searched anew for the name Frederic Sandoval online. The only thing that came up was the notice of his death. The police had said he had been found dead of natural causes. A memorial service was set for Wednesday at 10 A.M. at the Antioch Missionary Baptist Church.

For the remainder of the evening and into the early morning hours, Lila reviewed all the information, trying to look at everything with fresh eyes. There must be something obvious that she was missing.

Once again, she flipped to the Javier section of Teddy's database. How could there be nothing about his illegal doings in Teddy's exhaustive compilation of newspaper articles, tax returns, and earnings reports? How did Javier's secrets stay hidden even after his death? Did someone close to him know and protect his memory after his murder?

The image of Sandoval dying on the floor before her was flitting wildly around her brain, jumping out to surprise her at unexpected moments. She'd be reviewing notes one second and then suddenly think of Sandoval, desperate for air, pain flooding his body, the life draining out of his eyes.

Teddy had a file on Javier that contained scans of every document found in his office and on his desk after his murder. Lila had no idea how he'd managed to gather all this material. There must've been someone on the police force who sold him this stuff for the right price. Lila figured that somebody working for Javier had erased incriminating information from his computer after his death, but she reviewed the other documents just to see if Teddy had found something that she'd missed.

There were take-out menus, payroll forms, pieces of correspondence with buyers and artists. Lila scrolled through hundreds of pages. Then something strange caught her eye, something she hadn't seen before. It was the scan of a newspaper article, which, she surmised from the jagged edges now digitally immortalized on the PDF, had been ripped out of the paper.

Man Shot Outside South Beach Liquor Store

A Miami man was gunned down on December 26 in what was reported as a drive-by shooting on Lenox Avenue in South Beach, police said.

The victim, Dylan Rhodes, age 31, is currently in critical condition at Miami General Hospital.

Officers responded to a 911 call, which reported the shooting just after 2:00 P.M. They discovered the victim had sustained serious injuries. Emergency medical personnel transported him to a nearby hospital, where it was determined he had suffered a gunshot wound to the lower back, according to a police statement.

No witnesses have come forth, and no arrests were immediately made. The investigation continued into Friday night. "We have no updates at this point," a police spokeswoman said. "Every angle is being looked at."

Mr. Rhodes comes from a prominent Miami family. In 2008, Mr. Rhodes's father, Jack Rhodes, then CEO of Connachta Co., died, leaving his two sons controlling ownership of his company.

At this time, no relatives of the victim could be reached for comment.

Lila read the document again, not believing what she saw. Then she read it once more.

Frantically, she searched Teddy's endless files for more information. Did Dylan survive the shooting? Was the perp ever caught? But she couldn't find anything.

Hours later, after scanning so much information so quickly

that her eyes were bloodshot and her head was throbbing, she found a long profile in *Fortune* magazine on the Connachta Company—the business founded by Dylan's dad. It was dated May 31, 2016. Halfway through the article she read, "After the 2014 shooting and paralysis of company heir apparent Dylan Rhodes, Connachta faced a leadership crisis from which it never recovered."

Lila breathed a sigh of relief. At least he was alive! She continued reading, "Since the shooting, Rhodes has not been seen in public, refuses all interviews, and lives a protected and reclusive existence. A former family friend who asked to remain anonymous said that shortly after the shooting, Rhodes suffered a 'complete mental collapse.'"

Dylan? A recluse? Lila couldn't reconcile this description with the Dylan she knew. She kept rereading every bit of information she could find, hoping that somehow the words would magically change. But they didn't.

She felt tears on her cheeks before she even realized she was crying. The only voice she heard was one in her head that kept repeating, "No. No. No. No."

CHAPTER 23

FEW THINGS CALMED Lila down more effectively than driving at dangerous speeds along the Florida highways. With the top down so that the whipping wind would drown out the thoughts spinning around her mind, she shot along the road, trying to outrun her pain.

She drove west, cutting across the Florida peninsula toward the Gulf of Mexico. But no matter how fast she drove, she couldn't escape the despair about to consume her.

Everything felt like it was coming undone. Her friend Effie would die. A random act of violence would soon destroy the mind and body of the man with whom she was falling in love. Her own mother would succumb to the cancer that was gaining strength within her at this very moment. And there was nothing she could do to stop any of it. Somehow, Lila would have to stay strong if she was going to catch the killer and make all this heartbreak worth something.

As she sped through the Everglades, with all their hidden and obvious dangers, Lila thought back to years ago, when she'd kayaked through the labyrinthine mangrove tunnels in Big Cypress National Preserve. Paddling along the murky green water, accompanied only by alligators and the myriad calls of birds, Lila had lost her way. It felt like up became down and right became left in an instant. It took her hours of frantic paddling, in what she suspected was one big circle, to finally emerge from the quagmire just as the sun was setting. She vowed never to set foot in the Everglades again.

Here she was, lost once more, without any idea how to escape.

She had gotten into the car not knowing where she was going, but when she pulled up to a tiny bungalow with roses curling around the white lattice fence, she wasn't really surprised. She should've known she'd end up here. It was a little after nine, and the windows of the house glowed with an amber light. Lila saw a woman standing at the window, deep in her own thoughts. The woman's face looked very similar to her own.

"Hi, Mom," she whispered from the front seat of her car.

Lila ached to knock on her mother's door, to feel her mother's arms around her, to hear her voice and smell her perfume.

In less than a year from this moment, Lila's mom would die, a husk of herself, all alone. Tears flooded Lila's eyes. Her obsession with finding the Star Island killer had blinded her to her mother's failing health. She hadn't been with her at the very end, when it was most important.

Now, through this strange series of events, she was in the past, and her mother was alive again. But Lila couldn't undo the thing she regretted the most. If she knocked on that door and thrust her future self into her mom's life, who knew what would happen?

Her mother's head disappeared from the window. Lila got out of the car and crept around to the back of the house, smelling the fragrant jasmine bush that her mother had planted a week before Lila was born. And there was the tree swing that she and her sister had fought over when they were children, still hanging from the large oak in the backyard.

Lila knew her mother would be sitting on the living room couch with her feet up, reading a book, which she'd done every night for as long as Lila could remember. She tiptoed up to the window and watched her mom for a while, careful not to be noticed. She smiled every time her mom smiled at something in the book. She took in all of her—the warmth; the quick, intelligent eyes; the strength of her. This was as close as she would allow herself to get, and it was both wonderful and acutely painful to be so near and so far away.

After about an hour, Lila watched as her mom stood up and walked from room to room, turning off the lights, then retreated to her bedroom.

"Good night, Mom," Lila said aloud. It didn't matter what she said. There was no one there to hear her.

CHAPTER 24

THE DRIVE BACK to Star Island felt like an eternity. Lila kept the car's top down so that the cold December air would help her stay awake and alert, though it was bordering on unbearable. To keep warm she blasted the heat, enjoying the simultaneous fever and chill that glided over her skin.

Her phone buzzed. She glanced at the screen and pressed Ignore. Dylan. She wasn't sure how to talk to him knowing what she knew. How could she not warn this amazing man about the awful future that awaited him? So, for the time being, she decided it would be better for both of them if she stayed silent.

Her mind kept switching between thoughts of Dylan and thoughts of her mom. The memories, both joyous and sad, crashed over her like waves, ready to drag her under and swallow her whole. Seeing her mother again had been as excruciating as it was comforting. But that just about summed everything up these days—a mix of pain and pleasure. Lila felt that, no matter what she did, it was somehow wrong.

"Wherever you go, there you are," Lila said out loud as tears popped quickly into her eyes. It was a saying that her mother often repeated, always with a knowing smile. And, as usual, her mother was right. Lila had traveled farther than anyone had thought possible, she'd traveled back in time, and yet here she was, still blind to the same things, struggling in the same ways, failing to solve the same case. Even though she'd created a whole new persona for herself, she had never felt the burden of her own failings more than right at this moment.

As she drove, she realized that she needed to get away from Camilla Dayton's life and distractions in order to clear her mind. She needed to be away from Effie. She needed to take a break from maintaining this exhausting facade.

WHAT DO YOU mean you're leaving for the weekend? Where are you going?" Effie asked. It was Saturday morning, and Lila was putting several bags into the trunk of her car as Effie watched with a stunned look on her face. "I thought we'd go to Fisher Island today. I made plans for us." There was a whiny desperation in her voice, mixed with more than a hint of annoyance.

"Some of my old friends from the city are in Key West for the weekend. They invited me down at the last minute," Lila lied easily to Effie's pouting face. "I'd invite you, but they said the place is small and kind of shabby."

"Oh, and here I was worried that you didn't have any friends. I've gone all-out introducing you to mine—to every damn person in this city. But clearly it would be too much to ask for you to let me meet anyone you know." Effie paused, looking at Lila with her eyes squinted and her lips pursed.

Lila knew Effie was trying to bully her out of going, but she needed the space. Not to mention that it was hard to really feel pushed around by a hundred-pound blonde wearing a rhinestone bikini.

"It sounds like you don't really need my help anymore." Effie sniffed.

"You know, I think you're right, Effie," Lila said as she slammed down the trunk lid and got in the driver's seat. She was tired, but more than anything, she was fed up with being polite when she didn't need to be. She was here for a reason, to solve a case, and nothing in the world mattered more than that. Every moment she wasted on Effie's feelings, she was standing in her own way. In less than one month the Star Island killer would strike. If she didn't uncover the killer's identity, then this whole ordeal would be for nothing. "I'm not as helpless as you think, Effie. Never have been."

"Really, I beg to differ. You'd have nothing if it weren't for me. Nothing. But anytime I ask you for anything, you're busy."

"You know that's not true, Effie. I feel like all I do is repay you for generosity I've never asked for. It's like you give me things just to keep me on a goddamned leash."

With that, Lila shut the car door and drove away, not even looking in the rearview mirror to see Effie's angry face. As she was heading south, Lila was surprised to find herself still dwelling on their fight. She was genuinely hurt by what Effie had said. She shook her head. She needed to stop thinking of Effie as a friend, and remember that she was just a means to an end.

That part about visiting New York friends was a lie, of course, but the Key West bit was true. Key West, that perfect slice of weirdness, was just the escape hatch Lila needed to hide away, take stock of the case, and grab some perspective back from this long, tumbling fall down the rabbit hole she'd been on for the last couple of months. She'd booked herself a few nights in a cozy cottage, painted robin's-egg blue, on a sleepy street in Old Town. Now she raced toward it in her Maserati as if her life depended upon it.

Just as he'd said he would in their e-mail exchange, the owner of the cottage left the key under the large rock beneath the honeysuckle bush to the left of the white picket fence. As she brought her bags into the cottage's foyer, Lila exhaled with relief. It was relaxed and ramshackle, a little musty and a lot beachy. Unlike in the Star Island home she'd recently made her own, none of the furniture was worthy of being featured in *Architectural Digest* and none of the art hanging on the walls was "important." It was perfect.

The cottage was two stories, with a spartan kitchen and a tiny backyard canopied by magnificent palm trees. Lila picked the largest of the three bedrooms, on the second floor, to set up her office. She could sleep anywhere, but what she needed was space to think. In the large bedroom, she carefully removed the few pictures from the wall and moved the spare furniture to the center of the room.

Most of her information was on her computer or on Teddy's thumb drive, but she felt that the evidence, in its digitized form, was keeping its secrets hidden from her. On the long drive south to Key West, she'd stopped at a big box store to purchase a printer, which she set up now on the dining room table. Late into the night, she printed up hundreds of pages of documents and pictures while slowly sipping bourbon, with the windows thrown wide open so that she could feel and smell the humid ocean breeze.

When most of the printing was done, Lila moved to the bedroom on the second floor, making several trips up and down the stairs, hauling stacks of printed pages, photographs, and pages torn from her notebooks. On each of the four walls, she created a makeshift bulletin board, with every victim getting a third of one wall.

On the north wall, she put Effie Webster, Meredith Sloan, Vivienne Hunter.

On the east wall: Javier Martinez, Theo von Fick, Fernando Salazar.

On the west wall: Neville Crawley, Sam Logan, and Rusty Browder.

On the south wall: Chase Haverford, Adebayo "Johnny" Oluwa, and Khaled Fathallah.

Then she stood in the center of the room, regarding it all. The members of the Janus Society, with their messy lives—their pasts, their presents, and their futures—were all there, in fragments taped up on the wall. These twelve people had been her constant companions for more than three years, so much so that each face and each story felt as familiar to her as her own. Yet there was a riddle at the core of all of it that she couldn't solve. Why would someone murder this group of philanthropists, these people who gave so much to those in need? And who could the murderer be?

Lila was so absorbed in her thoughts that she startled when her cell phone rang. It was Effie calling. Lila didn't want to answer the phone at all, but she knew ignoring Effie would just make everything between them all the worse.

The moment she forced herself to pick up the phone, an assault of deafening sound greeted her. "Camilla? Camilla?!" Effie shouted over the loud hum of voices and throbbing club music in the background. Lila figured she was at one of her usual haunts, letting men buy her round after round of custom-made cocktails.

"You won't believe what I just heard," Effie squealed. She sounded high.

"Tell me."

"You made that offer on the house forever ago, right? And even though Meredith calls you, like, ten times a day, nothing's happened, right? Now I know why. It's Alexei Dortzovich's fault. He just closed on the house this morning! Can you believe it?"

In truth, Lila had known she'd never get the place. She'd put in low offers and followed up with even lower counteroffers. She'd requested various inspections and made inquiries about a million little ridiculous things just to keep dragging the process out. Lila was stalling and Meredith knew it.

That someone else bought the house was no surprise, but the fact that Alexei had swooped in and purchased it was perplexing. After the Star Island massacre, Lila had interviewed every person who was on that island on the day of the murder, and she'd investigated every single person who owned a home there—but Alexei was never interviewed.

"Hmmm . . . that's curious," Lila said.

"Why aren't you freaking out? I mean, that's your house! And what does that hideous Russian need with yet another mansion? It makes me sick. And not to sound too paranoid, but," Effie said, lowering her voice to a conspiratorial whisper, making it difficult to hear her over the pounding techno playing in the background, "I think Alexei is, like, obsessed with me. You've seen how he hits on me. And he's always totally staring at me. Now he's going to be living right next to me all the time? I'm seriously worried he's stalking me, Camilla."

As Effie continued to share alcohol-fueled speculations, Lila paced back and forth in the room, looking at the walls.

"I mean," Effie said, "the Russians are just so tacky. I'm not being racist or anything."

"I don't think Russians are a race, Ef."

"Whatever. You know what I mean. It's like the more garish the better with those guys. Am I right?"

This coming from a woman whose closet boasted enough sequins to turn Liberace's head.

"I don't know," Lila said carefully.

Effie chattered on as Lila surveyed the visual map of the case she had created. She had surreptitiously taken hundreds of pictures of the future murder victims at the Fisher Island Club, where all the Janus Society were members. As she looked at the photos she suddenly saw a pattern, something she'd never noticed before.

Alexei.

Now the words were spilling out of Effie's mouth at an ever-quickening pace. "And so I'm going to, like, build a moat or something, and fill it with alligators, and—"

"Effie. Stop. I gotta go. We'll figure out what to do about Alexei when I'm back, okay?"

"No, it's not okay. This guy is going to totally murder me, and you're just going to—"

"Bye, Ef." Lila hung up the phone. She hated to do it, but she knew Effie. In a state like this, she would go on talking all night, and she most likely wouldn't remember anything in the morning. And Lila needed to focus.

She ran down the stairs to the back porch, where she remembered seeing a few fishing poles. In a basket next to the poles, she found what she was looking for—spools of fishing line. She grabbed a fluorescent yellow spool and hurried back upstairs.

With the fishing line in hand, she went to a picture of Effie at the club frowning at a clearly drunken Alexei, who had his arm draped over her bare shoulder. Lila taped the line to the wall under the picture. Then she dragged the line to a photo of Alexei and Chase standing side by side at the bar, locked in what appeared to be a serious conversation. Then a picture with Sam Logan. Then one with Oluwa. Then Vivienne. With each new connection, Lila's heart pounded harder. After fifteen minutes of this activity, she stood back in the center of the room and marveled at what she saw. The yellow line wrapped around the room. She had a picture of every member of the Janus Society with Alexei. No one else could be linked to all twelve victims.

But what could it all mean? No one in the world knew who was in the Janus Society until their massacre revealed the truth.

Then she wondered, could Alexei have been part of the society? Why not? She hadn't considered the possibility of a thirteenth member, but it made such sense she wondered why she hadn't thought of it before. Maybe Alexei had snapped and killed all of his compatriots. After all, Effie, who wasn't afraid of anyone or anything, was terrified of Alexei.

Lila knew what she had to do. She had to pack all this evidence up, get in the car, and return to Star Island as fast as possible. She had a lead again, and nothing could stop her from chasing after it.

CHAPTER 25

THE MOMENT SHE got back to South Beach, Lila hurried to dig up every single bit of information about Alexei Romanovich Dortzovich.

It turned out that he was born on October 7, 1975, in a small industrial city on the Black Sea in what was then the Soviet Union. He was born into poverty and orphaned at the age of five, when both his parents died in a car crash. Alexei was raised by his uncle, an uneducated auto mechanic. When he was eighteen, he joined the newly formed Armed Forces of the Russian Federation, the penniless but highly trained military that rose out of the ashes of the Soviet Union. In the army, Alexei quickly rose through the ranks to serve in the Kremlin's elite special forces unit. He was a highly trained marksman.

After serving in the army for seven years, Alexei opened a small pig farm in Odessa. The pig business made him into a millionaire. Thanks to his riches and his strong connections to the Kremlin, Alexei then got into the booming oil business, which in a little less than a decade made him one of Russia's new class of oligarchs. Alexei relocated full-time to Miami in 2012, following his rumored connection to a Russian mafia money-laundering scheme that had moved four billion euros through one of his mining companies.

Lila rented a Ford Focus and tucked her blond hair up into a Miami Dolphins baseball cap, hoping to follow Alexei throughout the day and well into the night without being noticed. But that proved harder than she had anticipated. He had at least one bodyguard with him at all times, and his driver followed standard secret service protocol to avoid possible tails. Though she had years of experience keeping a mark in her sight, she had to really struggle not to lose Alexei's black Range Rover as it wove through Miami's streets.

On Thursday afternoon, Lila followed the SUV down to Ocean Drive. The car pulled over at Eleventh Street, and Alexei jumped out of the backseat, heading straight for the boardwalk. His two bodyguards followed him. Lila drove past then and, as quickly as possible, parked her car illegally on the next side street. She hurried back to the boardwalk on foot as fast as she could without drawing attention to herself.

The streets were clogged with the usual mix of tourists, drunken college kids, young bodies exhibited in barely-there bathing suits, and the eccentric derelicts and lunatics that make up the South Beach carnival of human beauty and grotesquerie. The glitter and doom of Miami were on full display.

Lila knew that Alexei wouldn't easily spot her in this mass of humanity, but she worried that he would, once again, elude her. It took her about twenty minutes of frantically searching the crowds before she caught sight of one of his bodyguards, an enormously tall and muscular man with dark black, pockmarked skin. Then Lila spotted Alexei. He was sitting on a park bench, flanked by his security, and talking to another man. Keeping her distance, she walked closer. She felt even more sure that her hunch about Alexei was right when she saw who he was sitting with—the one and only Chase Haverford.

Even with the crowds concealing her as they pulsed and pushed their way around her, Lila couldn't get close enough to the bench to overhear what Alexei and Chase were talking about. But she could see them well enough to know that they were arguing. Alexei's face was contorted with rage, his hands gesticulating wildly. Chase sat with his aviator sunglasses on and his head mostly down, never looking directly at Alexei. He appeared jumpy and self-conscious, like a man praying not to be recognized. Then Alexei sprang off the bench, spinning toward Chase.

Lila heard him shout, "You are not the one who refuses me, asshole! Fucking, cocksucking asshole!"

At that, Chase stood up and, without even throwing a glance toward Alexei, walked away. The Russian stood there, stunned, his arms hanging heavy at his sides. Lila hustled back to Ocean Drive, where she passed by Alexei's SUV. His driver was in the car, leaning out the window trying to grab the attention of any one of the bikini-clad girls strutting by on wobbly high-heeled shoes.

FOR A FEW frenzied days in early December, Miami Beach turns its distracted attentions to the Art Basel festival, during which every artist, collector, gallerist, and artsy wannabe descends upon the city to buy, sell, pontificate, posture, and drink headache-inducing cheap white wine, all while complaining vigorously about the degraded and debased state of the art world. The convention center becomes a roiling sea of people in ridiculous glasses, eye-rolling and air-kissing and arguing. No one loved it more than Javier Martinez, who always hosted a festival kickoff party at his gallery.

"Darlings! Hello!" Javier exclaimed as Effie and Lila walked into the packed gallery. The cavernous main room had no light save for a few glass-encased voodoo candles weakly flickering on the floor. Turkish psychedelic music played so loudly that Lila could feel it reverberating through her body. "So glad you could make it," Javier said as he gave them both perfectly executed air kisses.

As Lila's eyes adjusted to the dark, Javier finally came into clearer view. A dandy at the most casual of times, he was fully turned out tonight in a tight-fitting white suit with a robin's-egg blue silk shirt underneath, unbuttoned to his sternum, and a silver handkerchief tied jauntily around his neck. He looked like a perfect cross between Tom Ford and Tony Montana.

"Of course we're here!" Effie squealed. "Yours is always the best party of this whole dreadful week."

"No party is a party without you, Effie, darling. Enjoy yourself! Be back in a second," Javier called over his shoulder to them as he went on to air-kiss a tiny Japanese woman with a shock of red hair sitting stiffly upon her head.

Effie grabbed Lila's hand. "Let's circulate."

Lila was still anxious to figure out Javier's connection to Sandoval, but doing it at this moment was an impossibility. She could barely hear herself think, let alone pick Javier's brain for clues.

Scattered throughout the gallery were eerily realistic life-size wax statues of people that, like the candles, were slowly burning from the top down. The human candles gave the place a haunted feel as Lila navigated through the rooms in the semidarkness, not knowing which people were real and which would, upon closer inspection, reveal their lit wicks and collapsing skulls.

Lila heard Effie gasp and turned to find her pointing at Alexei, who was on the other side of the room sandwiched between two scantily clad women gyrating to the music.

"I fucking hate that about Miami," Effie said. "The moment you want to avoid someone, they're everywhere you look."

Though Lila pretended she was unhappy to see Alexei, she was secretly thrilled he was here. He was the first real break she'd had in the case since she stepped out of that North Miami warehouse, and she needed to get as close to him as she could.

"Let me go talk to him," Lila said. "I'll see if I can get any information out of him about buying the Star Island house."

Effie grabbed her arm. "Camilla, don't." Lila was taken aback when she saw that Effie actually looked frightened.

"You know me, right?" Effie asked. "There's not a lot of things that scare me. Not a lot of people I would back down from, right? Well, that man," Effie said, gesturing to Alexei, "that man scares the shit out of me. Yes, sure, I want to know about his plans for the house, but I don't need you to find that out for me. That's what my lawyers are for."

"Oh, quit it, Effie. Let me see what my feminine charms can do," Lila said, assuming the pose of an empty-headed sex kitten—single finger on her pouting lips, hips jutted out to the side.

"Please," Effie said, throwing her hands up in exasperated disgust. "Comrade Back Hair is all yours. Just know that I warned you."

As Lila crossed the room toward Alexei, she could feel his eyes on her even as he was groping the woman pressed up against him. Lila made eye contact with him, holding for a few beats too long, letting him know she was interested. She noticed a pulse of excitement run through him as he returned her gaze. Lila stopped a few feet away, pretending to admire one of the human candles but continually looking in his direction. The wax statue was of a man sitting in an office chair. He had on a gray suit, and his head was melted all the way to the bottom of his nose.

Lila was startled when she felt someone standing behind her wrap his arm around her waist, which caused her to flinch, which, in turn, caused the arm to wrap tighter. The stench of a body sour from too much alcohol flooded her nose.

"I see you looking at me," Alexei's thick Russian accent whispered into her ear.

"Don't flatter yourself," Lila said, using both hands to try to pry his arm off her body. "I was just looking at the art."

An enormous guffaw burst from Alexei's heavy lips. He still held her tightly. She could feel his crotch pressing into her. "This you call art?" he said, pointing to the flickering statue. He took his index finger and thumb, pinched them together, and shoved them into Lila's mouth, then withdrew them. Before she could say anything, he pinched the wick of the sculpture with his dampened fingers, extinguishing the flame.

"Hey, guy," a shaggy man in skinny jeans said as he put his hand on Alexei's shoulder, "you can't touch the art." Alexei whirled around, letting go of Lila, and forcefully pushed the man, who stumbled to the floor.

"And you can't touch me, you pig's cunt," Alexei shouted. As the man scrambled to his feet and was about to lunge back at Alexei, the Russian's two bodyguards stepped in to block his way.

Alexei turned back to Lila. His eyes were foggy and his face was slack from too much booze. Effie was right, this guy was completely frightening, but Lila needed to find out as much as she could about him. He put his hand on her ass.

"Whoa!" Lila said. "Do you always come on this strong? I don't even know you."

"Yes, you do. You know who I am. I am the man that stares at you in your little bikinis at the club. And you know me. That little bitch Effie has been in your ear whispering about the mean Russian man, no?" Lila nodded. "You know who I am. Why must American girls play dumb? It makes everything go so slow."

"I guess we're crazy that way," Lila said, leaning into him. Never in her life had she found a man as physically revolting and unlikable as Alexei Dortzovich, but she knew that she had to come at people where they had a weakness, and Alexei clearly had a blind hunger when it came to women.

Alexei looked back at the two women he had left, who were now pressed against each other, kissing deeply. "Until later," he said and quickly turned from Lila back to the undulating women. Lila watched as Alexei called over one of his bodyguards and barked something in Russian to him.

The bodyguard then approached to Lila.

"Be here at nine P.M. tomorrow," the man said to her, handing her a business card with only Alexei's name embossed on the front and the address of the Soho Beach House handwritten on the back. "Mr. Dortzovich will be expecting you."

Lila wrapped her fingers around the card, smiled slightly at the bodyguard, and nodded her head. "I'd be happy to," she said, though she knew it wasn't a request. It was a command.

CHAPTER 26

EFFIE WAS LYING horizontally across Lila's bed, watching her friend get ready to meet Alexei. Effie had been in a strange and hyper mood for the entire day, which wasn't helped by the steady stream of vodka and Red Bull she was continually drinking. It was a blustery night, and Lila could hear the wind whipping through the palm trees.

"I hope you're not going out with Alexei for my benefit," Effie said as she watched Lila put on a dress with a plunging neckline. "You're not going to wear that, are you?" she continued, her eyes widening. "That little Russian shit would hit on a woman in a burqa. He'll interpret that amount of cleavage as proof that you're a slut."

"Wow. You really don't like him."

"And you do? I mean, how could you? It is like a cold, hard fact that the man is repulsive. If I were as ugly as him, I'd really try to be at least a bit more charming." Effie paused. "And what about Dylan?"

What about Dylan? Lila thought. It had been days since she'd last seen him, but he'd been constantly on her mind. Yet, every time he reached out to her, she ignored him. She'd never worked so hard to push someone out of her mind.

"I won't argue with you. Alexei is a brute, but there's something kind of appealing in that," Lila said. In fact, she was dreading tonight. Her last encounter with the man had left her feeling violated. He had handled her like he was inspecting a prize hog. "But maybe you're right about the dress. Better to go with something less revealing."

Lila changed into a cream-colored Stella McCartney suit with a tangerine orange silk camisole underneath and a pair of red heels. She pulled her hair back into a sleek ponytail.

"How's this?" she said, as she twirled for Effie's approval.

"That's better. Very Bianca Jagger," Effie said, rolling onto her back and resting her drink on her stomach with her eyes closed. Lila regarded herself in the mirror with pleasure. Then she realized, with horror, that she was transforming into some kind of clotheshorse. Was her persona taking over her personality?

"Now you just need some Mace for your purse," Effie teased.

"It's not as bad as that, Effie."

"To be honest, Camilla, I thought you and I were so much the same," Effie said, hauling herself into a cross-legged slump at the foot of the bed. "But if Alexei is your type of guy, then it just shows how different we are. And I'm not saying that's a bad thing, but I've spent the last few months introducing you to proper society people, and now you want to run around with the Moscow Menace. It's confusing."

"It's one night, Effie."

Effie sighed and sucked back the rest of her drink. "If you're interested in his money, let me tell you, you'll never get near it. I've seen him go through countless brain-dead beauties all hoping to one day be Mrs. Asshole, but none of them lasted longer than a month."

"Jesus!" Lila exclaimed. This was becoming exhausting. "I got it. You don't think it's a good idea. Message received." She looked at her watch: 8:30. She had to be there in thirty minutes. "I gotta go."

"Fine. I'll leave," Effie said as she swayed to her feet. "Just one more thing, then I'll never say another word about it. You know he's trying to set up a drilling operation off the coast of Florida, right?"

Lila nodded, though she had heard no such thing.

"Literally everyone is against it. No one wants to risk, you know, sad little oil-covered pelicans scaring away the tourists. But that Russian maniac won't back down. And he's tight with the Russian mob. So he's sending these goons to strong-arm anyone who stands in his way." Effie lowered her voice to a conspiratorial whisper and leaned in close to Lila. She smelled like lime juice and tanning lotion. "Get this. There's this local congressman, cute guy, who's against the drilling. Two weeks ago he was found drowned. The police said it was a sea kayaking accident." Effie rolled her eyes. "Like, yeah, right. Everyone knows Alexei had him whacked. The guy is totally dangerous, Camilla. Just be careful."

"I promise," Lila said as they both left the guesthouse. Effie's attempt to dissuade Lila from seeing Alexei had the opposite effect. All her warnings and gossip did was make Lila more convinced that Alexei was the Star Island killer. This was a date she wouldn't miss for the world.

ALEXEI WAS SITTING alone at a table by the Soho Beach House's pool, flanked by his two bodyguards. He was smoking a cigar and wearing dark sunglasses even though it was night. When he saw Lila he frowned.

"Why are you dressed like man?" he growled in his thick Russian accent. He blew a thick cloud of cigar smoke up and toward Lila in her suit.

"Nice to see you, too."

"Sit," he commanded. Lila obeyed. Alexei sat silently, neither looking at nor addressing Lila. A young woman wearing a strapless black leather dress and five-inch platform heels walked by. Alexei watched her with great interest, turning his head as she passed. He then barked in Russian to one of his bodyguards, handing him a large roll of hundreds. The bodyguard left, and Alexei went back to smoking his cigar.

Since Art Basel had come to Miami, the Soho Beach House was the hub for the festival's who's who of attendees—millionaire artists, socialites, hoteliers, and midlist celebrities. Everyone was tan, everyone was drunk, and everyone was working very hard at appearing to have a great time. A model wearing a white tank top, gold lamé short shorts, and headphones was standing on a stage, DJing from behind a laptop, limply swaying to the music. Nineties hip-hop blasted from the hidden sound system. Chinese lanterns hung from the palm trees. The whole spectacle was dramatically lit, transforming the pool water into a shocking purple and the palm trees into an electric blue.

Everyone pulsed with the energy that came from knowing they were in the place to be. Lila, on the other hand, was feeling wary. Alexei had barely acknowledged her as he sat, drinking, smoking his cigar, and scanning the crowd. After five minutes of total silence between them, the bodyguard returned to the table holding something in his hand, which he gave to Alexei.

"Here," Alexei said, throwing the garment onto Lila's lap. "Go put this on."

It was a dress. A leather strapless dress. The dress she'd just seen on that young girl who walked by. "Wait, how did you get this?" Lila asked.

"I paid for it. Same as how you get anything you want." Alexei was still looking out into the crowd. He hadn't once even so much as glanced at Lila. "I want to spend the night with a real woman. Not a woman dressed up like a boy. Go put it on."

Lila wanted to laugh. Could this guy be for real? she wondered. She'd met a lot of epic assholes in her time, but Alexei's rudeness was downright sociopathic. She loudly exhaled. "Fine," she said.

"Sergei here will follow you. Don't take too long," said Alexei.

Lila wove through the undulating crowd of revelers with an enormous black-suited bodyguard trailing close behind her. She wished she had the reassuring weight of a gun on her, but she'd known better than to meet Alexei and his security crew with a concealed weapon.

The bathroom was stuffed full of women reapplying their dark lipsticks carefully in the mirror. Some were two to three in a stall, taking forever to get their fix. Lila stood anxiously, clutching the dress. The air practically pulsed with privilege and aggression.

Tiring of the wait for a stall, she undressed while still standing in line, quickly stepping into the tiny leather dress. As she zipped it up, she was surprised to find it fit her perfectly. She exited the bathroom with her white suit draped over her forearm. The bodyguard was waiting for her.

"Here," she said as she shoved the suit, top, and bra into the man's hands. "Try not to lose this."

Walking back to the table, Lila saw a stranger sitting with Alexei. He was a small man in his forties with dramatically receding dark blond hair. Even though he was sitting down, Lila could tell he was little taller than five four, with incredibly muscular shoulders and a linebacker-size neck. Lila sat down across from him.

"Much better," Alexei said, looking Lila up and down as if she were a sumptuous snack he was getting ready to sink his fangs into. Then he brusquely tore the elastic band out of her hair, ripping some hair with it.

"Oww!" Lila exclaimed, rubbing her scalp. "Guess you're no fan of the ponytail."

"Now you look like a woman. This," he said, pointing to the man next to him, "is Illya Smurov. Old comrade from Russia. This is Kim," he said, gesturing to Lila.

"Camilla," Lila corrected, stretching her hand across the table toward Illya, who practically crushed her hand in his. "My name's Camilla," she said to Alexei, who waved her away dismissively as if he didn't have time for or interest in such small details as correct names. Lila sat there, thinking what to do next. Her hand was throbbing.

"So, how do you two know each other?" she asked, making her voice rise up with the polite girlishness she knew these brutes would appreciate.

"Olympics," Illya said. His rather high-pitched voice took Lila by surprise.

Alexei nodded as a gloss of nostalgia washed over his face.

"True," he said. "We were in Barcelona Olympics together. Russian shooting team."

Lila tried to keep her face passive, but inside she felt like shouting. The evidence was adding up. She had known Alexei was an expert marksman, but an Olympic-level shooter was another thing entirely. Forensic evidence had shown that the Star Island killer was most definitely an accomplished sharpshooter. Who else but someone with Alexei's training could manage to execute so many people with such merciless swiftness and precision?

Lila felt her phone vibrate through her purse. Dylan was calling. She silenced her phone and turned her attention back to Alexei.

"So, Alexei," she said, snuggling up to him. As she pressed against him, a wave of revulsion swept through her. "Bought anything yet at Art Basel?"

"Da," he said, still chomping away at his cigar. "Today, I buy piece-of-shit painting for seven hundred fifty grand. There was a bidding war!" An enormous belch of laughter burst from his lips. "People fighting for this hideous crap made by a homosexual freak makes me laugh. Now it is mine."

"Why would you spend so much money on something you hate?" Lila asked.

Alexei leaned back from Lila, staring at her straight in the face with a look of disgust. "You look ugly when you're being a nosy bitch," he spit at her.

He grabbed the bottle of Grey Goose sitting on the table and poured shots for himself and Illya. They clinked the glasses together, poured the liquor down their throats, and then smashed the glasses loudly down upon the table in almost perfect unison. A synchronized drinking team.

"I tease you," Alexei said, putting his meat paw of a hand

high up on Lila's inner thigh. "I tell you why I bought shit painting." He poured himself and Illya another shot. "One of my spies told me Chase Haverford, that bastard, wanted paint-ing. He wants it. I want him not to have things he wants. I buy it to say fuck you to him."

Illya refilled their shot glasses and said something to Alexei in Russian that caused both men to nearly double over in fits of laughter. One of the glasses tipped, spilling vodka onto Lila. Alexei dipped two fingers into the pool of vodka that had formed on the lap of the leather dress Lila was wrapped in, then put those fingers in between her lips.

"Now look what I've done. I've made you wet," he said, re-moving the fingers from her mouth and then wiping them off on her bare shoulder. "My friend here just said funny joke. He said I should take painting and hang it in one of the plants where I slaughter pigs." He burst out laughing again, and he slapped a pleased and drunk-looking Illya on the back. "I'll do that. And I'll send Chase a picture of dead pigs on hooks going by the painting he so badly wanted."

"What do you have against Chase?" Lila asked. "He seems like an okay guy to me."

"An okay guy?" Alexei snarled. "Only a dumb bitch like you would think that. Which is why you need to keep your mouth shut. Let the men talk."

Lila, again, complied with the wishes of this sociopath. She sat there quietly, watching the two men get drunker and drunker, but her head was spinning. It was all finally coming together. Alexei had the skill to kill the members of the Janus Society. And he detested Chase. But why? What had caused this red-hot hatred between Chase and Alexei? And why would he kill the rest of the Janus Society?

She got up from the table and headed down to the beach. Alexei and Illya, consumed by a drunken oblivion, didn't even notice. Finding a quiet corner away from boisterous crowd, Lila checked the one message on her voice mail. It was from Dylan.

"Camilla?" he said in a bruised-sounding tone. Lila pressed the phone close to her ear, her heart racing from hearing his voice. "It's Dylan. I don't know why you've been avoiding me, but whatever it is, I know we can figure it out. But you've got to call me. It's too hard to go through so many days without hearing from you. Call me." Then the message was over. She listened to it again. Then again.

More than anything else, she wanted to call him back, to run into his arms, and to never, ever see Alexei again. So far, the best part of being Camilla Dayton had been meeting Dylan Rhodes.

She realized, at that very moment, that she wanted Dylan's love more than she wanted to find the killer. After all, once this was over, she'd be going back to the bleak, broken life she had left in 2018. Yet somehow, now, returning to that life would be even harder because she finally had a taste of real love.

But it was all so much more complicated than that. The Dylan she knew now would soon be gone. He would be gunned down, paralyzed, and forever changed. Knowing what she knew about his terrible fate made it impossible for her to face him. She felt as if she was drowning in lies, cursed by knowing the tragic futures awaiting the people she loved.

She let herself listen to Dylan's voice once more and then, closing her eyes, deleted the message. Nothing good could come from continuing contact with him. She knew she had to walk away. It would be easier for them both if he thought she'd simply lost interest.

But nothing could be farther from the truth.

CHAPTER 27

I'M ONE HUNDRED fucking percent not in the mood for one of these godforsaken charity events," Effie said to Lila as they walked down the hall toward the ballroom where the annual Platinum Ball Gala was, from the sounds of the loud music pulsating through the air, in full swing.

Lila looked questioningly at Effie, who, to her mind, was created for parties like these.

"You're a party girl who doesn't want to go to a party? That's like a bird who doesn't want to fly, Ef," Lila teased as she playfully grabbed Effie's hand, swinging it to the beat of the music.

The hallway was lined with candles, and pink lights crisscrossed in a tight pattern along the ceiling, giving attendees the feeling of entering some magical realm. The Platinum Ball was a black-tie event and one of the highlights of the Miami social calendar. Effie had spent weeks deliberating with Lila about what to wear and how to arrange her hair, so it was a bit shocking to hear this perfectly coiffed woman in a gorgeous Dior gown saying that she would rather be doing something else.

"Here," Lila said, grabbing a glass of champagne off a tray

held by an exceptionally well-formed waiter with a boy-band haircut. "Drink this. It'll make everything better." Effie gave Lila a fake grin and gulped the champagne down in one impressive chug.

"I'm going to need a few more of those." Effie put the glass back on the tray, then picked up a full flute. "I'm going to circulate. Catch up with you later," she said as she disappeared into a sea of gowns and tuxedos. As Lila walked the perimeter of the ballroom, she saw all of Miami society spread out before her. Among them, somewhere, were each of the twelve members of the Janus Society. Events like this were perfect opportunities for Lila to see all of the future murder victims interact in their most natural habitat—surrounded by other members of the financial and social elite.

When she'd been a lowly detective trying to find the killer, Lila had always felt as if this high-society world kept a giant fence around itself, prohibiting outsiders from seeing and understanding its inner workings. Now she knew it was even worse than that. Even now that she was an insider, one of them, she was continually encountering more walls, more secrets, more mysteries, the closer she got to the center of it all.

Then she saw Dylan.

Panic flooded through her. She had been worrying all day that he would be at the ball, and here he was, standing with Vivienne Hunter, whose arms were wrapped tightly around his right biceps. From the looks on both of their faces, they were having a rather serious conversation. Dylan's head was turned toward Vivienne, so Lila knew she had not yet been spotted. She needed to escape. Her heart racing, she stumbled blindly onto the veranda.

A strong tropical breeze greeted her, as did the mesmerizing sound of the waves rhythmically crashing on the deserted beach below. Out of the corner of her eye, Lila saw two figures huddled in the darkness, way out of sight. She heard them whispering, but the moment she spotted them, they must have also seen her, because they fell silent. She walked toward them and was shocked to discover Teddy Hawkins and Meredith Sloan.

"Camilla!" Meredith said, blinking at her with nervous eyes, her voice as tense as a wire. "How wonderful to see you."

"Yes," Teddy echoed, with a strained smile. "Wonderful!" His eyes were darting around, as if looking for the closest exit.

Meredith's hair, which was always silken perfection, like the hair of a silent movie star, was loose in a halo of errant strands. Even in the dark light, Lila could see her bright lipstick was half smudged off, and a bit of mascara was crawling down under her eyes.

"I came out here to admire the view," Meredith nervously explained. "And ran into Teddy."

"Indeed. I needed a bit of fresh air myself," he said quickly.

"Of course, darling, you've heard that someone else closed on your house, right? Sorry I wasn't the one to tell you."

"That's fine," Lila said. Teddy and Meredith were acting so strangely. She wondered what she had walked into. And then, as she saw the way Teddy's eyes flicked over to Meredith, she realized the truth.

Teddy and Meredith were having an affair.

"We'll find you another place in no time. Though I always suspected that you weren't all that interested in buying that house. After all, it did have its problems."

"Don't we all," said Teddy.

"But it's rather windy out here, isn't it? I feel as if I'll be blown overboard. So, I think I'll be heading back inside," Meredith said, and, with that, she scuttled away, leaving Lila alone with Teddy.

Lila stood there in silence, digesting it all. She still couldn't believe that this man was the same one who would send her into the past to catch the Star Island killer. But at least now Lila knew why. It was for Meredith.

Willow, the yoga teacher, had told Lila that Meredith was having an affair with a high-profile guy. Why hadn't Lila realized it earlier? Teddy would become obsessed with the Star Island murders because the woman he loved would die in them.

Encountering this Teddy, the Teddy that had yet to be devastated by the Star Island murders, still in love with Meredith and hopeful for the future, made her suddenly and unbearably sad.

Teddy grabbed her hand. "Enough of us standing on the sidelines," he exclaimed, energy filling his voice. "Why don't you and I take a spin on the dance floor?"

Lila took him in, the bright eyes, the contagious smile. How could she refuse this man anything?

"Sure," she said, as he pulled her inside.

Laughing, Teddy spun Lila, then put one hand on her waist and the other hand in hers. She looked around to see if Dylan was close by, but fortunately, he was nowhere in sight. She gazed up at Teddy. In the ballroom glow she could see that there were traces of lipstick around his mouth. Teddy's eyes were searching the room; then, when they caught something, an enormous smile spread across his face. His eyes were locked on Meredith, who was smiling back.

"Ummm, Teddy," Lila said gently as they danced. "You've got something all over your mouth."

"Really?" he said, producing a monogrammed handkerchief

from the inside pocket of his suit jacket. He wiped his mouth and, upon seeing the lipstick traces on the cloth, blushed a deeper shade of pink than the lipstick itself. "I was. I was"—he stumbled—"eating strawberries earlier. It seems I made a real mess of things." Lila felt the hand that held hers grow warmer and sweatier.

"Not at all," she said. "You're just fine." They smiled at each other. "All cleaned up now."

As the rest of the night unfolded around her in all its grandeur, Lila couldn't stop thinking about Teddy and Meredith, and Teddy's relentless pursuit of the man who had killed his love. For the entire time that Lila had been living as Camilla Dayton in this strange, upside-down world, she'd thought of Teddy's warnings not to change what had already occurred. Now she knew that he really, truly meant it. After all, Teddy hadn't sent her back into the past to stop the murders, to save the woman he loved. He'd sent her here to find out who had carried out this terrible crime, so that, finally, he could bring the killer to justice.

That was a kind of love that she admired. A brave love. She felt ashamed that she was too scared to share how she felt with Dylan. She doubted Teddy would be so frightened of a broken heart.

The song ended, and Teddy drifted away from Lila and back toward Meredith. Lila's cell phone chimed. As if he could read her mind, Dylan had sent her a text. *Why are you avoiding me?* She glanced up from her phone to see him looking right at her. She held his gaze, wanting to run to him, wanting to explain everything. Instead, she just texted him back: *It's for the best.*

She pressed Send, then hurried out of the ballroom. "It's for the best," she said aloud to the empty street.

CHAPTER 28

ALL MEN ARE bastards," Effie said to Lila as she walked around the pool topless, a cigarette in one hand and a tumbler full of vodka on the rocks in the other. "I want you to know that I know that. I'm not saying, 'Wait for your Prince Charming,' because I'm not an idiot. Like, screw Prince Charming, right? But Alexei? Really?"

Lila was outside, waiting for Alexei to pick her up in his yacht—or as he put it, "one of my yachts." It was their second date. Lila wanted to say to Effie: *This is the man who will put an end to your life in less than a month. I'm not dating him, I'm investigating him.* But instead she just played the dumb girl, a role that, to her horror, she was getting quite good at.

"Sometimes bad guys make for the best time," Lila said. Effie gave her a dismissive wave.

"You know what I don't understand," Lila continued, "is what Alexei has against Chase. I mean, the last time I saw him, he was ranting about Chase. It's like he has a personal vendetta against him or something."

Effie's eyes grew wide at this. "What exactly did he say?" she asked.

"Nothing much. But he really hates him. Do you know if the feeling is mutual? Does Chase ever say anything about Alexei?"

Effie laughed nervously, turning her back to Lila. "I have no idea who Chase Haverford likes or doesn't like," she said dismissively.

Over the last few months of living with Effie, Lila had been observing how she interacted with the eleven other members of the Janus Society, and what she saw puzzled her. Sure, she had seen them all at the same parties and country clubs, but it seemed to Lila as if they almost actively avoided one another. Keeping the society's membership a secret to the public made sense, to a certain extent. By not disclosing the names of its members, the society could avoid a continual bombardment of requests from people hoping to receive their massive annual donation. But why, Lila wondered, were the members themselves so cold to one another? Why did they all act like the society didn't exist? Why was everything shrouded in so much secrecy?

Suddenly a deafening roar pulled Lila away from her thoughts. She turned to see a giant cigarette boat pulling up at Effie's dock, an oversize Russian flag waving behind it.

"Oh, Christ, here's Prince Charmless." Effie sighed, putting her hands over her bare breasts. "I'm going inside. Just the thought of that creep seeing my tits makes me want to puke."

Alexei, who was impatiently watching Effie and his date talking, laid on the boat's horn in two long, loud honks. Effie, placing her left forearm across her entire chest, gave him the finger with her right hand. Alexei, smiling, returned the gesture.

"How lovely that the two of you are getting along," Lila said sarcastically. "But remember, you should play nice. He'll be your neighbor soon." She began walking toward the dock, bile rising in her throat as she took in the grotesque spectacle that was Alexei posing in his ostentatious boat.

"Please don't remind me," Effie called after her.

Alexei was wearing an unbuttoned white silk shirt, which revealed his tanned, waxed, and tautly bloated torso. He looked somewhat like a hot dog.

Steadying her nerves for yet another round with the Russian, Lila stepped onto the dock.

"Hi, Alexei," she said, her fake smile already exhausting the muscles of her face. "Thanks for coming to get me." Without an offer of help from her date, she stepped down into the boat. The moment her foot left the dock, the boat roared off, causing Lila to stumble forward.

"Buckle up," Alexei shouted above the twin engines' ear-splitting noise. "I don't want to have to fish you out of the water when you blow overboard."

The extreme speed of the boat caused its bow to push up almost out of the water, forcing Lila to practically crawl on her hands and knees to join Alexei at the front.

"Can you slow down?" Lila cried as she tried to get up into the seat next to his.

"Boo hoo," Alexei said in a mocking tone. "Is Little Miss Tough Shit finally scared? Well, check this out," he said as he made the boat go even faster. "I didn't pay half a million for this thing so I could go slow."

He steered the boat around the southern tip of Miami Beach and then up the coast, parallel to its bustling beach. Though the waters off the coast of Miami were never short of show-boating assholes, Lila had never seen someone drive a boat so recklessly. She cringed as he capsized two kayakers, almost collided with a couple in a small sailboat, and flipped off anyone unlucky enough to get in his way.

What troubled Lila the most was that the closer Alexei got to possible bodily harm, the more he seemed to enjoy himself. Whenever he glanced over at Lila, who was holding on to the boat for dear life, he would laugh uproariously and then drive faster. *He's a textbook sociopath,* Lila thought. For the first time since she'd been sent back in time, she was truly afraid.

About ten minutes north of South Pointe and a few hundred feet from shore, Alexei suddenly killed the engines.

"Why are we stopping here?" Lila asked, but Alexei cut her off with a hissing "Shh!"

Digging out a pair of binoculars from beneath his chair, he used them to diligently scan the shoreline, spending a long time with his gaze trained on the Grand Palm Hotel, Ocean Drive's largest and most profitable resort. And also, Lila knew, the crown jewel in Chase Haverford's hotel empire.

"What are you looking at?" she asked, wondering why all things with Alexei tended to circle around Chase.

Alexei let out an exasperated sigh but kept the binoculars pressed against his eyes. "I feel like I'm with a child," he said. "Always with the 'why, why, why.'" He put down the binoculars and glared at her. Then he moved toward her, thrusting his hand down the back of her underwear.

Without thinking, Lila slammed her elbow under his collarbone. Her police training was always there in her muscles, waiting to come out. She stepped back, worried that her cover was blown, but when she looked at Alexei, he seemed surprisingly pleased.

"I love women who put up a fight," he said.

"Why'd you shove your hand down my underwear?" Lila snapped.

"I was just checking to see if the little baby who asks so many questions had peed herself." A lascivious smile stretched across his face. "If you keep pouting that pretty face at me, I'll give you a spanking you'll never forget."

"Don't touch me," she said while she looked around the boat for something she could use against Alexei if it came down to it, which she was starting to think it might.

Alexei frowned at her in disbelief.

"Don't touch you? Why? You'll punch me again? Just try it. That's my kind of foreplay." He shook his head. "But don't play hard to get for too long. What else do you think you're here for? Conversation? You American girls are never worth your price."

"I'm not for sale."

"That's what you'd like to think, wouldn't you?" Alexei's face slackened, as if he pitied her and her innocence. He resumed his inspection of the Grand Palm. "You know who owns that hotel over there?" he said.

"I don't," Lila lied.

"A little gold digger like you? You know exactly who owns this place," he growled. "Don't waste my time pretending to play dumb. That cocksucker Chase Haverford owns it. This eyesore is that bastard's pride and joy."

"Again with Chase," Lila said.

"You're quite close with him, no?"

"Who do you want to fuck? Me or Chase?"

Alexei slowly lowered the binoculars and turned toward Lila.

"Both," he answered.

"What've you got against him anyway?" she asked.

"Why waste time speaking of things known by us both?"

Understanding she'd get nowhere, Lila dropped the subject.

CHAPTER 29

THE STARS WERE just beginning to show in the sky by the time Alexei dropped Lila off at Effie's dock. There was a hint of winter in the air. Lila wrapped her arms around herself in an attempt to keep warm.

Her mood was heavy. The evening had been a failure, and a brutalizing one at that. All Lila had learned about Alexei was that he was a sadistic monster who embraced danger and hated Chase. So, nothing new. Throughout their time together, she had asked him in as many ways as she could think of to explain this obsession he had with Chase, but she had gotten absolutely nowhere. Alexei was not a man willing to share his secrets with anyone, least of all a woman, whom he clearly thought of as one step below a dog.

Once she knew she had hit a brick wall, Lila had wanted to get away from the Russian as quickly as possible. So she'd feigned seasickness, even going so far as to fake-vomit off the side of the boat as he looked on in horror. She was back home within ten minutes.

Feeling windblown and battered by his crazy driving, Lila

went to give Alexei a kiss on the cheek before she got off the boat. He recoiled, turning his face away from her.

"You smell like vomit," he said. "Just go."

"I'll see you soon?" Lila asked. As much as she never wanted to see this man again, she knew that she needed to keep him close. "Next time, I'll make it worth your while," she added, smiling coquettishly.

"You better," he said, baring his teeth in a half smile, half growl. She could see in his eyes that he was buying her desire to see him again. His belief that she would come back for a second helping after he'd treated her so cruelly made Lila want to laugh out loud. But she refrained. Men like Alexei assumed all women wanted them, even if just for their money.

Exhausted, she dragged herself toward the guesthouse as she heard Alexei's boat roaring away. But then she stopped dead, all her senses on high alert. Someone was on the front porch.

Her heart thumped rapidly in her chest as she slowly walked to the house.

Then she heard Dylan's voice. "Camilla?"

She stopped in confusion. "Dylan? What are you doing here?"

He stepped toward her, his eyes searching hers.

"When I heard you were with Alexei, I couldn't believe it. I said there was no way in hell." He paused, as if choking on his words. "But now I see that I was wrong."

"I'm not with Alexei."

"That's not what it looks like."

"You've never been fooled by appearances, Dylan. Please don't start now."

"Explain it to me, then." He reached out and grabbed both

of Lila's hands. An electric shock ran through her the moment they touched. "I need to understand this."

Lila wished more than anything that she could tell Dylan the truth—all of it. But it was impossible. Even if she could, even if it weren't against all Teddy's rules, he wouldn't believe her.

"I can't tell you," she said. "But I will, someday. Just trust me when I say I'm not with Alexei."

"How can I trust you? You've totally disappeared. And from where I stand, it looks like you're having an affair with Alexei and you're just too chickenshit to own up to it. If you've moved on, then tell me and you'll never see me again."

Here it was. Her opportunity to let Dylan go. She inhaled, and just as she was about to say, *Yes, please go,* something reached up into her throat and snatched the words away. She stood there, her lips slightly parted, staring at Dylan, speechless. She couldn't push him away, no more than she could force her heart to stop beating.

Without stopping to think, to breathe, she rushed into his arms and kissed him, relishing the feeling of his body pressed against hers. Finally he pulled back and looked into her eyes with a combination of relief and confusion.

"Camilla, I . . ."

Lila couldn't let him say any more, so she interrupted him with a kiss.

Tonight, there would be no more talking. Words were too dangerous. She couldn't tell him the truth, she couldn't warn him about the future, and she couldn't stand lying anymore. Instead, she took his hand in hers and led him into the guest-house, up the stairs, and toward the bedroom.

As she undressed Dylan, and he undressed her, in the soft

blue light of early evening, she thought that this precious time with him was worth any and all pain it would bring either of them.

And since she couldn't let herself say it aloud, she said it the only way she could—with her lips, her hands, every fiber of her being whispering *I love you* as the tide of her feelings swept her under.

CHAPTER 30

DYLAN LEFT HER bed early in the morning, after which Lila couldn't get back to sleep.

The psychological toll of working undercover was getting to be too much to bear, especially now that she'd met someone with whom she wanted to share everything. Nothing was more exhausting than living a lie.

To quiet her thoughts, she turned on the television and was surprised to see the face of Sam Logan on the screen. The image then changed to footage from that summer's Wimbledon finals, of Logan and Pedro Bolivar battling it out.

The TV anchor said, "Pedro Bolivar announced today that he would not be competing in the upcoming Australian Open. That's good news for his number one rival, Sam Logan, who is expected to cruise through the tournament and pick up his fourth major title. Bolivar said he would return to the circuit in the spring."

Lila practically leaped up to grab her laptop. She opened a search engine and typed Pedro Bolivar and Frederic Sandoval, but she already knew what she would find.

Sandoval was Bolivar's estranged father. In order to grieve

for him, Bolivar was taking some time off from tennis. This move would be good for Logan, of course. No one else in men's tennis had any chance of beating him. But what did that have to do with Javier? And why was he having Sandoval followed?

Teddy's database had nothing on Bolivar or Sandoval. Was there a link between Sandoval and Alexei? Lila made furious notes, trying to see the connections, but she was distracted by the faint hint of Dylan's smell still clinging to her sheets. She buried her face in the pillow and inhaled his scent as the sun rose slowly from its hiding spot beneath the azure horizon. Even though her mind was running in circles, she was overcome by a deep sleep.

Hours later, Lila was awakened by a piece of clothing landing softly across her stomach. Blinding morning light hit her like a wall. She picked up the garment, blinking in confusion. A blood-orange silk dress. Effie stood across the room, her back to Lila, rooting around in her closet.

"What time is it?" Lila asked. She couldn't believe she had fallen back into such a deep and dreamless sleep.

"Around eleven," Effie said. "Here, put this on." She balled up a strapless cream-colored dress and threw it to Lila. "I've got plans for us." She crossed the room, snatching the orange dress up. "This one's for me. You've got an hour to get ready. We'll take the boat."

"And where are we going?" asked Lila. She had planned to spend the day looking into Alexei's businesses to see if there were any economic motives connecting him to the Star Island murders. Now it seemed as if she was going to get roped into one of Effie's vortexes of sun, alcohol, and oblivion. "Because I've already made plans."

"Then cancel them! I'm sure that hideous Russian has something else to do besides ruining your reputation."

"I wasn't aware that I had a reputation, much less that it was being ruined."

"Well, it's time you knew the truth." Effie sat down on the bed next to Lila with an expression of grave seriousness on her face. "Everyone detests Alexei, and if you continue to hang out with him, I'm afraid that they'll hate you, too."

"Who cares?" Lila asked, putting a pillow over her face to get some respite from the oppressive sunshine.

"I care!" said Effie.

"South Beach society is junior high with bank accounts," Lila said.

"Exactly!" Effie exclaimed triumphantly. "Isn't it fun?"

Leaping off the bed, Effie returned to Lila's closet to pick out shoes to match her dress.

"There are rules, Camilla, and you're breaking every one of them," Effie said in the measured tone one uses to address a naughty child. "Usually I approve of a little lawlessness, but not in this case. Your Alexei phase is nothing short of bananas."

"So how, may I ask, are you planning to rehabilitate my sullied name?"

"There's a little who's who of all the fabulous people happening today at Fisher Island. I thought spending time in the fresh air with handsome men who aren't psychopaths would help you see the light."

Effie's phone vibrated. The moment she looked at it, her bright face went dark.

"Who's that?" Lila asked.

"It's nothing." But judging from Effie's changed demeanor,

it was far from nothing. "Okay, be at the dock in an hour. Got it?" She quickly left the room.

Effie was right. The party at the Fisher Island Club was a who's who of Miami's elite. It was thrown by *Ocean Drive* magazine to celebrate their upcoming January issue. The country club was packed with perfectly toned women in high heels and bikinis swaying next to men outfitted in flip-flops, swim trunks, and tank tops. The club elders, not wanting their surgery scars to be seen in unfiltered daylight, stayed by the bar. A band made up of four men who all looked like the preppy villains in a John Hughes movie were playing their vaguely calypso music with the detached, superior air typically adopted by young men desperate to be rock stars.

"You're right, Ef. This certainly is the place to be," Lila said to Effie, who was clutching her phone while nervously looking around the room. "Ef? . . . Earth to Effie!" Lila said, waving her hand in front of her friend's face.

"Oh, sorry. What?"

"I was saying that—" Lila started, but then Effie's phone vibrated again.

"Got to take this," Effie said as she answered her phone. "Hey," Lila heard her say, before she once again went skittering away. Her curiosity piqued, Lila decided to follow.

Lila stayed a few steps behind as Effie wove her way through the undulating crowd of swimsuit models, hairdressers, socialites, financiers, and self-described entrepreneurs. She watched as Effie ducked into an empty bathroom, closing the door behind her. But Lila was disappointed to find that she couldn't hear anything, even standing in the hallway right outside the bathroom door.

She jumped when someone grabbed her arm.

"Whoa! Easy, girl," Javier said from behind her. He was wearing white linen pants, a white wife beater, and a paisley scarf tied jauntily around his neck.

"Javier!" Lila exclaimed.

"Look at you." Javier ran his hands along the sides of her hips. "You are absolutely delectable. I've been meaning to call you. Tell me what they say isn't true."

"Tell me what the great 'they' are saying, and then I'll tell you if it's true."

"Well, when I saw you with Dylan those many ages ago, I was thrilled. I mean, really, rich, gorgeous guy falls for rich, gorgeous girl. It's proper. Then I hear about you and Alexei Dortzovich. Are you serious?"

"We're just friendly. It's nothing."

"It's a lot more than nothing. Trust me. That man doesn't do friendly."

"What do you know about him?"

"Enough to know that he's someone to avoid."

It suddenly dawned on Lila that maybe Alexei wasn't just at war with Chase. Could his conflict be with the entire Janus Society? She needed to find out more.

"I have heard him bad-mouth Chase Haverford," she admitted. "Has he ever done anything threatening to you?"

"Please," Javier said with a dismissive wave. "I'm a lot tougher than I look. No backwoods Russian hick is ever going to push around Javier Martinez."

Says the man who will be dead in two weeks, Lila thought. Suddenly, the bathroom door was flung open by a red-faced Effie, who looked shocked to see Lila and Javier huddled right there.

"Christ," Effie muttered under her breath. Her mottled skin

and swollen, makeup-free eyes made it clear that she had been crying. Effie nodded curtly to Javier, who nodded back. Then she grabbed Lila's hand. "I need a drink, or several. Let's go to the bar."

"Effie," Lila asked in concern, once they had arrived at the bar. "What's wrong?"

Effie shook her head, her eyes tearing up, but said nothing. They stood together in silence. When the bartender finally came their way, Effie ordered a vodka soda, downed it, then ordered another.

"Please, Effie, talk to me," Lila pleaded. She was really starting to worry about her friend.

"Okay," Effie said, "but not here. Let's go down to the beach." Drinks in hand, they walked away from the crowd toward the quiet of the water. When they were finally alone, Effie turned to Lila.

"What I'm about to tell you can go no farther than you and me."

"Okay."

"You promise on your life?" Effie asked. "Because if this gets out, it's all over."

"I promise."

"It's my dad," Effie said, collapsing into the sand. "He told me like two hours ago that he's under investigation by the SEC. When we talked, he sounded hysterical. It was scary, hearing my dad like that," Effie said, reaching up to Lila. "I'm worried that he'll do something crazy like hurt himself. I mean, if any of this gets out, if even a whiff of this comes to light, he's finished."

Lila was taken aback. This was not what she was expecting Effie to say. She sat down in the sand next to her friend and put her arm around her, her brain working on overdrive. Effie's father, Winston Webster, was an international hedge-fund titan, a self-proclaimed soothsayer of the markets. But Lila knew for a fact that whatever investigation the SEC was conducting, it would not go far—because in all her years of investigating, she'd never heard anything about it.

"I'm sure it'll be fine," Lila said, but Effie wasn't consoled.

"Can you imagine if my dad is the next fucking Bernie Madoff?" With a groan, Effie lay back on the beach. "I asked him if there was anything to worry about, and he just kept telling me, over and over again, that he was innocent. And I guess I believe him, but why would he sound so crazy if he had nothing to hide?"

"We all have something to hide," Lila said quietly. "But if anything happens, I'm here for you. You know that, right?"

Effie nodded. Lila brushed away some of the mascara-tinged tears that were on her friend's cheek.

"Okay." Effie sniffed. "Let's go back."

Lila stood, pulling Effie up with her, and the two women walked back to the club hand in hand.

When she entered the room, Lila immediately saw Dylan. "Effie," she said, unable to take her eyes off him, "I'll be right back."

Lila almost ran to him. She couldn't help herself. She threw her arms around his shoulders, and he wrapped his arms around her waist. She could feel all the eyes of South Beach on them. This was the first time they'd been affectionate in public.

"What are you doing here?" she asked.

"Looking for you, of course."

Lila felt joy well up inside her. "Lucky me," she whispered into his ear.

Out of the corner of her eye, she saw Effie and Chase cross the room together and disappear down a hallway. They both had very serious looks on their faces. Something was wrong.

"Dylan," she said, leaning her head against his shoulder. "Effie's in a bit of a crisis at the moment."

"What else is new?" he said, exhaling loudly.

"I know. But just humor me, all right? I'll be back in a minute."

Lila left Dylan's side to follow Effie and Chase. She went through an empty dining area and stopped when she heard shouting down the hall.

As she tiptoed toward the commotion, the voices grew louder, but she couldn't make out what was being said. Suddenly, Effie ran out of the room, with Chase behind her. They whooshed by, rushing out a back door that led to the tennis courts, not paying Lila any mind.

Chase Haverford and Effie Webster? As far as Effie had let on, they barely knew each other. But Lila had already known that was a lie. Lies, it seemed, were crumbling all around her. Lila set out to find Effie and figure out exactly what was going on.

It took a fair bit of searching, but she finally found her in her boat, which was moored to the dock. Effie was passed out, reeking of booze, and slumped over the steering wheel, with only one shoe on.

Lila put her hand on Effie's shoulder, and the girl roused slightly, lifting her swaying head. She saw Lila, then started crying again.

"He's going to ruin me," she whispered.

"Do you mean Chase?" Lila asked. Effie put her head back down and let out a big, shaky sigh. "How's Chase going to ruin you? Does he know about your dad?"

Effie was beyond talking. She was reduced to gasps, sighs, and sobs, a tiny, drunken, broken mess.

CHAPTER 31

IT WAS HARDER than Lila had thought to get Alexei to agree to see her again.

"Are you going to vomit this time?" he asked over the phone, his voice dripping with disgust. She felt as if she could hear his lips curling into a sneer.

"I'm not planning on it, but you never know," Lila replied. Earlier that morning she had gone back over her notes, reviewing her files and compiling the information. In fifteen days, the Star Island killer would strike. More than ever, she was convinced that Alexei was the murderer, but everything remained unproven. She needed more evidence.

"I'll be at Club Madonna at ten tonight. If you want to see me, I'll be there. If not, then all the better. I do not give a rat's ass at this point." With that, he hung up the phone.

"And they say chivalry is dead," Lila muttered to herself.

At a quarter past ten, she pulled up to Club Madonna, Miami Beach's only strip club, handing her car keys over to a Dominican boy who couldn't have been older than fifteen. She figured there was at least a 50 percent chance she'd never see her car again. The marquee, with its tempting deals of two-for-one lap dances and BYOB, signaled that this was the place for sleazeballs on a budget.

"Oh, God," Lila said to herself with a sigh before paying the ten-dollar cover and entering the darkly lit, dismal club. House music blared as two bored girls lazily ground against each other on the stage.

Alexei and his crew were in the back of the club, surrounded by many bottles of vodka and at least six completely naked strippers. As she walked toward him through the fog created by fake smoke and strobe lights, Lila could see him funneling vodka off a woman's nipple and directly into his mouth. *This should be a fun night,* she thought. If Dylan could see her now, he'd think she was crazier than he already did.

When Alexei spotted her, he put the stripper's nipple deep into his mouth, staring directly into Lila's eyes. Then he got up and reached for Lila, pressing his lips to hers. He tasted like booze and sickeningly sweet perfume. Lila tried to pull away, but he grabbed her by the waist and pulled her flush against him. His eyes were droopy and drugged—by lust, vodka, madness, Lila didn't know.

"I know how you like to tease," he whispered loudly into her ear. "But tonight you came to me, so don't pull away like some silly virgin. See this girl," he said, pointing to a brunette with enormous implants pushing out against her seemingly tortured skin. "You think you are better than her, with your fancy clothes and all your money."

"I don't," Lila said, still trying to get out of his grip.

"But you are nothing compared to her. She is honest. You lie. You act like you've never had a cock in your mouth before."

But I can tell you have. I can tell you like to play hard to get. I just like to play hard. Do you know who will win?" he asked as his fingers dug into her flesh. Lila winced in pain. "I will."

Lila was holding her breath, her eyes darting around the room. She was trying to assess how she could escape if she needed to, which she probably would any minute now. But all she saw were barriers. Alexei's bodyguards were there by the back exits. He had five supersize comrades sitting with him at the table, and Lila knew they were all armed. She had miscalculated the situation. If he decided to get violent with her, she was outnumbered and in big trouble.

She made a split-second decision. It was the only way she could think of to get out of this place. She stopped pulling away from Alexei and leaned into him.

"It's a bit crowded in here," she purred. "Plus, I don't like it when you look at other women. Why don't we go back to your place, alone?"

By going to Alexei's she was putting herself in the lion's den, but at least there she would be with only him. She figured she had a better chance of fighting off Alexei, if it came to it, than of battling his entire cadre of coked-up and drunk psychopathic sycophants.

Alexei released Lila, who exhaled in relief to be out of his clutches. He went over to one of his bodyguards and said something to him in Russian. Then the two bodyguards quickly ushered Lila and Alexei out of the club and into the idling black SUV waiting for them outside.

The bodyguards sat in the front, with Alexei and Lila in the back. Alexei poured himself a vodka from an open bottle sitting in a silver bucket between them. The car raced through the streets of Miami.

Alexei regarded Lila with a drunken smirk. "You don't fool me for a minute," he said. His speech was slightly slurred.

"Excuse me?"

"You don't fool me!" he shouted with such force that he spilled some of his vodka on the car floor. "Dumb whore, look what you've made me do."

"Alexei, calm down. Nobody's trying to fool you."

Alexei began to laugh. It was a cackle that made Lila's skin crawl. There was so much hate in him. "I'm sick of playing this game with you. You think you're playing me. But I'm the one playing you. I know you're just Chase's spy. He couldn't send his little bitch Effie, so he sent you instead."

"You've gone crazy," Lila said. She tried to make eye contact with either of the bodyguards, but they both kept looking forward. She knew they'd do nothing to help her. "I barely know Chase."

"Liar! You fucking lying cocktease. You think I believed you wanted to be with me? You think I don't feel you shudder when I touch you? And all these dates we still haven't kissed. Well, I'm going to get my kiss from you now."

He leaned toward Lila. She was thankful that the bottle of vodka was sitting there between them, giving her some kind of barrier against him. She imagined smashing the bottle over his head, but instead she moved closer to him, closed her eyes, and readied herself for a kiss from a monster. *Will I have to sleep with him tonight to prove that I'm not Chase's spy?* When nothing happened, she opened her eyes to see him laughing at her.

"Even worse than a tease is a whore who'll fuck her way out of a problem." Alexei sneered. "Sit back and shut the fuck up. I'm taking you back to my place for a real surprise."

Now Lila was seriously afraid. If she punched his windpipe,

she knew she could disable him, but she'd have to do it the moment the car hit the next stoplight.

"Not such a tough bitch now, are you?" Alexei said, seeming to relish the fear on her face.

Without him seeing, Lila kept her hand on the door handle. The second the car came to a stop at an intersection, she started to frantically turn the handle, pushing her shoulder against the door. She was ready to bolt. Nothing. She tried again. The door didn't budge.

Again, Alexei laughed. He was really enjoying himself now.

"How much of a fool do you think I am? That my security doesn't know to lock the car doors?"

The light turned green, and the car began moving again. Lila sank back into the leather seat. A feeling of defeat overwhelmed her. She was trapped.

After a long drive north up Miami Beach, the SUV turned onto La Gorce Island and pulled up in front of Alexei's gigantic white stucco mansion. The bodyguard driving the car exited the vehicle, opened Lila's door, and dragged her out.

She kicked and screamed, but he outweighed her by almost two hundred pounds. The other bodyguard and Alexei silently followed them into the house. This was it. What she had feared her entire life and had come close to several times as a cop was going to happen at this very moment. She didn't know what form the pain and violence would take, but she was sure it was coming. As sure as she'd been of anything for her entire life.

Her body went limp, and the bodyguard, holding his arm around her waist, tossed her onto the floor of the main living room. Then the two giant men flanked the front door as Alexei disappeared into another room.

When he came back, he was holding a bottle of champagne

in one hand and two flutes in the other. He was smiling from ear to ear. He set down the glasses on a side table next to the black leather couch and picked up a remote control. The TV clicked on to CNN.

"You're here to be a witness to my victory. My triumph," Alexei shouted as he uncorked the champagne. He poured some in one glass and set it in front of Lila, who was still crouched on the floor. "Drink," he said to her. "And listen. The deal was announced at midnight, so it should be coming on any minute now."

Lila had never been more confused. What was happening?

On the screen, a young blonde in a coral-colored blouse and matching lipstick was reading the business news. "The Dow Jones was down over one hundred points over investor concern about the continuing decline in housing prices." Lila looked at Alexei, who was transfixed by the TV. "And, in breaking news," the woman on the screen continued, "the hotelier Chase Haverford has announced that he has sold his hotel conglomerate to a holding company controlled by an Israeli businessman identified as Nakaleni Suka. Suka has agreed to buy a controlling stake of the Haverford empire for a reported one point six billion dollars. Next up, how can economic uncertainty work for you . . ."

Alexei turned the television off, downed his champagne, then greedily refilled his empty glass.

"Drink with me!" he shouted at Lila. "Toast your friend Chase's big news-making business deal." She sat still, her glass untouched. "Drink," he commanded.

Lila brought the champagne flute to her lips and took a small sip. Her hand was shaking.

"I can see him now. Celebrating somewhere. Thinking he is the king. But what Chase doesn't know is I am the one who bought his hotels. Me. The Russian pig farmer. The man he thinks is beneath him. He thinks some man named Nakaleni Suka bought his hotels. Well, you know what *na kaleni, suka,* means in Russian? It means 'On your knees, bitch.' And that's where he's going to be, on his fucking knees."

Alexei picked up a pile of papers from the table. "It's all here. Signed and certified," he yelled, waving the pages around, his eyes bulging and wild. "That idiot thinks he's still in control. But I'm the one who runs things now. Little does he know, I'm about to dismantle his entire life's work, piece by piece, and sell it to the dogs. He'll have to watch helplessly while I tear down everything he's spent his entire life building."

"Why would you do that?" Lila asked, trying to piece everything together, but nothing quite made sense.

"You still want to act as if you know nothing?" Alexei asked.

"It's not an act," Lila said, finally standing up. She was done with cowering.

"Sit down," Alexei said, his voice suddenly cold and dangerous. "And I will tell you."

Lila sat. Alexei poured himself another glass of champagne and downed it in a single gulp. "I grew up in a small city on the Black Sea," he began. "It was Soviet era. A dark time, and we were all very poor. Every year a circus would come to town for a few days. It was all that mattered to the children. One year, when I was six, I saw a circus lion rip apart his handler. He grabbed the man's arm with his jaw, then devoured his face. My uncle tried to cover my eyes, but I pushed his hand away. I wanted to see. Do you know why?"

Lila shook her head.

"Even though I was a little boy, I knew what I was seeing. I knew what it meant. Life is cruel. A battle between weak and strong." Alexei was pacing the room, his hands balled into tight fists. "Chase thought he could order me around, making me dance like a circus animal, all so I could be part of his stupid club."

The Janus Society? Lila wondered.

"And then he tells me I'm not good enough. Me! Alexei Romanovich Dortzovich, who is one hundred times more man than him! Now I own him. Now he is the one who does not belong."

"Belong to what? Are you talking about the Janus Society?" Lila asked.

Alexei rushed toward her. Before she could duck out of the way, he shoved her to the floor. "Why do you continue to play games? The game is over. I have won. Don't pretend to know nothing. I was as good as in, then that asshole Chase, your spymaster, told me I was out. Now he acts as if I'm a stranger to him."

He placed his foot on Lila's upper thigh and pushed her along the floor toward the door. "Now, leave. Go back to Chase. Tell him what I've told you. As much as I will miss seeing his face when he learns what I have done, I want you to be the one to tell him. And I have better things to do."

Lila scrambled onto her hands and knees, trying to crawl toward the front door, but she was knocked back to the floor when Alexei's foot pushed her over.

"Look at you now, princess," he said, laughing. "Get out. You are no longer of any use to me."

One of the bodyguards opened the door as two barely dressed women from the strip club sauntered in. "Ah, here are some real women. Come to me, my lovelies. Pay no attention to this dog on the floor."

The two bodyguards approached Lila, picked her up by her arms, and tossed her out of the house, slamming the door behind her.

Her palms and her knees were skinned and bleeding. Lila sat on Alexei's front stoop catching her breath, somewhat shocked to find herself alive.

CHAPTER 32

LILA LOOKED OVER her shoulder to make sure she wasn't being followed by any of Alexei's goons as she hurried to the bridge that connected the cloistered opulence of La Gorce Island to the real world. No one was following her. She was alone.

It wasn't until she was on the other side of the bridge that she fully exhaled.

It was as cold as a Miami night could get, and she shivered in the frigid air. Her tiny cocktail dress and stiletto heels provided little protection against the elements. She walked for at least twenty minutes before she was able to begin to calm down. As the veil of shock slowly lifted, she realized that her body was in pain, and a debilitating headache was blooming in her skull.

Star Island was a long, cold, two-hour walk away, but Lila wanted to walk. She needed the time to collect her thoughts and settle her nerves. As she headed south toward home, she began to sift through what Alexei had told her. Here she'd thought she was seducing him in order to prove her overwhelming suspicion that he was the Star Island killer. But the whole time, he was using her to get to Chase. Yet again she had been wrong, all wrong.

Alexei wasn't the killer; he couldn't be. He would never have spent so much time and money buying Chase's empire if he was going to kill him in just two weeks.

And then there was the business with the club. When Alexei had been railing against Chase rejecting him, he had to have been talking about the Janus Society. It was the only thing that made any sense.

That explains why I've seen him with every member of the society, Lila thought.

Of course, she realized, Alexei had met with all twelve members of the society because he was being considered as a new member. But then Chase must have rejected him, which explained the argument she'd overheard on the South Beach boardwalk.

Alexei wasn't going to murder Chase, or any of the rest of the society. He'd carried out his revenge by taking away what Chase valued most: his company.

But this new revelation left Lila more lost than she'd ever been. Instead of finding the killer, she'd found another dead end. She was, once again, lost in the maze.

By the time she stepped into Effie's driveway, it was a little past two in the morning, but Effie's bedroom light was still on.

Lila was desperate for answers, and she couldn't wait until the morning. Time was running out. She needed to dig deeper into what Effie knew. Maybe Lila's telling Effie about what had happened with Alexei would prompt Effie to be more honest about her involvement with the Janus Society.

And then Lila remembered what Alexei had said, about how

he'd thought Chase sent Lila to spy on him because he couldn't send Effie. Lila wasn't sure what that meant.

As Lila climbed the stairs toward Effie's bedroom, she heard voices. She tiptoed to the door, curious.

"Please don't leave," Lila heard Effie plead.

"Never beg. It's beneath you," a man said. Lila instantly recognized Chase's distinctive voice.

Effie and Chase? So they were together. Hiding in the darkened hallway, Lila listened.

"How could you be so cold?" Effie sobbed. "You won't even look at me!"

"Just calm down. Here, take this," said Chase, in a tone as measured as Effie's was wild.

The sound of glass shattering exploded from the room.

"I've told you, I won't swallow those tranquilizers anymore," Effie screamed. "I don't want to be calm. There is nothing to be calm about."

"You're weaker than I thought you were." Lila didn't have to see Chase's face to hear the sneer in his voice.

"You're not who I thought you were either. You're cruel."

"I'm not cruel. I'm in control. I take care of my business. Why don't you take care of yours?"

"I told you I can't do it anymore."

"Then you know what I'll be forced to do."

"No one is forcing you."

"You spoiled child," Chase said. "How can you say that?"

"But I love you." Effie let out a large, mournful sob. "And you said you loved me."

"Of course I love you." Chase's voice was rough. "What matters more than anything is that you do your job. And we won't ever have to have this conversation again."

"Why can't you help me, just this one time?" Effie wept. She sounded trapped and desperate.

"I should never have exposed myself like this. Rules are made for a reason, right?" Chase paused. "Now go wipe your face, and then let's go downstairs and fix you a drink."

Quickly, before she could be discovered, Lila slipped off her high heels and moved away from the door, running down the stairs and out the back entrance, wondering what she had heard.

CHAPTER 33

LILA HURRIED ACROSS the lawn, her bare feet racing over the dew-heavy grass, making her way as quickly and as quietly as possible to the guesthouse. She got inside and locked the door behind her. Safe.

Needing to wash the miseries of the day off her skin, she took a long, burning-hot shower. She winced as the water hit the scrapes on her hands and knees, watching the blood circle down the drain. Then she wrapped herself in a terry-cloth bathrobe, poured four fingers' worth of Wild Turkey in a tumbler, and collapsed on the couch.

Her head was spinning. She felt as if she were a pinball, bouncing off of one concussive surface only to be propelled to another. The moment she hit one wall, she was sprung back into the fray for another round. Nothing felt in her control. Each lead had only set her off in the wrong direction. Now she was thoroughly lost, and couldn't see the big picture.

Taking a sip of bourbon, she tried to settle her spirit and sort through her tumbling thoughts. Several things had become abundantly clear to her tonight. Alexei had been vetted as a possible member of the Janus Society. But he was rejected, and, in revenge, he carried out a raid on Chase's hotel conglomerate.

She now knew that Alexei wasn't the killer, and that Chase, the ringleader of the society, was Effie's lover. But what were Effie and Chase fighting about? And why did Effie think she had to keep their relationship a secret?

Lila sighed. Effie was such a puzzle. For every true thing that could be said about her, the exact opposite could also be true. She was cunning, yet ditzy. She was generous, yet thoughtless. She seemed like an open book, yet Lila was slowly realizing that she barely knew her.

Was her dad really being investigated by the SEC, or was that just another lie? Lila was 100 percent sure that Winston Webster was never indicted by the SEC for investor fraud. That juicy fact would've been revealed during her investigation into the murder of his daughter. So either the truth about Webster's thievery was buried or he had been able to dig himself out of whatever financial pit he had found himself in. Or, Lila wondered, was that story all a lie, something Effie came up with in order to hide the truth about what had really upset her that night at the Fisher Island Club?

Lila finished her drink, then went back to the kitchen for a refill. The accumulating futility of her investigation over the course of so many of her days and weeks and months was wearing her down.

Whatever the truth was, Lila knew for sure that Effie was unraveling. She said she loved Chase, but they were obviously on the rocks. It sounded as if he was threatening to kick her out of the Janus Society, which clearly meant a great deal to her. And if the story about her father was true, then Effie was also living in fear that he might go to prison, stripping Effie of both her wealth and her reputation, transforming her overnight from princess to pariah.

It seemed like Effie would do anything to keep her world from crumbling. Maybe, Lila realized with a shock, kill for it.

Was it possible? Could Effie be the Star Island killer? In all her years of investigating the case, Lila had never truly considered that one of the victims could also be the perpetrator of the crime. The gunshot wounds and forensic evidence at the crime scene had never led her in that direction. But what if she'd had it wrong all along? What if one of the Janus Society members was the murderer?

The society operated in total secrecy. Every person that Lila had interviewed who had connections to the twelve dead stated that they had had no awareness of any of the victims' involvement with it. And no one had known about the secret meeting at Chase's Star Island estate except, of course, the members themselves.

So what happened? If Effie or another of the club members was the killer, then what went wrong?

The bourbon had begun to catch up with Lila, and she felt simultaneously heavy and light, exhausted and exhilarated. Her thoughts drifted away from the case and toward Dylan. Just as she was telling herself to concentrate her mind on finding the Star Island killer, her hand picked up her phone and dialed him.

From the sound of his voice, her call had pulled him out of a profoundly deep sleep. She looked at the clock. It was 3:23. She hadn't realized it was so late.

"Camilla?" Dylan said, his voice shifting instantly from sleepy to worried. "What time is it? Is everything okay?"

"I woke you," Lila said. Only once she heard Dylan's sober voice did she realize just how drunk she was.

"Are you okay?" he asked, still concerned.

"I'm fine." She paused. "I just needed to hear your voice. It's been a very long day."

"You sound strange." He paused, and Lila could hear him getting out of bed. "I'm coming over."

"You don't have to."

"I know I don't have to. I want to. I'll be there in fifteen minutes."

True to his word, in fifteen minutes Dylan was at her door, in her arms, in her bed. As he removed her robe, she saw his eyes linger over the scraped flesh on her knees and hands. But he didn't ask her what had happened, just leaned over her body, gently kissing around the edges of her cuts, while she lay back, running her hand over his back, wondering how, amid all her bad luck, she had had the fortune to meet such a man.

But he will be taken away from me, she said to herself. In less than two weeks, life as they both knew it would be over. Her love for Dylan wasn't a blessing. If anything, it was just one more heartbreak waiting to swallow her up.

Dylan looked at her. "What's wrong?" he asked.

"Nothing," she said. "I was only thinking how happy I am to have met you. It's just—" She paused, needing to swallow the truth that she couldn't share. "I wish it had happened at a different time."

He pressed his lips to hers.

"I was thinking the same thing today. I wish I could've met you years ago. My life maybe could've been different. Better."

This made Lila laugh despite her sadness. "Your life is perfect. How could I make it better?"

"I told you. Things . . . aren't always what they look like from the outside." Dylan's face grew grave. He continued, "There are things I've done that I'm not proud of. Decisions I made when I was younger. Things I would never do today."

She took his beautiful, melancholy face in her hands. She realized he was lost, just like she was. But now they had found each other.

After they made love, Dylan fell into a deep sleep, but Lila was wide awake. She had made up her mind. She didn't want to give in to fate anymore. Why must she always follow the rules? Where had that gotten her?

Well, she thought, *not any longer.*

She cared more about the man she loved than any warnings from Teddy about changing the shape of the universe. Hadn't her very presence here in the past already changed the course of the future? She had befriended Effie, fallen in love with Dylan, held Frederic Sandoval as he took his last few breaths. She had certainly left some kind of mark. How much risk was there in making sure that Dylan wasn't shot?

The truth was, whatever the answer, she didn't care. Some things were worth the risk.

Before Dylan left Lila's place late Friday morning, she made him promise that they would go for a long sail on the day he was supposed to be shot. The fates be damned. Together, they'd outrun destiny and create a new future.

CHAPTER 34

NOW THAT EFFIE had become her primary suspect, Lila decided to start with a thorough search of her house. During the daylight hours, the doors to Effie's estate were typically unlocked. Even if she wasn't home, at least one of the several people tasked with caring for both the property and its mistress was working busily on something.

When Lila entered the kitchen on Friday morning, one of Effie's cooks was at the counter, feeding heaps of kale into a riotously noisy juicer.

"Is Effie in?" Lila shouted over the ruckus. The woman turned toward Lila and shook her head no while she continued to fuel the machine with vegetables.

"Miss Effie is out shopping. She'll be back later," the cook shouted.

"I have to borrow something from upstairs," Lila said, pointing at the ceiling as if the noise of the juicer made gesturing a necessity. The cook shrugged and turned back to her duties.

Lila had been in Effie's master suite plenty of times, but never alone. As she took a step inside, she quickly locked the door behind her, then flipped a switch on the wall that brought blackout curtains automatically down on the windows. She turned the lights on and began her search. If someone stumbled upon her surreptitious snooping, she knew she'd have no credible excuse. She would have to work quickly, quietly, and diligently.

Effie's room struck Lila as what a young girl's fantasy of an adult bedroom might look like. Large windows overlooking the ocean and the cityscape of Miami took up two sides of the bedroom. There was a small sitting area, with European furniture that had been reupholstered in animal print fabrics. The chairs and the side tables were so delicate-looking that it seemed as if a heavy gaze would crumple them. And on the west wall sat Effie's most prized possession, a sofa created by Salvador Dalí, which, with its bright pink cushions and dual arched back, was meant to resemble Mae West's lips. Only five had been made by the artist, and Effie had one of them.

Lila's first stop was the closet, though it wasn't so much a closet as an expansive, bright room that resembled an incredibly chic boutique. The all-white space was punctuated by a custom-made hot pink sofa and a pink pony-hair area rug. Her hundreds of shoes took up one entire wall, while the rest was devoted to her enviable wardrobe.

Lila began searching the various drawers, finding only piles of sunglasses, cashmere everything, and an incredibly extensive collection of lingerie. Running her hands through a bunch of silk slips, Lila jumped when she touched something metallic. *A gun,* Lila thought, but it was only a thin gold vibrator. She turned it on, turned it off, and placed it back in the drawer where she had found it.

She searched the bathroom, examining shelves upon shelves

of creams, unguents, and ointments from all over the world that promised to keep time at bay, but found nothing. Then she moved to the two antique mirrored bedside tables that flanked the bed, opening each drawer and giving every object a thorough once-over. There was nothing besides a silk sleep mask, a bottle of Ambien, and a cream that, according to the label, was for the "décolletage." Still nothing.

But years of experience as a detective had given Lila a pretty sharp instinct. She moved the side table to see if there was anything between it and the wall, and bingo: there in the floor was a barely perceptible change in the wood grain. She felt around the edges of the area and, after some experimenting, found that when she pressed on one of the corners, a secret door popped open.

The hidden compartment contained a Wilson Combat customized .45 handgun with a titanium suppressor, built to muffle the sound of a gunshot, along with several boxes of ammo. "Bingo," Lila whispered. This wasn't a weapon that someone like Effie might have for self-defense. Lila had seen a gun of this make only once, when she found it in the dead hand of one of the Mexican cartels' most notorious assassins.

"What in the world are you up to, Effie Webster?" Lila whispered.

Time was ticking. Every minute she was in this room by herself, Lila risked being discovered. She returned the gun to its home and moved the table back to its proper place. At that moment, she spotted Effie's laptop sitting atop a bunch of art books on an antique bookshelf. In less than a few minutes, Lila had copied the entirety of Effie's computer onto the external hard drive she'd used to do the same thing to Javier.

A moment later, the blinds were up, the door was unlocked, and Lila was bounding down the stairs with one of Effie's L'Wren Scott cocktail dresses held high in her right hand as her cover, just in case Effie asked why she'd been in her bedroom without her.

Now Lila knew that, this whole time, she'd been living in a hornet's nest. She needed to be more careful than ever. As Lila was walking back to the guesthouse, she couldn't help feel, amid the shock, that she had been completely betrayed by a woman she had come to think of as a friend.

LATER THAT EVENING, Lila sat on the couch with her feet up and a glass of white wine within arm's reach, sifting carefully through the contents of Effie's hard drive. Everything appeared fairly normal until she encountered a number of files that were under the same type of military-grade data encryption that she had found on Javier Martinez's computer. She wondered if all of the members of the Janus Society had their data protected to this extent.

Just as she had done before, Lila sent the files to Shadow, the hacker. Within two hours, he had cracked the data protection.

There was a long correspondence between Effie and someone who called himself "the Facilitator." The Facilitator had sent Effie daily in-depth reports on the comings and goings of a person identified only as "the Target." The information reminded Lila of the surveillance she'd found of Sandoval on Javier's computer.

Then Lila's heart jumped; she saw who the Facilitator was sending his surveillance reports to: camilla_dayton@gmail .com. She looked at the e-mails again. Effie had been carrying on the correspondence with an unidentified spy under the name Camilla Dayton.

Lila then looked deeper into the files and was shocked to discover that numerous flight itineraries had been booked under the name Camilla Dayton. The first flight was taken on October 10 to Costa Rica, just a few days after Effie had invited Lila to stay with her at the guesthouse. Not only had Effie lied about the destination of every trip she'd taken since Lila moved in, but it appeared as if she'd been carrying out an elaborate scheme to set Lila up. But why? Was Effie planning on framing Lila for the Star Island murders?

Lila knew what she had to do next. She had to shadow Effie in order to uncover the identities of the Facilitator and the Target.

Lila unearthed the black wig she'd used to impersonate her old self on Thanksgiving night at the police station. She rented a nondescript car that she parked at a construction site a few doors down. And then Lila trailed Effie around the streets of Miami.

After four exhausting days of tailing Effie as she went from the Delano to the Soho Beach House to Club Deuce to the shops of Bal Harbour and every Ocean Drive hot spot in between, Lila was losing patience. She now had only a little more than a week before the Star Island killer would strike, and she didn't want to waste it watching Effie pick out shoes.

Finally, on the fifth day, Christmas Eve, she caught a break. Lila was watching as Effie tried on sunglasses at Barneys when Effie got a text that sent her hustling out of the department store and into her car. Lila followed, two cars behind. Effie drove south on Collins, across the MacArthur Causeway, then north on Bayshore. Lila watched as she pulled her car over at a small park, got out, and removed a shopping bag from her trunk. Lila drove past and pulled her car over a few hundred feet ahead, keeping her eye on Effie through the rearview mirror.

Apart from Effie and four retirees practicing tai chi, the park was empty, making it hard for Lila to stay close without being detected. Effie was visibly nervous, and seemed acutely aware of every inch of her surroundings. She was constantly swiveling her head, like a mouse searching for a hawk.

As Effie walked toward the water, a man stepped out from behind a tree and approached her. Lila quickly sat on a bench about thirty feet from where, she assumed, "Camilla" was meeting with the Facilitator.

Wearing a motorcycle jacket and jeans, the man was wiry and bald, and he walked with the rigid posture that comes only from years of military training. From where Lila sat, it looked like he had scarred skin and tattooed eyebrows. Effie handed the shopping bag over to the Facilitator, and then the meeting was over.

Effie spun around and, with her head down, walked back toward her car, right past Lila, who shielded her face with her hand as if to block out the sun. The moment Effie passed, Lila jumped up and set off to follow the bald man.

Holding the bag, he walked along the water toward the Grand, a monolith of a hotel that rose high up into the sky. Lila followed. But she must have been getting too close because, in an instant, the man began running. Making a split-second choice between maintaining her cover and pursuing her suspect, Lila took off after him.

The man, clutching the bag under his arm like a running

back cradling a football, made a sharp right up the Grand's staircase and entered the hotel lobby with Lila in hot pursuit. But when she entered the cavernous lobby, all traces of him had disappeared. Weaving among the meandering tourists, Lila searched to no avail. Her heart was racing, and drops of sweat were streaming down her face from the itchy heat of the wig atop her head.

Lila stood by the revolving doors that led out to the main street, trying to catch her breath and hoping to pick up the scent of the Facilitator. Five minutes later, she knew the trace had gone cold. She exited the building, planning to sweep its perimeter, when she suddenly spotted him across the street, walking toward a red Pontiac. When he saw that he'd been found, his lips curled into a murderous scowl. He jumped in the car and tore out onto the road. There was no chance of catching him. But through the smoke of burned rubber left from his tires, Lila had been able to identify the license plate. Relief washed over her.

That was all the information she needed to hunt him down.

IT WAS ONE in the morning on Christmas Day when Lila, still wearing her wig, walked back into the Miami police station. Just as he had been on Thanksgiving night, Kreps was dozing off behind the front desk, his chin on his uniformed chest. Lila tried to pass by into the back office undetected, but Kreps snorted awake. In thirty years on the force, not much had gotten past him.

"Back so soon?" he asked. "Thought you went home for the night."

"I forgot something at my desk," Lila replied. "Just gotta go and grab it."

"Sure, and while you're getting that, why don't you also get yourself a life?"

"Good one, Kreps," Lila said, smiling despite herself. With a little bit of distance, even Kreps's corny jokes and grumpy demeanor made her nostalgic for her old life.

Lila walked through the desolate halls to her empty desk, flicked on the lights, and sat down. She logged in to her computer and opened up the Department of Motor Vehicles database.

Lila discovered that the Facilitator was driving a car registered to Esther Johnson, age eighty-six, of Ambrose, Georgia. This didn't surprise Lila. No criminal worth his weight would drive a car that was registered under his own name. More typically, either the license plates were stolen or the vehicle was registered to a relative. Seeing that neither the vehicle nor the plates were listed as missing, Lila hoped that she could make a connection between Esther Johnson and the man with the tattooed eyebrows.

After a few hours searching IRS records, Lila was able to compile a list of dependents the old woman in Georgia had claimed, long ago, on her tax returns. From there, Lila could find the children of those dependents. Then she cross-checked the names of Esther's sons and grandsons—there were eight of them between ages fifteen and sixty-three—with the Veterans' Service Records, because she would bet her life that this guy was ex-military. That was when she hit the jackpot. She found him. His military photo showed a much younger man, with hair and eyebrows intact, skin unscarred, but it was definitely him.

He was Shane Johnson, age forty-seven, and from what Lila could dig up, he'd had his thumb in almost every nasty black ops plot that the government perpetrated, from running guns to the Contras when he was in his teens to supervising soldiers at Abu Ghraib. He was granted an honorable discharge in 2008 after sustaining second-degree burns on his face and torso from a roadside IED while in Baghdad. Most likely, that was what had left him bald and without eyebrows.

After he left the military, the trail went fairly dark. In 2010, he was picked up for assault in New Orleans, but the charges were later dropped. According to his tax returns, from 2010 until 2013, Johnson was an employee of Xe Services, the army of mercenaries known to supplement U.S. military operations.

The only possible reason Effie would have to get mixed up with a man as shady as Shane Johnson was if she needed a murderer for hire. Had the transaction at the park today been Effie giving Shane money to carry out the Star Island murders? But, if that was the case, how did Effie end up dead? Maybe the deal Effie had made with this killer would somehow go sour. Or was someone else paying him, too?

Johnson had one credit card that he used regularly. Pulling up those records, Lila noticed that there were frequent charges made to a bar in Little Haiti. She knew the place—a dive familiar to any cop who worked that beat. It was too late to go there tonight, but she'd stake the place out tomorrow.

ON CHRISTMAS NIGHT, Lila drove by Shane Johnson's local bar. Sure enough, he was there, sitting at the bar by himself. He had seen her as Lila Day, and though she was back to looking like Camilla Dayton, she didn't dare go inside. Instead, she sat watching him from her idling car for three hours until he stumbled out into the night. She got out of her car and followed him, careful to keep a conservative distance though she suspected he was too drunk to notice her.

He walked west for three blocks until he arrived at a small run-down bungalow on a trash-strewn block: Northeast Sixty-Fourth Street. The red Pontiac was parked outside.

"I see you," Lila said softly as he unbolted his front door. "I've got you now."

CHAPTER 35

IT WAS THE day after Christmas. There were seven days left until the Star Island massacre would take place. After so many dead ends, Lila 's case had momentum. Shane Johnson must have been hired by Effie to assassinate her fellow society members. Lila still hadn't figured out Effie's motive, or what would go wrong, but she knew she would continue to wait and watch and build her case. Just not today. Today, something else was taking priority.

Dylan.

On this day, Dylan Rhodes would be shot in front of a convenience store on Lenox Avenue around 2:00 P.M. But Lila had decided that this was not going to happen, consequences be damned. She was going to save the man she loved.

She was surprised by her own conviction. Once she'd made up her mind, no other choice seemed possible.

Stopping the shooting wouldn't be all that difficult. She just needed to make sure she was with Dylan all day, and never let him get near the corner where his life would be forever altered by one terrible moment.

At first, when she'd suggested they spend this day together,

Dylan had objected. But she refused to take no for an answer. Finally, they agreed that he would pick her up in the morning and they'd go to the Sunset Harbor Yacht Club, where Dylan kept his boat. They'd spend the entire day sailing down to Boca Chita and back.

She'd be with him. She'd keep him safe.

At 10:30, Dylan pulled up in his silver Mercedes. The main house was empty. Effie had left the day before for New York, to spend Christmas with her father and his family. Or at least that's what she had told Lila, who needed to continually remind herself not to believe one word Effie said.

Lila ran out to greet Dylan, holding a small, cheerfully wrapped package. He got out of the car and swept her up in his arms. He held her close for a very long time, as if they'd been apart for months and not a week.

When she pulled away from his embrace, she saw his face was shadowed with worry.

"Everything okay?" she asked. Silently, he nodded yes, but his grim expression went unchanged.

Lila was anxious to get Dylan away from the streets of Miami. Never before had she been so eager to get out on the ocean.

They drove, top down, across the causeway, then north up Alton Road. Lila tried to get Dylan to talk, but he seemed uncharacteristically quiet. She hoped he wasn't upset with her about anything.

When Dylan turned right on Sixteenth Street, and then made a left on Lenox, Lila began to panic. This was the street where, if fate had its way, he would be shot.

"Where are we going?" she asked, her voice shrill with nervousness.

"There's a liquor store up here at the corner. I just want to grab some champagne for us, for the boat ride."

"No!" Lila shouted. "I mean, we don't need any, it's fine, let's just go." She was babbling and she knew it, but she couldn't help it.

Dylan looked at her with concern. "I'll just be a minute."

He pulled the car over at the corner of Lenox and Seventeenth Street. Lila looked at the clock. It was 11:18 A.M., a little less than three hours before the shooting would take place. Someone else would be shot today, she tried to tell herself. The culprit wasn't anywhere near here yet. But still, deep in her gut, she had a feeling that this was all wrong.

As if he sensed her concern, Dylan took her face in his hands and kissed her. "Hey," he said, stroking her hair. "I just want you to know that"—he paused, catching his breath, and she noticed his hands had begun to lightly tremble—"I love you."

"I love you, too," she murmured.

He kissed her on the lips, then jumped out of the car before she could stop him.

As she watched Dylan run to the liquor store on the other side of the street, all Lila could think was *Please, keep this man safe. Please, keep him safe.* She sat diligently surveying the scene, ready to jump out of the car at the slightest sign of danger.

He disappeared into the store, and then time did something funny for the second time in three months. It stopped. The minutes he was out of sight felt like an eternity. She checked her watch. He'd been in there for five minutes. It seemed too long. She was just about to get out of the car to make sure he was okay when he emerged with a bottle of Veuve Clicquot under his arm.

She started to wave at him, relieved.

And just then, a car roared out of nowhere, swerved to the other side of the street, and screeched to a dead stop in front of Dylan. Lila saw that the man driving the car had on a mask. In his hand she saw the metallic flash of a gun. She was so close, but too far to stop it.

She opened her mouth to scream, but nothing came out. The sound of two gunshots blasted through the air. Lila jumped out of the car and started running, the shots echoing in her ears. She bolted across the street, barely dodging a car that swerved to avoid her. With his face covered, the gunman was impossible to identify. All Lila saw as she rushed forward were three red birds tattooed on his left forearm. As she bent down to Dylan, the gunman tore down the road, took a sharp right, and disappeared.

Dylan lay sprawled in a rapidly growing pool of blood, the neck of the shattered champagne bottle still clutched in his hand. Lila fell to her knees in front of him. All of her surroundings went black. Nothing existed except him and her own all-consuming fear of losing him.

"Dylan!" she cried. He wasn't able to respond, but his eyes were open. He was still breathing. Thank God, he was still breathing.

People began to hover around both of them. What they were saying to her didn't matter. He was breathing. She heard sirens in the distance. And that's when she realized she had to go.

The moment she was connected to an attempted homicide, even as a witness, was the moment her cover was blown. Leaving Dylan as he lay bleeding on the sidewalk was the hardest thing she had ever done. But she couldn't risk being found out, not when she was so close to catching the killer.

She leaned down and kissed Dylan on his trembling lips. "I can't explain," she whispered into his ear, "but I've got to go. I love you. I love you."

Then she got up and started running, ignoring the voices from the crowd shouting after her, begging her to stop.

CHAPTER 36

IT WASN'T UNTIL her breath gave out that Lila stopped running from the scene of the crime. Then she collapsed on the sidewalk, gasping for air.

How could it have happened? She had done everything in her power to stop the shooting, but in the end it didn't matter. Everything she knew about the universe must be wrong. Those grand notions of fate and destiny were real—as real as bullet, bone, and blood.

An out-of-body sensation overcame Lila as she walked back toward Star Island. Everything felt surreal. Because it was the day after Christmas, there were almost no cars or people on the streets, which heightened her feelings of isolation and strangeness.

She didn't have long. If Dylan was conscious enough to give his account of the crime, he'd tell the police that she was an eyewitness. Then they'd come looking for her. She couldn't risk that. She'd have to go underground.

The walk to Star Island took half an hour. When she got to Effie's house, she was relieved to see that there were no police cruisers out front—not yet, at least. In fact, the day seemed absurdly serene. The sky was azure blue, with picture-perfect cumulus clouds peppered here and there. The sun was shining and the songbirds were singing sweetly. There was no sign of the tragedy that had just cut her heart in two.

Lila hurried to the guesthouse. She grabbed two suitcases and quickly stuffed them full of clothes, her computer, her notebooks, her wig, and her gun. She brought the luggage to the top of the driveway, got in one of Effie's cars, which she would ditch later, and sped away.

She spent some time just driving, trying to get her head straight. She needed a place to think things through, and she knew that she couldn't go to any of the high-end hotels in the area. If the cops were looking for her, those were the first places they'd check once they discovered she'd fled the guesthouse.

Lila remembered a motel in Little Haiti that she knew from her time on the force. It was a dilapidated place built in classic old Miami style, off the beaten track just enough for her to briefly slip into obscurity, gather herself, and plan her next move. The fact that it was close to Shane Johnson's house made it all the better.

That night Lila couldn't sleep. Every time she shut her eyes, she'd hear the gunshots again, and then she'd see Dylan lying helpless and bloody on the pavement. She paced back and forth in her small room, clutching a tumbler of Wild Turkey and trying to wrap her head around how she had, once again, failed.

Throughout the night, Lila monitored the local news channels and websites, hoping to get some word of Dylan's condition. One story on the eleven o'clock news caught her attention. It mentioned a police search for a suspect in a shooting that had taken place on the corner of Ocean Drive and Fourteenth

Street. The TV anchor identified the victim as "Willow Morris, a twenty-four-year-old South Beach resident and employee of the Four Seasons hotel." On the screen was a picture of that doe-eyed mistress of Scott Sloan. The TV anchor continued, "According to eyewitnesses, the shooter fled the scene in a red sports car."

It felt to Lila, at that moment, that everyone around her was going to wind up dead.

It wasn't until later that there was any news about Dylan. At 2:36 A.M., *The Miami Herald* posted an article that read:

Man Shot Outside South Beach Liquor Store

A Miami man was gunned down on December 26 in what was reported as a drive-by shooting on Lenox Avenue in South Beach, police said.

The victim, Dylan Rhodes, age 31, is currently in critical condition at Miami General Hospital.

Officers responded to a 911 call, which reported the shooting just after 11:00 A.M. They discovered the victim had sustained serious injuries. Emergency medical personnel transported him to a nearby hospital, where it was determined he had suffered a gunshot wound to the lower back, according to a police statement.

No witnesses have come forth, and no arrests were immediately made. The investigation continued into Friday night. "We have no updates at this point," a police spokeswoman said. "Every angle is being looked at."

Mr. Rhodes comes from a prominent Miami family. In 2008, Mr. Rhodes's father, Jack Rhodes, then CEO of Connachta Co., died, leaving his two sons controlling ownership of his company.

At this time, no relatives of the victim could be reached for comment.

Lila compared this article with the one in Teddy's database. They were identical except for the time of the shooting, which had changed from around 2:00 P.M. to 11:00 A.M.

THE NEXT MORNING, Lila drove to Northeast Sixty-Fourth Street—Shane Johnson's house. His red Pontiac was outside. Lila parked a little farther up the street and sat watching his front door. She stayed there for over two hours until he finally left.

Lila remembered how her old police chief used to tell her, "Good detective work is five percent bravery, five percent intelligence, ten percent stubbornness—and eighty percent patience." She had seen him proven right over and over again. Cases often went unsolved because most detectives bored too quickly. But Lila, to the ruination of her life, would stick with a case until the bitter end.

She followed Shane's car as he headed south, then onto the expressway west toward the Miami airport. He then took a left on West Flagler Street and pulled into the parking lot of Charlie's Armory, a gun dealership and shooting range. She watched as he got out of his car, removed two sniper rifle cases from his trunk, and went directly to the outdoor shooting range.

"He's practicing for New Year's Eve," she said aloud, her voice full of rage. She took out her binoculars so she could get a good look at him, checking his forearms to see if he had the tattoo of three red birds that she had seen on Dylan's shooter. But his arms were bare.

Lila could tell from the types of guns he had and the expert way he handled them that Shane Johnson was a well-trained killer. She focused the binoculars on his cold, dark eyes, observing that he registered no emotion as he fired off his rounds. This wasn't a fun day at the shooting range for him. This was strictly business.

Over the next couple of days, Lila kept close watch on Shane. She learned his routine. The five-mile run in the morning. The afternoons at the shooting range. Evenings in front of the television. Nights at the bar. She never saw him talk to anyone except in a perfunctory way. No one ever dropped by his house. He was as faceless and disconnected from his surroundings as a trained assassin should be. As she watched him, she couldn't wrap her mind around the fact that Effie Webster, a woman she had, as improbable as it was, considered a friend, was the Star Island killer. Had it been because of what happened with Chase? Or were there other factors? And what went so wrong that New Year's Eve that Effie herself wound up dead? But more than to Effie, Shane, or anyone else, Lila's thoughts turned to Dylan. It seemed like she couldn't close her eyes without picturing him lying on the sidewalk in a pool of his own blood. The weight of her guilt was so intense that it felt, at times, like it would crush her. She called the hospital several times, posing as different relatives, but never succeeded in getting a nurse to give her an update.

Then, at 5 A.M. on December 30, four days after the shooting and one day before the Star Island murders, Lila decided she couldn't take it anymore. With her hair tucked up into a baseball cap and oversize sunglasses on her face, she snuck into Miami General to see Dylan.

She hesitated at the door to his private room, overcome by

nerves. How would she explain leaving him bleeding on the street? How could she look at him, knowing that she had failed to save him?

Taking a sharp inhale, she stepped inside the room, only to gasp when she saw him sleeping. He had an oxygen tube beneath his nose and several IVs hooked into his arm. His skin was pale, and his mouth was slack, slightly open. His breath came in quick bursts, almost as if he was panting in pain.

Taking her cap and sunglasses off, Lila stood at his bedside, delicately curling her fingers around his. She couldn't stop the tears from falling down her cheeks.

"Dylan," she whispered.

He stirred, then opened his eyes and looked at her. It took a while for his eyes to focus, but once he knew it was her, he pulled his hand away and turned his face from hers.

"I can explain," Lila cried. "Please, let me try to explain."

"You left me lying there on the street alone." Dylan's voice was small and weak. "I'm lucky to be alive."

"I didn't want to leave you."

"It doesn't matter now," he said. He turned to look at her. "I'll never walk again. That's what the doctors say. So, count yourself lucky. You wouldn't want to be stuck with a paraplegic, would you?"

Lila put her hand on Dylan's arm. "I love you. If you can't walk, so what?"

"So what?" he spat angrily.

"That's not what I meant. I meant that I love you no matter what."

"Sure you love me," he sneered. "Enough to leave me bleeding on the street, surrounded by strangers."

"Dylan, I'm sorry. If you just—"

"Just go," he said with a painful sigh. "And don't worry, I didn't tell the police you were a witness to the shooting. It was them you were running away from, wasn't it? Or was it me?"

Lila stood there, speechless. There was so much to say, but the pure anger in his eyes made it impossible for her to speak.

"Fine," he said dismissively. "You don't have to explain."

Just then, a doctor walked into the room. "How are we feeling today, Dylan?" he asked in a booming, cheerful voice. Then he saw Lila, with her pale and tearstained face. "Sorry, I don't think we've met," he said, extending his hand. "I'm Dr. Verma, and you are?"

"Leaving." Dylan interrupted Lila, who was shaking the doctor's hand. "She's leaving."

"Yes," Lila said, sneaking a side glance at Dylan, who avoided her eyes. "I'm leaving."

She walked toward the door, then turned to see him one last time. "Good-bye, Dylan," she whispered.

Dylan said nothing in return.

On her way out of the hospital, Lila felt something inside her snap. The man she loved believed that she had betrayed him. He gave his heart to her, and she paid him back by abandoning him. Then, as he lay there in a hospital bed, he asked her to explain herself, and she was too busy drowning in her lies to speak.

Who had she become? In pursuit of the Star Island killer, she'd ended up hurting far more people than just herself. Lila got in the car and slammed the door, blinking back tears. She'd had enough. She was sick of all the lies, of the charade. It was time, once and for all, to end this. It was time to confront Effie.

CHAPTER 37

BY THE TIME Lila drove up to Effie's house, she was in a boiling rage. She rushed through the front door. Effie was slumped at the kitchen counter with a cup of coffee by her elbow and her head in her hands. Hearing the footsteps, she looked up to see Lila.

"Where the hell have you been?" Effie said, her voice raw. "I was worried. I heard about Dylan. Is he okay?"

"I find it impossible to believe that you care, Effie," Lila snapped.

"Excuse me?" Effie shot back. "I know your boyfriend is in the hospital, but you don't have to bust my ass about it."

"Just cut the shit, Effie."

"What?"

Lila shook her head in disbelief. She hoped she wasn't making a huge mistake, but she couldn't wait on this anymore. She was going to show her hand.

"I know everything. I know about the forty-five in your bedroom with the silencer."

Effie bolted up from her chair, a confused and wide-eyed look on her face.

"I know about Shane Johnson."

Effie started to speak, but Lila kept talking over her.

"I know that he thinks you're Camilla Dayton. And that you've been traveling under my name on a fake passport."

Effie turned her back to Lila and looked out over the lawn to the ocean. The sun was slowly rising, the sky a mix of bruised blues and purples. It would be the second-to-last sunrise Effie would ever see.

"I've got you, Effie. Any one of those things will have you in prison for a decade, at least."

"I underestimated you," Effie said. "I guess you're not the boring little lamb I thought you were."

"Effie, listen to me." Lila grabbed her friend's arm and spun her around so that they were face-to-face. "I won't say a word of any of this. Just promise me one thing."

"Oh?" Effie sneered. "And what's that?"

"The Janus Society," Lila said. "I know what you're going to do."

"I have no idea what you're talking about," Effie said icily. "I'm going to pretend we never had this conversation."

"You can call off Shane. And this will all be over. But you have to do it right now."

Effie began to laugh, which caused her to hold her head in pain. She stopped laughing and groaned. "Laughing doesn't mix well with a hangover. Neither does listening to a stupid, raving bitch."

"Effie, please. Just tell me why. Why are you doing it? Is it because of Chase? Because your dad's under investigation? Tell me."

Effie gave her a confused look. "It's already been done. You think you know what's going on. But let me tell you, you're in so far over your head, you're already drowning. You're asking me to stop? Me?" Effie tapped her fingers on her chest. "Well, let me tell you as simply as possible," she said, leaning close to Lila's face. "Back. The. Fuck. Off. Do you understand?"

"I'll go to the police," Lila said.

"Something tells me you won't, because you can't. Otherwise you would've already done it." Effie walked away toward the staircase. "So, I'm glad we had this little talk. Now, get your ass out of my sight and your shit out of my house. It's been a pleasure having you."

With that, Effie climbed the stairs and slammed her bedroom door.

IN LESS THAN seventy-two hours, Lila would be back in Teddy's time machine with nothing but the clothes on her back. She knew what she had to do to salvage any meaning from this whole experience. She had to stop the Star Island massacre. She had to at least try.

As she drove out of Effie's driveway, she passed three police cruisers pulling in. She kept her head low and watched as two officers got out of the cars to knock on the front door. She assumed the cops were after her about Dylan's shooting. She left Star Island in a hurry, relieved to see that her rearview mirror was free of black-and-whites.

A half-hour drive later, Lila pulled up to Shane's house. His car was in the driveway. All his lights were on, but she couldn't see any movement through the windows. Her first thought was to knock on his door and, once he answered it, to shoot him dead. But Teddy had stressed that, above all else, no one could die by her hands. And the more she mulled it over, the more she realized that she didn't want to play it that way, regardless of the impact it might have on the future. She didn't want to just stop the Star Island killer. She wanted to bring him, and Effie, to justice. And she needed to know why Effie was carrying out this plan, and what had happened to make Effie a victim, too.

IT WAS NEW Year's Eve, and the streets of Little Haiti were full of celebratory parties. Every other lawn was hosting a barbecue. People wandered happily down the street, red plastic cups in their hands. Firecrackers periodically exploded in the sky.

Lila sat in her car, waiting, watching Shane Johnson's house. Hours passed. Growing anxious, she looked at her watch. It was 11:30. Though the exact time of death at the Star Island murder scene could never be determined, forensic evidence suggested the victims died between midnight and 3 A.M. on January 1, 2015. She knew that Shane would leave his house within the hour.

Sure enough, at 11:55, he left. He was dressed in all black and was carrying a large duffel bag and a camouflage sniper rifle drag bag. He started up his car and headed southwest toward the highway, with Lila in close pursuit. This time, she wouldn't let fate cheat her.

When the clock struck midnight and the arrival of 2015 was celebrated up and down the Eastern Seaboard with cheers and kisses, Lila didn't take any notice. She was four cars behind Shane, going south on I-95, headed straight for Star Island. The closer they got, the more the adrenaline coursed through her body. She was finally going to get all the answers she'd waited so long for.

She watched as Shane's car approached the intersection to Bridge Road, the only way to get to Star Island by car. Then, to her horror, he passed the intersection.

"Where the hell are you going?" she yelled, her hands gripping the wheel.

She kept up with him past Star Island, but she immediately sensed something was off. As she barreled down the causeway toward Miami Beach, Lila was shaking in shock, confusion, and disappointment. Could she have been wrong?

"Where are you going, goddamnit!" she screamed, slamming her hands down on the steering wheel, as she followed Johnson's red Pontiac across the causeway and over to Collins Avenue, where it made a left. Lila let out a primal yell of frustration. It was 12:23 A.M., and she didn't know whether she was trailing the killer or had, once again, followed the wrong path to yet another dead end.

She needed to choose, now. If she stopped tailing Shane, she would be giving up on all the time she had invested in following him and abandoning any opportunity she'd have to stop him from killing the members of the Janus Society.

Should she stay the course, or cut and run? Lila felt the frustration boiling up in her, an infinite scream about to pour from her mouth. After driving five more minutes north, still keeping a two-car distance from Johnson, she made a snap decision.

With a screeching U-turn, she headed back to Star Island, her heart racing. Shane Johnson couldn't be the killer. But she was on her way to finding out who was.

CHAPTER 38

LILA PULLED UP to the stone-lion-flanked gates of 21 Star Island Drive, Chase Haverford's six-acre, $45 million estate, which was about to be transformed into the blood-soaked crime scene of the century.

After frantically buzzing the gate intercom for what felt like an eternity but was most likely thirty seconds, Lila gave up and, taking only her gun with her, climbed over the six-foot-tall gates.

From all her time surveying the crime scene and studying the property's blueprints, Lila knew Chase's estate like the back of her hand. Her gun at the ready, she kept close to the stone-wall perimeter in order to stay out of sight.

Lila remembered that the single sign of forced entry to Chase's home was a broken basement window on the northeast side. Keeping as low as possible, she sprinted across the property until she reached that side of the house, hoping to find the broken window and use it to sneak inside. But the window that should've been broken was intact.

He's not in the house yet, Lila thought. She still had a shot at stopping the murders.

But to get inside the northeast side of the house, Lila would have to break the window herself. With the butt end of her revolver, she hit it until it shattered. Then, with her sweatshirt hood up over her baseball cap to protect her skin from the shards of glass, she crawled into the basement, careful not to leave any fingerprints.

She blinked in the sudden darkness. All the lights were out, and Lila struggled to see. But her memories of the place quickly kicked in, and, as she rushed down the hall toward the wine cellar, her eyes adjusted. The only sound was that of her feet against the floor. Then her ears were assaulted by a bout of screaming, and the noise of a gunshot ricocheting down the halls. Immediately after, there was another. And another. The noise was so powerful, she felt the pain of it rip through her.

Instinctively, she hit the floor. Then the fourth gunshot exploded. Lila sprang back up to her feet and started running as fast as she could toward the bone-chilling screaming that was growing louder with each step. Then she heard a fifth shot. The sixth. Then another. Still running. Fighting her body to go faster. The throbbing veins in her head making her feel she was about to explode into a thousand jagged pieces. Then the eighth shot. She was counting. Was she still running in the right direction? Then another. Then another.

Finally, she stood at the wine cellar door. She moved to open it, but it wouldn't budge. She threw her body against it. Another shot rang out. One wall stood between her and the murderer. She put her entire weight into the door, screaming bloody murder. Then another shot. Twelve.

"I'll kill you," she screamed at the murderer behind the door. She kicked at the door, feeling no pain, only panic, only rage. She took the butt of her gun and brought it down, over and over, on the door's hinges and handle, attacking them fe-rociously until she heard something give. Then, with one final kick, the door fell into the room. The smoke from the gunshots poured out. And there they were, the Janus Society members, all dead on the floor. The killer was nowhere in sight.

She rushed past the dead bodies and through the rest of the cavernous wine cellar, her gun in her hand, searching for the murderer. She spotted an open door. She ran through it, then up the stairs and out onto the large lawn overlooking the ocean. Scanning the property, she didn't see any movement.

"Where are you?" she whispered into the night sky.

For the next two hours, Lila searched everywhere, but she found nothing.

CHAPTER 39

A STRAY SLANT of sunlight peeking from between two heavy motel curtains forced Lila awake. The clock read 9:36 A.M. The moment she opened her eyes, she closed them again and rolled over into a fetal position. She was still in last night's clothes. The smell of spilled bourbon clung to the stagnant air.

She didn't think she had the strength in her to ever get out of bed again. It felt as if the entire weight of the world was pressing down upon her bruised, aching flesh. But in a little under seven hours, she needed to be back at the warehouse in North Miami so that she could go back to 2018. Back to her ruined life. And she would be going back empty-handed, knowing nothing more than she had when she arrived.

What if I don't go back? she thought suddenly. The very notion of running away released a bit of energy inside her, energy she didn't think she had. There was nothing waiting for her in 2018. Suddenly, the thought of returning to that life, its isolation and its numbness, was unbearable. What if she just stayed here? What would happen if she and her past self were coexisting like that? Would one of them flicker out of existence at some point, like a ghost?

Lila knew that if she stayed in the past, she would have to remain hidden. But she still had plenty of Teddy's money left, more than enough to disappear forever. She could get in the car and drive south, buy a place along the rugged Pacific coast of South America, and live out the rest of her life on her terms.

Yes, she thought, that was what she would do. Either way, she was letting Teddy down. He had put his faith in her, and she had failed. There was no point in going through the excruciating exercise of telling him that she'd spent months following false leads while spending his money and wasting his time.

And then there was Dylan, lying broken in a hospital room, thinking that the woman he loved had abandoned him when he needed her the most. How could she explain the truth to him when so much of what he knew about her was a lie?

It all added up to one big, hopeless mess.

Soon Lila had packed up her things, loaded the car, and headed north. She'd drive up, out of Florida, and then go west, clinging along the southern underbelly of the United States, through Alabama, Mississippi, Louisiana, Texas, then head down into Mexico.

Alone in the car, her mind made up, she finally felt a slight semblance of control, and with that came a bit of peace. When she saw the exit to Fort Myers, she took it without thinking it through. Before her brain processed the turn, her instincts had kicked in. She was going to her childhood home.

Two blocks from her mom's house, Lila pulled the car over. She needed to hide any lingering evidence of Camilla Dayton. Looking in the rearview mirror, she pinned up her blond hair and pulled on a baseball cap. She looked like shit. She hadn't looked this bad since 2018, she thought wryly.

As Lila pulled up to her mom's, she spotted her outside, hunched over her rosebushes. Lila was shocked by how thin she'd become. Her usually full, pink cheeks were sunken and sallow.

When she got out of the car, her mother didn't recognize her at first because of the baseball cap she wore to conceal her changed hair.

"Mom?"

"Lila, is that you?" Lila's mother ran toward her daughter and threw her arms around her. "What a marvelous surprise!" But mother's intuition kicked in instantly. She knew something was up with her youngest daughter. "What's wrong? You don't look so hot."

"Oh, I'm fine, Mom. I'm heading out on a trip and was passing by. Thought I'd stop in for a moment."

Her mother took her hand, and together they walked toward the humble home. They sat down silently on the cement front steps, still holding hands, letting the warmth of the winter sun wash over them.

"How are you feeling, Mom?"

"I'm a bit run-down today, but mostly okay."

Lila squeezed her mother's hand tighter and rested her head on her mom's shoulder. Every day since her mother died, Lila had prayed to do the very thing she was doing at this moment—seeing her mom once again, feeling her touch, hearing her voice. She didn't want the moment to end, even though she knew it had to.

The pure agony of losing her mother, on top of everything

else she'd lost recently, came crashing over Lila. She inadvertently let out a long, pain-filled sigh.

"Oh, don't worry, my baby," Lila's mother said, putting her arm around her weeping daughter. "Things will be just fine."

"I don't think so, Mom. I think I'm done being a cop. I just can't take it anymore."

"That's not the Lila I know." Her mother paused, looking closely at her daughter. "Is this about a man?"

Despite her sorrow, Lila had to smile. Her mom had always known things about her without being told. "Yeah," she admitted. "There is someone, but . . . I messed it up. Now he won't even talk to me. And I don't know what to do."

"Love hurts the most the first time, my darling," her mother said, knowing that her daughter had never before let a man into her heart. "Shhh," she murmured, stroking Lila's hair, letting her cry.

Now that Lila had started crying, she couldn't find it in her to stop. She couldn't bear the thought that this was the last time she would ever see her mom.

Her mother held her tighter. "You've got to remember that life and love are worth fighting for, Lila. I know you'll remember that when it counts." She held her daughter's face in her hands and looked softly into her eyes. "Life is *always* worth fighting for."

The women sat together in silence for a while as the sun rose higher in the sky. Lila didn't want to leave. But when she looked at her watch, she was shocked to see that it was almost 2:00 P.M. Suddenly, she knew she had to go back. To 2018. Her mother was right. She couldn't give up on her life, not yet.

She jumped up from the stoop. "I've got to run, Mom."

Her mother stood up and hugged her tight. "I love you so much, my girl. Now, go knock 'em dead. And remember how proud I am of you."

"I will. I always will. I love you, Mom."

Lila ran to her car. She'd have to hurry. She didn't have much time before the window to the future was closed forever.

CHAPTER 40

LILA KEPT HER eye on the clock as she raced eastward, back to Miami. She was running out of time. In order to make it to room 2867 of the storage facility by 4:16 P.M., as Teddy had instructed, she tore across Florida at dangerous speeds, paying no mind to the startled, honking cars that she zoomed past. Nothing mattered more than returning to her life, becoming Lila Day once again. Enough hiding. Enough retreat. She'd go back and face the future.

It was 4:02 P.M. when she arrived at the storage facility. Fourteen minutes left. She pulled the car up to the exit and sprang out toward the building, leaving the engine running. Nothing from this time was of any use to her anymore. She ran up the stairs to the second floor and sprinted along the hall, scanning the numbers on the doors, her heart beating in her throat, until she arrived at 2867. 4:06 P.M.

She paused, stunned, and stood staring at the door. There was a giant padlock on it. She looked at her watch. 4:08 P.M. She raced back down the halls, down the stairs, and to her car, which somehow, miraculously, was still running, not yet stolen. She reached into the glove compartment for her old police revolver and sprinted back up the stairs.

With four minutes left, she aimed her gun at the lock, and fired. The explosion rang in her ears, and the bullet, which grazed the lock, ricocheted off the metal door. She aimed again, then fired. Fired again. And fired once more. She lunged toward the lock. It was pulverized. She tore open the door. Once inside the tiny storage space, Lila looked at her watch. 4:15 P.M. Just in time.

She stood in the middle of the room. The only sound she heard was her own frantic breathing. 4:16. Taking a sharp exhale and closing her eyes, she waited. For what? The rapture? Beam me up, Scotty?

Inhale. Exhale. Okay. Still nothing. She opened her eyes and looked around the four cinder-block walls. How was this supposed to work again? When she'd traveled back in time, Teddy and Conrad had been there to guide her, but now she was alone, without any idea what to do.

Still 4:16 P.M.

And then there was an instant change, as if drugs had just kicked in. The contours of the room suddenly began to blur. It was as if all the molecules around her were trembling and stretching. The room started to vibrate, and a high-pitched screech filled her ears until it felt as if they'd pop. Lila crouched down on the floor, closing her eyes, cringing, and covering her head with her arms.

Then.

Total silence. Profound darkness. She couldn't feel her body as different from the space she was inhabiting.

Then.

The return of sound. The return of light. She felt her body heavy in space and looked around to see that she was, once again, in the leather-and-steel cockpit of the time machine. The door unfurled, and there at the bottom of the stairs was the hollow face of Teddy Hawkins, his eyes flickering with hope.

Before she could climb out of the jade dome, she blurted out, "I'm sorry." She was unable to bear the sight of anticipation. "I failed you." She kept her eyes closed so that she wouldn't have to see his hopes crashing down around him.

After Conrad ran her through a series of tests to check her vitals, the two men brought her up from the subterranean lab to sit, once again, by the pool.

Everyone was quiet.

"You changed your hair," Teddy finally said, before falling back into silence. He seemed to be at a loss for what to say.

"I went back in time and all I got was this lousy haircut," Lila said, her voice edged with bitterness and fatigue.

Teddy stood up, agitated. "Just tell me now. What happened?"

Lila put her head in her hands. She felt dizzy and angry and sad. "I got close, so many times. I thought I had him. Then I thought I had her. But now I'm back empty-handed." She paused and looked up at Teddy's face. He was crestfallen. The small amount of hope he had summoned instantly drained out of him. "I'm so sorry," she said. "I know what a disappointment it must be for you."

He took a few steps away from her, as if he was already distancing himself from this failure. "You were the best person for the job," he said. "If you couldn't solve it, then no one could."

"I appreciate you being kind. I really do. But I know what it meant to you. I know about Meredith. That you loved her."

He looked at her in surprise. "I thought you might figure it out," he admitted.

"There's so much I uncovered, but the puzzle pieces didn't come together."

"Then perhaps we can talk things through. Maybe together we can figure it out."

He returned to his seat, and Lila once again marveled at how different he was from his earlier self, how he seemed to be missing that energy and sparkle that had made him the center of the universe that afternoon at the Fisher Island Club.

They sat by the pool for hours as Lila told him everything. About Scott Sloan's affair. About all the files Javier had on Frederic Sandoval, but that Sandoval had died before Lila managed to talk to him. About his connection to Sam Logan's tennis rival, Pedro Bolivar. About Javier's arms dealing. About Alexei Dortzovich's schemes, his destruction of Chase Haverford's hotel empire. About Effie and Chase's dangerous liaison. About the hit man.

When Lila gave Teddy the abbreviated version of how her relationship with Effie went from friendship to framing for murder, he was astounded.

"But even if Effie was setting me up to take the fall for the Star Island murders, a lot of questions are still unanswered."

"Like what?" Teddy asked. His eyes were bewildered, as if all this startling information had caused his brain to fry slightly.

"Well, I saw her pay a hit man whom I know for a fact wasn't the Star Island killer. So, what did she pay him for?"

"Let's try to think this through. Did anything else suspect happen around the time of the murders?"

Immediately Lila's mind went to Dylan, shot down in the middle of the day. But she didn't say anything. There was already too much for them to discuss, plus he had nothing to do with the Janus Society.

"Wait!" Lila said, remembering. "Scott Sloan's mistress was killed just a couple days before the murders on Star Island. And"—Lila paused, trying to recall the exact information—"I remember witnesses reported seeing a red sports car speed away from the scene of the crime."

Teddy looked pensive. "I remember her death quite well," he said softly.

Lila was on a roll. "Maybe Effie paid this hit man to use my car when he murdered Scott Sloan's mistress. The last time I left her place on Star Island, three police cruisers were pulling in. What if they were looking for Camilla Dayton? What if they were there to inspect the car? Wait." She sprang up from her chair. "We've got to go online."

Teddy handed Lila a tablet and she typed, "Willow Morris death." Up popped several newspaper articles about the accident and the subsequent police search for Camilla Dayton, owner of the Maserati GT spotted at the scene of the crime.

Teddy read off the computer screen, "Police were unable to track down the suspect, Ms. Dayton, who was a houseguest of social fixture Effie Webster. Ms. Webster's recent murder is also currently under police investigation."

Lila and Teddy both stood silently, processing this information.

"But why would Effie want Scott's mistress killed? And then who was the Star Island killer?" Teddy asked.

"I have absolutely no idea," Lila said. All the facts were so jumbled in her head that she couldn't think straight. "I need a drink."

Teddy went to the poolside bar and poured two glasses of Wild Turkey over ice. He handed one to Lila. At first, she was surprised that Teddy knew what she drank, but then she remembered that he knew everything. Well, almost everything.

She took a deep gulp of the bourbon. "You know what I keep thinking about? Right after the murders in 2015, when I was investigating the case, the clues I was most fixated on were a broken basement window, a battered-down door, which led to the wine cellar, and this short video from the one operational surveillance camera that had two seconds of footage showing a figure dressed in all black. Aside from the bullets lodged in the brains of the victims, that was literally the only physical evidence at the scene of the crime that I had to point me in the direction of the killer. And now"—Lila began to laugh, a slightly hysterical, rueful laugh—"I know it was me who broke the window and busted the door. Me! It was me in that footage. Which means for years I was hunting myself."

She took another giant swig of the bourbon, letting the burning sensation travel down her throat. "It's enough to make you think you've gone crazy," she finished.

Teddy was looking off toward the ocean. Lila wondered if he'd heard anything she just said.

"Have I lost you?" Lila asked. Her mind was spinning, and she needed Teddy there to tether her to reality.

"Oh, sorry." He shook his head, as if trying to wake himself from a dream. "It's just that . . ." He let out an enormous sigh. "Willow. Well, Meredith talked about her a lot. I mean, she was her husband's mistress. So it's not a big surprise that Meredith was fixated on her. But I never really understood it, if I'm being honest. I mean, we were in love. Why waste time thinking about that terrible husband of hers with his stupid mistress? But in Meredith's mind, Willow was the one that stood in the way of us being together."

"Why?" Lila asked.

"Meredith and I were discreet about our relationship. Incredibly discreet. But Scott found out, and he told Willow. Meredith knew it was just a matter of time before Willow made this very private information public because it would be her best shot at breaking up the marriage and getting Scott all to herself. Of course, I secretly thought this would be great. If the cat was out of the bag, Scott could be with Willow, and Meredith and I could also be together. But Meredith wouldn't have it. She knew if her infidelity came to light, even if Scott's was also revealed, the divorce settlement would be millions of dollars less advantageous."

"Why couldn't Meredith use her knowledge of Scott's affair against him in court? After all, they were mostly living off her family's money."

"She couldn't risk it. She knew if she took him to court, our affair would surely come to light, and she felt we had more to lose. I could never convince her otherwise," Teddy said sadly.

"But where does Effie fit in? Would she kill someone for Meredith?"

"Are you implying that Meredith may have had something to do with Willow's death?" Teddy asked, his lips pressing into a tight grimace. "Because if you are, I will ask you to leave immediately."

"I'm sorry," Lila quickly said. "I didn't mean to imply anything. So, did you and Meredith talk about Willow's death?"

"Of course. I mean, I hate to say it, but news of that poor girl's death made me incredibly happy. I knew we'd be together. Finally."

"But then . . ." Lila said.

"But then, five days later, Meredith was killed. And the only thing that's kept me going since then is the hope of finding the person who robbed me of my happiness."

Lila finished her drink, then went over to the bar, grabbed the bottle, and brought it back to where she and Teddy were sitting. She filled both of their glasses. Teddy's experience was painfully reminiscent of what had happened to Lila with Dylan.

"I'm sorry I couldn't save her for you." The alcohol was beginning its work on her, opening her up and loosening her tongue. "But even if I tried, I learned that you can't change fate."

Teddy, his red-rimmed eyes on hers, shot her a quizzical look. "Fate? What does that mean?" he asked. "I told you that you are not allowed to alter the course of events. You could neither kill anyone, nor prevent anyone from being killed."

"But I tried," she said in a barely audible whisper. "I tried to stop someone from being shot and I found out that I couldn't."

"What do you mean?"

It was getting late. They sat together in the gentle light of the blue hour, that luminous transition when day becomes night. Lila had never felt so tired in her life. Slowly, fumbling over her words, she told Teddy the story of Dylan. How she fell in love with him. How she knew he was going to be shot and paralyzed. How she tried to save him. And, finally, tragically, how fate intervened three hours early.

"Fate is fate, I guess," she said bitterly. "Our destinies have already been written." She felt her head grow heavy with fatigue. She closed her eyes.

"Why don't you stay the night?" Teddy suggested. "You're clearly exhausted, and I hate to send you back to that little spider's nest you call home. I'll have one of the guest rooms fixed up for you."

If she hadn't been so tired, Lila would've protested. Instead, she allowed Teddy to guide her toward a bedroom and pour her into bed. In seconds, she was asleep.

CHAPTER 41

THANKS AGAIN FOR the ride," Lila said as she stepped out of Teddy's midnight-blue Bentley. Conrad, of course, was at the wheel, as silent and watchful as ever.

"Are you sure you feel all right?" Teddy asked. "You were in the past for quite some time. Your old life may seem strange to you at first."

She looked up at her run-down apartment building on this shitty block in Little Havana. All she could think was how broken everything looked—the cracks in the building walls, the trash on the sidewalk, the yellowed undershirt of one of her neighbors hanging out on the stoop.

"Strange," she said. "That's one word for it." *Shithole is another,* she thought.

"Let's talk in a few days," Teddy said. "It's not over yet, remember that."

Lila nodded in agreement, but she'd had enough. She was done chasing after ghosts. And from what she could see, she suspected Teddy was done, too. This was their last shot, and she had blown it. Time to move on.

When she opened the door to her apartment, a wall of heat and humidity hit her. It was over a hundred degrees inside her spare little place. She regarded it with mostly embarrassment. How had she ever lived like this? It wasn't just that she'd been living in luxury for the past three months. It was something more. That time away from the present had allowed her to see how low she'd let herself fall and how little she'd come to expect from herself and from her life.

One thing was clear. She needed more than this.

She needed Dylan.

She knew it was best to leave him in the past. He had made it clear that she had done something he could never forgive. So much of their relationship had been built upon a foundation of lies. But Lila knew it wasn't *only* lies. There was also love there, a connection she'd never known before and doubted she'd experience again.

Lila moved quickly to her desk, opened up her laptop, and typed his name into the search field. Dylan Rhodes. Thousands of articles came up. She searched through them ravenously, eager for any news about him. Most of the information was about the Rhodes Foundation, founded by Dylan and Dr. Arun Verma, the doctor she'd met when she visited Dylan at the hospital. She looked up the foundation online. The mission statement on the website read: "The Rhodes Foundation is dedicated to curing spinal cord injury by funding innovative research and focusing on improving the lives of those living with paralysis."

Through his foundation, Lila read on in awe, Dylan had raised tens of millions of dollars for research on spinal cord injuries. There was an article about how Miami General Hospital had recently opened a Rhodes wing dedicated to treating patients with injuries similar to Dylan's. Hoping to see a picture of him, Lila searched the article in vain.

The article said that "Dylan Rhodes did not attend the opening of the wing named in his honor." The journalist went on to make note of his "strange, solitary life." "Although," Lila read, her eyes glued to the computer screen, "he was once a fixture on the Miami social scene, Rhodes withdrew from the public eye following the robbery that left him permanently unable to walk. Today, he lives in almost complete isolation on a three-hundred-acre mangrove preserve by the Biscayne Bay on the outskirts of Miami."

Lila tried everything she could think of to get Dylan's address online. But her efforts were futile. She bit the bullet and phoned one of her old partners at the police station. She hated calling in favors, but this was important. Within two minutes, she held his address in her hands: 1 Black Point Peak, Homestead, Florida.

She couldn't believe it. He was only a thirty-minute drive away. What would happen when he saw her? It had been only five days since she'd seen him, but years had passed since he'd seen her. Maybe he'd met someone else. And even if not, there were so many obstacles in their way.

She looked outside. A summer storm was blowing in. Low, dark clouds hung ominously in the sky. The palm fronds tossed around in the increasing wind. Just then, the rain started to fall. Lila didn't let the downpour stop her. She dashed to her car and set off to find Dylan.

The storm picked up speed as she drove south, but she barely noticed. All she could think of was the fact that soon, she'd see his face once more.

The rain had stopped by the time Lila pulled up to the

wooden gates that let onto Dylan's estate. She was almost sick with nervousness.

The gates were about ten feet tall and studded with iron rivets. Lila got out of the car and looked for any intercom or way of requesting entrance. There was nothing. As she continued searching, the gates opened slightly, and a portly and sun-creased man with a hunting rifle slung over his shoulder waddled out to greet her.

"Can I help you, ma'am?" he asked. His face was kind, but Lila's nerves, already taut in anticipation of seeing Dylan, were put on edge by the gun.

"I'm here to see Dylan Rhodes."

"He expectin' you?"

"No, but I'm an old friend of his." The wind whipped noisily through the forest of palm trees that grew wild beyond the gate.

"He don't got a lot of friends calling these days."

"Can you let him know that Camilla Dayton is here to see him?"

The man with the rifle eyed her skeptically. It seemed as if in all his years guarding this gate, not one unannounced visitor had ever made it by him.

"Wait right here," he said, as he squeezed his giant belly back through the tiny opening. After a few seconds, Lila peeked through to see him in a little shed on the phone. The call didn't last longer than a minute.

The gates slowly opened all the way.

"Mr. Rhodes will see you now," the man said, quite grandly. "The road to the main house is a bit bumpy thanks to all the rain we got, but keep straight for about ten minutes and you'll find your way."

Lila thanked him and climbed back into her car. She felt light-headed with anticipation.

"A bit bumpy" was putting it mildly. It wasn't so much a road as an unpaved collection of giant potholes and muddy puddles. Lila eased her little car through the difficult terrain very slowly. About two minutes from the gate, she saw a Land Rover barreling directly toward her.

"Oh no," she cursed. This car was going to run her right off the road, which had fairly deep gutters dug next to it. If her car was forced to veer off in order to avoid this maniac, she'd never manage to get back on. Yet the car kept coming. She was caught in an unwanted game of chicken.

With the Land Rover about twenty feet away, she came to a complete stop, and the SUV, with enviable ease, went off-road around the left side of her car.

Lila scowled at the reckless driver as he passed. But he just smiled at her, giving her a little two-fingered salute as his car drove by and quickly retreated in her rearview mirror.

There was something familiar about him, but her mind was too focused on seeing Dylan to dwell on anything else.

A few minutes later, she pulled up to Dylan's house. It was a grand stone mansion, with beautiful tall, arched windows and a terra-cotta roof. Her heart jumped. There he was, waiting for her on the front porch. Though he was sitting in a very advanced-looking mechanical wheelchair, he looked exactly the same as she remembered. Unlike Teddy, who had aged in the face of tragedy and loss, Dylan looked as robust and as youthful as ever. He was beaming from ear to ear. Her heart leaped when she saw that smile. Against all odds, he seemed happy she was there.

The moment she got out of the car, she heard him call her name. "Camilla!"

She ran toward him, then bent down and threw her arms around him. The chair made the embrace awkward.

"It's you," he said softly, putting his hands on her face, as if to make sure she was real. "I can't believe it's you."

Lila felt relieved, drunk with happiness.

Dylan was looking up at her, reflecting all that she felt right back. "I've wondered about you every day. And now you're here." He laughed with joy. "Please, come inside."

Lila followed Dylan into the home's intimate main room. It had stone walls and exposed beams on its vaulted ceilings. Although it was the middle of summer, the smell of fireplace smoke hung in the air.

Dylan couldn't stop smiling. "I never thought I'd see you again," he said. "Where have you been? And why now? After so many years, what made you decide to see me today?"

"I came as soon as I could," she said. "I came the moment I realized my life didn't make sense anymore without you." She paused, then walked over to him and put her hand in his. "Plus, the last time I saw you in the hospital . . . it couldn't be the last time."

"I said things that day that I've regretted every day since."

"You shouldn't," Lila replied.

"Yes, I should. It doesn't matter now why you left me. Or why you left Miami. You did leave town, didn't you?"

Lila nodded.

"Thank God. It was either that or I had consecutively hired four of the most incompetent private detectives in all of history. None of them could find a trace of you, here or anywhere."

"I can explain—"

"I don't want you to," Dylan said, interrupting her. "Here, sit down." Lila settled into a leather chair. Dylan scooted so close that their knees were touching. "For the past three and a half years I've been here, mostly on my own, and I've had a lot of time to think. First, I was shot. Then all those people on Star Island. And you were gone. It felt like the world was just one empty and treacherous place. So I came up here to figure it out. But all I could think about was you. You won't believe me, but I made a deal with God, or whoever it is that runs the show, that if I ever found you again, there'd be no questions, no need for explanations, and no past. All we'd have was that very moment. And then the next moment. And then the rest of our lives together."

Lila ran the tips of her fingers along his glorious face. Along his eyebrow, down his cheekbone, then to his full lips. "I like that plan," she said.

"Plus," he went on, "there's hope I won't be in this damn wheelchair forever."

"Really?"

"I hope so. You remember meeting Dr. Verma at the hospital, when you visited me?"

"I don't want to think about that horrible night ever again," Lila said.

Dylan reached for her hand and ran his thumb lightly over her knuckles. "Well, that man has been my guardian angel from the moment I got shot. We've known each other since we were children and went to the same boarding school. When I arrived at the hospital, he was there to meet the ambulance. Since then, he's dropped everything to devote himself to my case."

Looking at Dylan now, drinking all of him in, Lila could believe that he might fully recover. His vitality had in no way faded. He was wearing a cotton T-shirt, which showed off his muscular chest and arms, and jeans. Even his legs looked powerful.

"Dr. Verma has been here every day, working with me," Dylan continued. "I'm not going to lie and say it's been easy. For the first few months after the accident, I didn't even want to get out of bed, but he was there to keep me on track. If it wasn't for him and my brother, I don't know where I'd be."

"Your brother?" Lila asked, distracted. The upward splatter of mud on Dylan's jeans had momentarily caught her attention.

"Sure. My brother's here almost every day. Actually, you just missed him. He left a couple minutes before you arrived." Lila got up from her chair, walking over to the window. There was a beer perched on a shelf around the height of her shoulder. Beads of condensation clung to the glass bottle. The window looked out onto the mangrove forest, a dense riot of overgrown tropical green. There were two sets of muddy footprints that went up the stairs, and two hunting guns resting in the rifle rack.

Lila heard Dylan behind her. "There's a lot to look forward to."

She leaned down to kiss him. She tasted beer on his breath. By the door she saw a muddy pair of shoes.

"In a few years, I may be able to walk again." Something else in the room caught her eye. It was an ancient-looking tapestry hanging over the fireplace.

"What's that?" Lila asked, pointing to the tapestry. It was exquisite, made of wool and embroidered with metallic and silk threads.

"It's beautiful, isn't it? When my dad died, it was the only thing of his that I wanted. It's the Rhodes family coat of arms. It's been in my family for many, many generations."

Lila stared at it. The coat of arms consisted of a blue shield, a knight's helmet, and three red birds. Something about it was bothering her, tugging at the edge of her consciousness. Then an electric charge shot through her body as she suddenly remembered: the three red birds that were tattooed on the shooter's forearm when Dylan was shot outside the liquor store. The same three birds that she saw before her. The same ones she had seen out of the corner of her eye on that man's—Dylan's brother's—arm when his Land Rover drove around her just minutes ago. She had been so focused on seeing Dylan that the connection didn't register.

Calling on all the cocktail party skills she'd picked up as Camilla Dayton, Lila settled her face into a smile, like a mask, trying to be as casual as possible even though a scream was ricocheting around in her head. She crossed the room toward the rifle rack, where she slowly picked up a hunting gun. The sharp smell of gunpowder filled her nose.

When she turned back toward Dylan, she trained the gun on him, trying to steady her trembling hands.

She finally knew who the Star Island killer was.

CHAPTER 42

CAMILLA? WHAT ARE you doing?" Dylan asked, sitting in his wheelchair with a stunned look on his face.

She opened her mouth, but she couldn't speak.

"Please, put the gun down," he said in a calm, measured tone.

"I . . . I . . . ," Lila stuttered, "I know."

"Know what?" Dylan said. His eyes darted around the room.

"I know that your brother was the one who shot you."

Dylan laughed nervously. "You've lost it, Camilla."

But Lila stayed still, the gun pointed straight at him.

"I saw the blood after you got shot," she said. "I know it was real. But you and your brother are real marksmen, right? So he shot you, but in a place where it wouldn't cause any real damage."

"Are you suggesting I'm faking? That I've been faking paralysis for years?" He was shouting now. His hands gripped the arms of his wheelchair. He narrowed his eyes and clenched his jaw. "You're being crazy. Please, put the gun down."

"I'm not suggesting it, Dylan," she said, shaking her head as she went on. "Your friend Dr. Verma was in on it, too, wasn't he? That's why he's been your only physician. That was the only way to keep your secret. You bought his silence by putting him in charge of the hospital wing. And, when you walk again, he'll be the genius that fixed you."

"Camilla, stop this. For your own good." Dylan's voice was barely a whisper.

"Then you moved down here, hidden away on this big piece of land, able to live your life without anyone discovering your secret."

"And why, exactly, would I have myself shot and fake years of paralysis? What would be the point of this elaborate plan?"

"Because you," she said, the words sticking like knives in her throat, "because you killed those innocent people on Star Island that night. And you knew that no one would suspect you if they thought you were a paraplegic confined to a hospital bed."

"Innocent!" Dylan said, with an indignant roar. "You think that I would murder twelve innocent victims for no reason? I guess you didn't know me at all."

He moved his wheelchair toward her.

"Put the gun down," he said.

"Stay back!" Her hands were shaking violently.

In a flash, Dylan sprang out of his wheelchair and lunged toward her, wrapping his arms around her legs and knocking her down. She felt her feet go out from under her and crashed hard to the floor. As her right hand collided with the floor, she accidentally squeezed the trigger, sending a stray bullet flying.

Dylan, who was on top of her, clutched his hand around her wrist and ferociously banged it on the wood floor until the white-hot pain caused her to drop the gun.

He picked up the rifle and trained it on Lila, who lay shaken and prostrate on the floor as her ex-lover hovered over her, a wildness in his eyes that she'd never seen before.

"Looks like I wasn't the only one telling lies. Or would you still like me to believe that you're who you say you are? Now, get up and sit in this chair."

From all her years on the force, Lila knew that the best way to get out of a bad situation was to follow orders—at first.

She sat on the chair.

"I won't hurt you," he said with a familiar tenderness in his voice. "But you have to tell me how you figured it out."

Lila sat there silent. She was too stunned to speak.

"Tell me," he said again, sternly. "Does anyone else know?"

"It was your pants," Lila said finally.

Dylan, confused, looked down at his pants.

"Mud only splatters up like that if you're walking around in it, which you can't do if you're paralyzed. Then, there was the beer that I tasted on your breath when we kissed. I saw the bottle was set on a shelf that was too high for you to reach from a wheelchair. You must've been drinking it before I arrived because it was still cold when I got here."

"That's absurd. I could've been using a walker outside, and someone could've put that beer up there for me. I may be isolated, but I don't exist out here without others."

He sat on the windowsill, never letting his eyes or the mouth of the gun stray away from Lila.

"It wasn't just those things. It was your family crest. Those three birds up there." Lila gestured toward the tapestry with her head, concerned that any sudden movement with her hands would be taken as a challenge. "I saw the same birds tattooed on the forearm of the man who shot you. Today I saw that your brother has the same tattoo."

"I love my brother," Dylan said with a wry smile. "But he's always been a bit sloppy."

"But I still haven't figured out one major thing."

"What?"

"Why you killed those people. I never pegged you as a cold-blooded murderer."

Dylan shook his head sadly. "Just trust me when I say that each and every person I killed that night deserved to die. Their murders were a gift to the world."

"How can you say that?" Lila asked, stunned.

He stood up, grabbed a chair, and placed it directly across from where Lila sat. He settled nervously onto the seat, with the gun resting on his knee.

"You don't have to look at me like that. I'm still the man you fell in love with."

"The man I loved was a lie," Lila said as she leaned as far away from him as she could.

"And it's becoming increasingly clear that Camilla Dayton is a lie, too. The woman I fell in love with would never be up here waving a gun around and piecing together crimes. So, let's call it even. Please," he pleaded. "Let me tell you a story. And, at the end, I promise you'll understand."

Lila said nothing. She sat still, waiting.

Dylan exhaled deeply. "I grew up in an incredibly wealthy family. But my parents and grandparents always stressed the importance of charitable work. My grandmother constantly spoke to my brother and me about the noblesse oblige of the wealthy. We were honor- and duty-bound to give back some of the incredible gifts that we were given."

Lila broke eye contact with Dylan. A murderer talking to

her about giving back? It was enough to make bile rise up in her throat. He saw the disdain in her face but continued anyway.

"So when Chase Haverford, whom I'd known for years, started talking to me about becoming part of the Janus Society, I couldn't have been more honored. No one was doing better work around the world. They were the world's premier philanthropic organization, bar none. Of course, the identities of the members were secret. I was stunned that someone I knew was part of this elite group, and when he said that I, too, could be a part of it, I jumped at the chance."

"When was this?"

"Two thousand five. I had just turned twenty-two. I think about that time a lot. I'd give anything to go back and stop myself from saying yes to Chase's offer. My life, even our lives together, could've been so different. Better."

Our lives? Lila thought in shock. But she smiled at him, cautiously. If he still believed in the fiction of their love, she would play along. It might keep her from getting killed.

"I told Chase I was interested. But I didn't hear back from him about it for a couple years. When we had that first conversation, Chase said I could never mention that he was a member of the Janus Society. So when nothing came of it, I dropped the whole thing from my mind and never raised the issue with him again."

"Did it make you angry that you never became a member?" Lila asked, wondering if Dylan had had the murderous reaction to rejection that she'd suspected of Alexei.

"I did become a member. But it took about two years. During that period all of these people came out of the woodwork to befriend me. I gained many intensely close friends at that time. Little did I know, each and every one of them was a member of the Janus Society. They were secretly vetting me to see if I was up to snuff."

Lila was listening attentively to Dylan. None of it was making any sense to her.

"Once I got in the club, and found out what was really at the heart of it, I desperately wanted out. But it was too late. Once you're part of the society, you're in it for life."

He sighed. "It was my first meeting. Two thousand seven. New Year's Eve. The secretiveness surrounding those meetings is mind-blowing. Always a different location that we would find out literally thirty minutes before we were supposed to be there. None of us could tell anyone where we were going. Most of the members are major corporate heavyweights, and most have families. Disappearing for even an evening is a big deal for all of us. Disappearing for New Year's Eve is half the fun. At first, I found the whole cloak-and-dagger routine exciting."

He paused and stood up. Keeping the gun pointed at Lila, he walked to the shelf and grabbed the beer. "None of this is easy for me to say, Camilla. But it's important that you understand. You of all people."

She nodded, anxious for him to continue.

"When I arrived, I was assigned to kill someone. A complete stranger."

"What?" Lila asked. She was sure she hadn't heard him right.

"See that reaction you're having? That's exactly how I felt. They expected me to kill? Me? I couldn't believe it. Then Chase took me aside and explained that it wasn't a random murder. The person I was eliminating was an enemy of one of the Janus

Society members. And now that I was in this society, any enemy of my fellow society members was an enemy of mine."

"But why did Chase think you could murder someone?"

"The thing is," Dylan said, with a hint of shame creeping into his voice, "it wasn't that far-fetched an idea." He took a long swig of beer.

"Why?"

"I was constantly getting into trouble. A lot of bar fights when I was younger. I was stupid, fearless. Violence wasn't something that ever frightened me. It's part of the reason I think Chase approached me. He recognized that there was a darkness in me before I realized it myself."

"How did he know you wouldn't run to the cops?"

"Simple. I knew they'd kill me. And Chase told me that anyone I killed always deserved it. And so I did as I was told. I didn't know what else to do."

"How many people did you murder? For the club, I mean."

"Only one," Dylan said quietly. Then he paused and looked out the window. The sun was beginning to set. "Well, two, actually."

"Who were they?" she asked.

"I've really missed you, Camilla," he said, crossing the room toward her. He put his hand on her cheek. "I wish today had gone differently."

Lila didn't flinch. "Tell me who they were," she said again.

Dylan sat back in a chair opposite her and looked up at the ceiling. Lila eyed the gun.

"To explain that, I'll have to start at the beginning of the club itself." He stood up again and walked to his desk, where he poured a glass of scotch from a crystal decanter into a glass.

"The club was founded by Chase's great-grandfather, a little after the turn of the twentieth century. Chase said the idea came to him when he and his fellow robber barons were sitting around discussing how life would be better if certain people could be gotten rid of. Of course, no one wanted to kill their enemies themselves. And hit men could never be truly trusted. They were always ready to sell out their employers to a higher bidder. The risk of being caught was too great. Then one of the robber barons came up with the idea of killing each other's enemies. That way each of them would have an airtight alibi for the murder of the person he was connected to. At first it seemed like a joke, but the more they considered it, the more they liked the idea. It just needed rules and structure. And so, the Janus Society was born."

Lila began to understand. "You're saying that the Janus Society is a murderers' club?"

"That's one way to put it. Have you ever seen images of the Roman god Janus? He's almost always shown as having two faces, just like the society's two faces. Only one was ever shown to the world." Dylan shook his head and stared off into the distance before continuing. "In two thousand seven, I killed Javier's mark, a Bolivian drug kingpin who was encroaching on Javier's gun-running business. That was my first hit. I could swallow that. The man was a sadist who left bodies in his wake."

Lila could tell that recounting this was taxing for Dylan. He began to look gray.

"But Chase said that, at the next meeting, I'd have to offer a name of my own. When I protested, he assured me that my life depended on it. I can't tell you how much I agonized over this. I contemplated running away, but I knew they'd find me. For a few months, I thought I'd kill myself, but I couldn't follow through. I wasn't as brave as I thought. Finally, I decided who I would have killed.

"It would be my father."

"Your father?" Lila was shocked. *If he's capable of that level of cruelty, he's capable of anything,* she thought.

"I see how you're looking at me," Dylan hurried to say. "But, again, I can explain."

"There's no way to explain killing your own father."

"He was a very sick man!" Dylan protested. "No one knew other than our immediate family, but my dad was in the advanced stages of Alzheimer's. He could've lived a bit longer, but his mind was gone. And he was such a proud man that I knew he'd rather be dead than be so dependent on others. In a way, the father I knew was already long dead."

"So you had him murdered?"

"I had no choice."

"There's always a choice."

"I don't expect you to understand. But you're right. I did make another choice that night, when I killed those twelve people on Star Island."

"What made you finally do it?"

"They asked something of me that I could not do."

"Worse than killing your father?"

"So much worse. They wanted me to do the unspeakable. They wanted me to . . . " He paused, then gave a long and angry sigh. "They wanted me to kill a child."

Lila was shocked. "Why a child?"

"Precisely. It was Neville Crawley, that sick fuck. He said the little girl had seen him commit a crime, and if she told anyone, he'd be ruined. But when I investigated her, I found out that she was his own daughter, and that his ex-mistress was blackmailing him."

"He wanted his own child murdered?"

Dylan nodded. "The moment I found out, I knew that there was nothing but pure sickness at the soul of the Janus Society. We had lied to ourselves that the huge charitable donations outweighed the crimes, helped balance out the damage. But I saw that was just a way we were trying to keep our consciences clean. I knew how much the bad outweighed the good. I could either kill the girl, kill myself, or kill the society. So, I decided to wipe the slate clean. One hundred years of the society was long enough. You see now that I did the right thing, don't you? I couldn't just cut down the tree. I had to rip the roots from the earth as well."

"But *how* did you do it? Why didn't anyone stop you?"

"It was simple, really. I brought night-vision goggles, so when I cut the lights, I was the only one who could see. They were all so defenseless. There was something so haunting about seeing villains like them groping around, cowering and whimpering for their lives."

Lila didn't know what to say. After all this time, she had finally learned the secret of the Janus Society. The world's most prestigious charity organization was just a cover for a bunch of killers. The truth was more horrifying than she could ever have imagined.

"You can't even look at me," Dylan said, as he emptied his glass of scotch. He was so overwrought that the vein in the middle of his forehead was visible and bulging. He walked toward the desk for a refill.

"I'm not turning away from you. I'm much stronger than

you think," Lila said, her voice small. "It's just . . . a lot to take in. I could use a drink, too, you know." In truth, she was terrified.

He shot her a suspicious glance, filled up his glass, and walked back to Lila.

"None for me?" she asked.

"We can share," he said, handing her the scotch. "I can't very well carry two glasses and a gun, after all."

"Yeah," she said. "About that gun."

"What about it?"

"What's the plan? You can't keep that thing pointed at me for the rest of our lives."

"I know. But if I were you, I wouldn't rush me. I'm holding all the cards."

Lila took a sip of scotch, then dropped her chin onto her chest and began softly weeping.

"Don't," Dylan said. His voice was concerned and tender. "Please, Camilla."

He went to her. He gently touched her face and then lifted her chin up so that he could look in her eyes. But as his gaze met hers, his expression changed from tenderness to surprise. Lila hadn't been crying at all.

Right at that moment, she spit scotch in his eyes; then, with all the force that she could muster, she kicked him, jamming her heel into the side of his kneecap. He cried out in pain.

She watched as the man she'd loved collapsed to the floor, the gun falling from his hands. Lila swooped down, picked it up, and pointed it at him.

Suddenly, someone burst through the door. She spun around with the gun in her hand, ready to shoot.

It was Teddy.

"Lila!" he shouted. "It's Dylan. Dylan is the killer!"

"Thanks for that, Teddy."

"Who's Lila?" Dylan asked, gasping in pain.

"That's me," Lila said. "My name is Lila Day."

ONCE TEDDY AND Lila had bound Dylan's hands and feet, they called the police.

As they waited for the cops to arrive, Lila turned to Teddy. "How'd you figure out that Dylan was the killer?"

"Something you said about his shooting bothered me. You said it was his fate, and you couldn't have prevented it. But the universe doesn't work that way, Lila."

"Now you tell me," she said.

CHAPTER 43

DYLAN RHODES'S TRIAL captivated the globe. At first, Dylan refused to testify, and there wasn't enough evidence without his testimony to convict him. But then Lila visited him in jail. She never told anyone what she said during that conversation, but, when she left, he had agreed to tell his story.

She still couldn't believe the man she loved was the killer she'd spent years pursuing. The last time she saw him, she needed to find out, above everything else, if anything real had existed between them.

Lila had tried to convince herself that Dylan was a sociopath who'd tricked her into feeling something that wasn't there. But despite everything he'd done, as she sat with him in his cell, she still felt something for him. And it was clear from his desperation and sorrow that he still loved her, too.

"Will you ever forgive me?" Dylan asked, reaching out for Lila. But she pulled away.

"First I have to forgive myself for falling for you. But I know what will help."

"What?" he asked desperately.

"I need you to tell the world the truth," Lila whispered. "If you love me like you say you do, then I know you'll do it."

And so he did.

Through the court testimonies of Dylan, Alexei, and Lila, the true nature of the Janus Society was finally made public. It was clear to everyone who saw Dylan on the witness stand that he held nothing back. He had lost everything. All he had left was the power to tell the entire truth, to pull back the curtain on the horror show. He even testified against his brother, who was convicted of three counts of fraud, a firearms charge, and perjury.

The revelation that the world's most revered charitable organization was a cover for a murderers' club shook the world to its core. It seemed as if anyone who was aided by the Janus Society unwillingly had innocent blood on their hands.

Every day of the trial, Lila and Teddy sat together in the courtroom, listening to the prosecution's case, though it was hard to hear. Teddy's heart, already broken by the loss of Meredith, was now destroyed by the knowledge that the woman he loved had been a killer.

Lila knew how he felt.

What she and Dylan had shared made it all the more painful when she had to testify against him. She hated being on the witness stand, but finally she had the chance to tell the truth—or at least a version of the truth. There was so much that could never be revealed. That she had traveled back in time. That she was Camilla Dayton. That she was in love with the man guilty of mass murder.

As the story of the Janus Society unfolded, it became clear that the Miami Police Department would have to reopen many of their closed cases, starting with the murder of Willow Morris. Shane Johnson was tried for and convicted of first-degree murder.

In an attempt to reduce his sentence, Johnson testified that Effie had flown to Costa Rica to meet him, then set him up in a house in Miami, gotten him a car, which he registered in his grandmother's name, and paid him twenty thousand dollars in cash to get rid of Willow. The reasons were now clear—Meredith wanted her gone so she could be with Teddy. So she had been Effie's mark for the Janus Society that year. And Effie hadn't had the heart to kill Willow herself.

Like Dylan, Effie must have been tiring of the murder game. Lila realized that her unwillingness to take care of Willow herself was what she and Chase had been fighting about the night Lila overheard them. Effie knew that if Willow didn't die, she herself would be killed. That was one of the ironclad rules of the society—kill or be killed. By hiring a hit man, Effie was breaking the code upon which the society was built. But it must have been the most desirable of all the terrible options available to her.

The death of Frederic Sandoval was reclassified as a homicide. His body was exhumed, and a toxicology report found trace amounts of potassium chloride in his system, a drug that, if injected, could cause massive heart failure. Based on new evidence, Javier Martinez was posthumously convicted of murder in the first degree. Sam Logan had assigned Javier to kill Sandoval in the hope that Bolivar would drop out of the 2015 Australian Open, which he did. After finding out the truth surrounding the death of his father, Bolivar went on to win three Grand Slam championships in the 2018–2019 season. He dedicated each of them to the memory of his dad. The International Tennis Federation posthumously stripped Sam Logan, Janus Society member and four-time Wimbledon champion, of all his victories and records, essentially writing him out of the sport that he had dominated for years.

COVERAGE OF THE Janus Society and the Star Island murders consumed the attention of the international press corps. For months it seemed as if no other news existed. There were endless front-page stories reporting on the crimes and countless editorials examining the moral, social, and cultural implications of the Janus Society revelations. Every cable and network station was clamoring to get a made-for-TV movie of the story on air before their competition beat them to it. Screenwriters were busy pitching their screenplays, and writers were pitching books to their anxious editors.

Standing at the center of this maelstrom was Lila Day, the beautiful young detective who had cracked the case wide open. To the dismay and astonishment of every journalist on the globe, she turned down each interview request, no matter how big or lucrative, with a simple "No, thank you." Lila had had her fill of the Star Island killer and wanted nothing more than to put the case behind her.

While she shunned the media spotlight, Lila did enjoy one aspect of the aftermath of the Star Island case—the restoration of her reputation as a detective. And the one invitation she didn't turn down was a celebration held by the mayor of Miami in her honor. While her former boss, her old colleagues, and the chief of police looked on, the mayor gave Lila keys to the city.

During one of the final days of Dylan's trial, Lila was standing outside the courthouse when her old boss, Police Chief Barker, approached her.

"I've got the mayor of Miami calling me, asking why you aren't on the force," he said, his puffy eyes shining brightly.

"And what did you tell him?" Lila asked. She was going to make Barker squirm, and she was going to love every second of it.

"What can I say? Mistakes were made."

"You can say that again."

"We can make it up to you, Lila. We want you back," he said.

She'd been waiting for Barker to say those words for years, but now that she was hearing them, they left her cold. It was only when she was invited back to her old life that Lila realized she wasn't interested in it anymore. She was done being a company girl.

She graciously declined the chief's offer with a smile.

CHAPTER 44

ONCE THE TRIAL was over and Dylan Rhodes was behind bars, it took several months for the rhythms of Lila's life to return to some kind of normalcy. The world eventually moved its attention on to other things, but it took Lila longer to pick up the pieces.

She thought a lot about Dylan. She thought a lot about Effie, too. For all their unforgivable sins, they'd both gotten stuck in a nightmare that they couldn't escape. Effie tried to buy her way out of it by hiring a hit man. Dylan tried to murder his way to freedom by ridding the world of a monstrous club. They were villains, but they were also victims. And, in her own flawed way, Effie had been Lila's friend.

But now everything had changed for Lila. Catching the Star Island killer and uncovering the secret of the Janus Society had transformed her into the hero of Miami. Her once quiet, isolated life was now a riot of phone calls, street cheers, high fives, free drinks, and marriage proposals. She found it both exhausting and exhilarating.

It seemed that everyone in her life, from old grade school

teachers to her high school prom date, was getting back in touch. Everyone except the one person she wanted to hear from: Teddy Hawkins. The two of them hadn't spoken since they parted on the courthouse steps on the final day of Dylan's trial. The only reason she answered the phone or opened the door was the hope of once again hearing Teddy's voice and seeing his smile.

She and Teddy had shared so much: the pain of loving the wrong person, the joy of a secret adventure, and, ultimately, a profound friendship. She felt that she had seen two different sides of Teddy—when he was in love in the past and when he was grieving in the present—and she understood and related to all of it. After all, no one else knew what Lila had gone through.

So when the knock on her door one steamy summer night turned out to be him, she was delighted.

"Teddy!" she exclaimed, giving him a good once-over. "You look great." He looked vibrant, clear-eyed, and full of life—just as he had when she met him as Camilla Dayton, that glorious afternoon on Fisher Island.

"As do you, Lady Day," Teddy said. "Mind if we go for a drive? I have a proposal for you."

"I'd be delighted." She followed him down to the street, where Conrad was waiting in the car. They both climbed into the backseat.

"Conrad," Teddy said. "Shall we?"

The car headed east toward Indian Creek Island.

"So," Teddy said tentatively, testing the waters. "I see you didn't go back to your job at the police department."

"That's right," Lila said. She was surprised at how giddy she was to be back with Teddy and Conrad. Not long ago, she'd thought they were two of the world's most insane men. Now, in a strange way, she considered them family.

"I guess you're no longer interested in the crime-solving racket?"

"It just didn't feel right for me anymore."

"So, you've got a lot of time on your hands, then?"

"Loads," Lila said, smiling at Teddy.

"Think you'd be up for another adventure?"

Teddy's car shot across the causeway. Lila looked out the back window at the moon's reflection shining brightly on the tranquil waters of Biscayne Bay.

"What do you have in mind?" she asked, smiling.

For the first time in a long time, she knew she was headed in the right direction.